Repenting at Leisure

A Hal Westwood Restoration Mystery

JULY 1666

by Jemima Norton

TUDOR GATE
PRESS

LARGE PRINT EDITION

ISBN 978-0-9801660-3-3

LARGE PRINT EDITION

You will find the other books in this series at:
www.jemimanorton.com
www.halwestwood.com

For ordering information visit:
www.tudorgatepress.com

This book is dedicated to:

Ian,

with many thanks for his help

Repenting at Leisure

July 1666

Sir Henry (Hal) Westwood, 27
  Guardian of the bride, Justice of the Peace, gentleman
Justin Danvers, 24
  Lawyer, Joint Guardian of the bride, Hal's brother-in-law
Sophia Redcroft, 19
  Hal & Justin's Ward, bride of Gervase Harcourt
Cordelia Sandys, 19   *Hal's ward, Sophie's friend*
Gervase Harcourt, 25
  bridegroom, elder son of Sir Edgar Harcourt
Sir Edgar Harcourt, 58
  wealthy landowner, father of the groom
Lady Harcourt, 40   *Sir Edgar's 2nd wife*
Katherine Harcourt, 17   *Sir Edgar's daughter*
Anthony Harcourt, 24   *Sir Edgar's 2nd son*
Jane Harcourt Selby, 27
  widow, Sir Edgar's daughter from his first marriage
Endurance Southgate   *land agent of Sir Edgar*
Pip Beniston, 22   *friend of the groom*
Kit Withiam, 24   *friend of the groom*

Jamie Brownlow, 25	*friend of the groom*
Sir Charles Wicliffe, 50	
	friend of Sir Edgar, local Justice of the Peace
Joshua Swarby, 45	*sheriff for the village of Harton*
Jem Styles, 36	*constable for the village of Harton*
Gabriel of Skirbeck, 28	*tenant farmer at Harton*
Michael Skirbeck, 23	*tenant farmer at Harton*
Raphael Skirbeck, 26	*tenant farmer at Harton*
Jack Hollingshead, 25	*kin to Cordelia Sandys*
Madeleine Hollingshead, 47	
	kin to Cordelia Sandy, Jack's mother
Thomas Kingscott, 49	*kin to Sir Henry Westwood*
Lady Mary Fanshawe, 45	*betrothed to Tom Kingscott*
Margery Kingscott, 61	*Hal's aunt*
Katherine Westwood, 41	*Hal's aunt*
Molly Brewer, 17	*village girl*
Mistress Tempy, 48	*the cook*
Reverend Berwick, 52	*minister of Harton*
Robin Lawrence, 16	*groom of Hal Westwood*
Ned Westwood, 20	*Hal's brother*
Hetta Shearsby, 17	*Hal's sister*
Will Shearsby, 18	*Hetta's husband*

Mary Armstrong, 28	*Hal's elder sister; Guy's wife*
Guy Armstrong, 29	
	Mary's husband; brother-in-law to Hal
Bess Danvers, 21	*Hal's sister; Justin's wife*
Harry Westwood, 6	*Hal & Libby's son*
Libby Westwood	*Hal's first wife (deceased)*

Glossary

OED- Oxford English Dictionary
BD Brewer's Dictionary of Phrase & Fable

banns
public notice given in church of an intended marriage, in order that those who know of any impediment thereto may lodge objections   *1440 OED*

boon companion
good fellow, jolly convivial   *1566 OED*

the bones
dice   *ME OED*

broadcast
sowing seeds by throwing them widely.

calumny
gossip, false accusation   *1504 OED*

cast away
rejected reprobate   *1526 OED*

character	a detailed report, especially one given to servant by employer *1645 OED*
cogent	appealing to the intellect or powers of reasoning; convincing strong *1659 OED*
Common law	the general law of a community as oppose to local or personal customs, the unwritten law of England *1551 OED*
cupping	the operation of drawing blood by scarifying the skin and applying a cup *1519 OED*
cutpurses	one who steals a purse by cutting it from the girdle by which it was formerly suspended *ME OED*

Glossary

Dogberry

the constable in Shakespeare's *"Much ado About Nothing"* —thence allusively, an ignorant consequential official

1600 OED

dower (house)

the portion of the deceased husband's estate, which the law allows his widow for life (the house thereof)   *ME OED*

done up

used up, worn out   *ME OED*

drab (cloth)

a kind of hempen, linen or woolen cloth   *1541 OED*

drab (fallen woman)

a whore   *1602 OED*

footpads

a highwayman who robs on foot   *17th century OED*

fop　　　　　　　a fool or simpleton　　*1664 OED*

fustian　　　　　a coarse cloth made of cotton
　　　　　　　　　　or flax, also inflated or lofty
　　　　　　　　　　language　　　　　　*1590 OED*

goodwife　　　　the mistress of the house
　　　　　　　　　　　　　　　　　　　ME OED

green-sick　　　an anemic disease, which
　　　　　　　　　　mostly affects young women
　　　　　　　　　　about the age of puberty, which
　　　　　　　　　　gives a pale, green tinge to their
　　　　　　　　　　complexion　　　　　*1585 OED*

groat　　　　　　a denomination of coin from
　　　　　　　　　　13th century equal to 4d. Circu-
　　　　　　　　　　lation ceased in 1662　*ME OED*

gull　　　　　　　a dupe, simpleton or fool
　　　　　　　　　　　　　　　　　　　1594 OED

Glossary

guttered
(applied to candles)
to melt away rapidly by becoming channeled on one side

ME OED

hair clubbed short
stylelessly and inexpertly shortened; rough cut;

17th century OED

hem
damned   a noise, cough-like, rather than using oath

1526 OED

ipso facto
by that very fact, by that fact itself (Latin)   *1548 OED*

Jezebel
name of infamous wife of Ahab, King of Israel, hence a wicked and abandoned woman

ME OED

Lady Day	March 25th, the Feast of the Annunciation *ME OED*
lawn	a kind of fine linen resembling cambric *ME OED*
loving cup	a large drinking vessel, often of silver; passed from hand to hand to drink from *OE OED*
Michaelmas	September 29 Third of four Quarter Days when rents fell due
nil nisi bonum	speak no ill of the dead (Latin) *ME OED*
petticoats	a skirt as distinct from a bod-ice, worn either externally or beneath a gown. *1602 OED*

Glossary

Quarter Day	the four dates in each year on which servants were hired, and rents were due
quo bono	Who benefits? (Latin) *1595 OED*
quoits	sport of playing at quoits *late ME OED*
sack	general name for a class of wine from Spain or the Canary Islands *1597 OED*
sen'night	seven nights *OE OED*
settle	a chair, wooden bench, usually with arms and a high back, having a box or locker under the seat *1553 OED*

Simon Peter	apostle	*The Holy Bible AD*
simples	a medicine or medicament composed of or concocted from only one constituent, especially one herb or plant— hence a herb or plant used for medicinal purposes	*1593 OED*
Sirens	one who, or that which, sings sweetly, charms allures or deceives like the Sirens of Greek mythology	*1590 OED*
at sixes and sevens	a state of confusion *(Brewer's Dictionary of Phrase and Fable)*	*1542*
stepping into the breach	to do someone's task when they are unable to	*OE OED*

trenchers	very thick slices of stale bread used as a plate; later wooden plates *ME OED*
truckle bed	a low bed, usually pushed un-der a high or standing bed when not in use *1495 OED*
virgo intacto	untouched virgin *Latin*
yeoman	a countryman of respectable standing; a farmer *late ME OED*

Chapter One

July 1666

The sun shone brightly, a faint balmy breeze rustled the leaves of the trees which lined the path, the sky was a clear cloudless blue, the grass a perfect green sward. The birds sang for joy, bees buzzed industriously, God was in his Heaven, all was right with the world.

The wedding party which walked the path was equally satisfactory. The bride was bright-eyed and beautiful, the groom young and handsome. The bride's maidens were happy and attentive, the groomsmen sprightly and jocular, and the wedding guests for the most part well-disposed to enjoy themselves at someone else's expense as they followed the newly-wedded couple cross the park to the handsome house on the hill.

"What was that scuffle as we left the church, did you notice?" asked Justin Danvers as he walked beside his widowed brother-in-law Hal Westwood.

"I did not," he replied. "I was receiving Sir Edgar's congratulations on acquiring so excellent a husband for our ward."

Justin snorted. "It looked like some of the local tenantry, they were certainly armed with clubs and sticks, but the groomsmen saw them off in no uncertain fashion."

Hal glanced ahead to their host. "Sir Edgar is reckoned a warm man. Likely he is hard on his tenants."

"He certainly doesn't appear to be overflowing with the milk of human kindness," agreed Justin, recollecting the older man's stern visage and gimlet eye.

"A companion-at-arms of the late Oliver Cromwell, I believe," remarked Hal maliciously.

"I doubt he is any the worst for that," snapped Justin swiftly. Then, as Hal only smiled thinly, he glanced to him sidelong and added, with an uncomfortable attempt at sympathy: "This must be difficult for you."

"Difficult?" repeated Hal. "How so?"

"Well, was 'twas but six months ago Sophia Redcroft was declaring undying love for you and vowing she'd marry you."

"I don't recall her ever saying she'd marry me," he replied distantly. "As for swearing undying love, she is but nineteen, emotions are rarely fixed at so early an age."

"Bess was but eighteen when we were wed," remarked Justin evenly.

"Dear Bess," Hal smiled at the thought of his sister. "She may have been eighteen in years, but she was at least thirty in common sense."

Justin grinned his agreement. "Aye, but I was convinced Sophia wouldn't alter," he said.

"Plainly Aunt Margery was correct," said Hal. "She said Sophia merely needed to enlarge her acquaintances to meet and fall in love with another younger man. One much more suitable all round."

"I don't care for the fellow," observed Justin.

Hal shrugged. "You don't care for Sophia either," he said blandly.

"No, but this Gervase Harcourt is somehow, different."

"How so?" repeated Hal.

Justin frowned. "I don't know, I mean, he is in essence quite perfect, don't you think? He has good looks, charming manners, he's educated, affable, cuts a good figure on a horse, talks hunting with Ned, law with you, family with your Aunt Margery, children with Bess, as I say, quite perfect."

"All two guardians of an heiress could require," agreed Hal.

"Yet something, something doesn't smell right," continued Justin. "Do you know when you pick an apple from a tree, and you look at it and see its rosy and plump, smells crisp, yet somehow you have an uneasy feeling as you bite into it, and sure enough, you find a worm at its heart?"

Hal smiled faintly. "You sound jaundiced to me, Justin. You drank too much ale last night."

"There was too much ale last night," he remarked. "Far too much."

Hal glanced up to the house, noting how the bride and groom paused at the threshold. "I think we begin to feel our years," he said. "They were, for the most part, young men, all of Gervase's own age."

"Aye," he agreed. "Too many of them, too!"

"Too much of everything in fact," murmured Hal, and then fell silent as they mounted the steps and the moment he was dreading approached. So it was over, truly over, and all the trouble and turmoil of the past year could be put behind him. All the pain and grief, joy and ecstasy which he had experienced since Sophia Redcroft burst unceremoniously into his life could be categorized, and then shut away forever.

It was strange how one became used to pain, he'd noticed it in sick people of course, how a cripple soon managed to accommodate a damaged leg and walk again, albeit with a shuffling gait. Well, he was like that, he supposed, an emotional cripple. He'd not been lame for long, none had noticed, and he could walk forward again even if it was with an ungainly mental limp.

The dreaded moment over, congratulations and compliments expressed and exclaimed, they joined the groom's parents in a place of honour and the wedding feast proceeded along conventional lines, with much gaiety brought about by copious amounts of wine, so that after a time even Hal's pain dulled a little and he was able to make a speech of such eloquence and erudition as to bring tears to Sophia's eyes and thunderous bursts of approval and gusts of laughter from the other guests.

This over, and the meal brought to a somewhat tedious and wine-sodden conclusion, it seemed to Hal that events began to move out of his control. Before he knew it, the bride and her maidens were withdrawing and the groom and his fellows indulging in overexcited horseplay and yet more drink. Suddenly he felt once again his years as he stood alone and contemplated a rather bleak future.

Justin, seeing his expression, moved to join him, a wine jug in his hand. Wordlessly, he refilled his cup and began a monologue about a recent case which was notable for its circumlocution and the grasping natures of both parties.

His ploy had the desired effect, Hal drank and listened, occasionally nodding as Justin recounted his steps and his protagonists' actions, but although he added the odd comment or two, his attention was but poorly given. Only the surface of his mind was dealing with the actuality of the moment, deep down, he was miles away, back in the halcyon few days of last spring and deeper even than that he was conscious of his heart creaking and bending in pain.

It was much later, as the short summer night was fast becoming dawn that Justin's attention was finally taken by another guest and Hal's mind was free to wonder. He stared into the bottom of his wine as recollections of the evening came to him. The ceremony of putting the bride to bed with its attendant laughter and ribaldry was long past. Neither he nor Justin had been of their riotous number, there were some duties he found it best not to attempt. Instead he'd sought solace in a jug of wine, aided by Justin, and now as he emptied the last of it into his cup; he knew he was stone-cold sober. He glanced restlessly about him, noting with distaste the feast was fast reaching its natural conclusion. The table was a wreck of broken meats and wine stains with dogs snarling over a bone. Two guests, more energetic than their peers still danced in the centre of the scuffed floor to the strains of a viol player, whilst the rest of the musicians had long lain aside their instruments and were talking and drinking in a corner amongst themselves. In the far corner a goodly crowd of youths were gathered about a game of dice, betting heavily on each fall and over by the old front door, which had been set open wide to let in some cooler night air and a panoply of moths into the over-heated chamber, sat several older and more earnest looking men who were discussing politics with an avid air.

He felt an overwhelming weariness with himself, his companions and the world in general. He drunk off the remainder of his wine, and noting that Justin had been caught up in talk of the dreadful events in London, he got up. Passing two over-tired children squabbling over sweet meats he went out through the open door and into the velvet night.

He paused looking up into the sky, the stars still twinkling but less brightly and already dawn's pink glow was predicted in the eastern sky. Resolutely he walked towards that faint light between an avenue of chestnut trees and only when he'd reached the ornamental gates a clear mile from the house did he falter and turn round.

It was over and his heart was breaking. Sophie was another man's wife and he had never felt so alone in his life. He'd read all the poets, heard many men speak of being in love, but never until he'd met Sophie had he fully comprehended how the experience could alter a man. The affection he'd felt for his late wife, Libby, the love he had for his children, they were nothing beside the blind adoration he had for this girl he'd met just one short year ago.

In the last year since this momentous event had occurred he'd felt as if his life had been turned asunder. He'd lost all sense of direction in his life, and could not find any clear idea of what he wanted for the future of what he should do. He, who had prided himself since his return from exile in having purpose and order in his life, had found his plans and dreams in ruins. All he'd known in all that time had been an empty void where his heart was an overwhelming longing to be with Sophie at all times. All he wanted was to see her, to hear her sweet voice, her step, her laughter, to see her lovely smile and to feel the infinite comfort of her presence.

He'd allowed none of this to show of course. As her reluctant guardian, and a married and later bereaved man, how could he have possibly done so and retained but a vestige of honour. He may have stumbled many times, especially in the beginning, but eventually he'd schooled himself to conceal the depths of his love. The result of which had convinced Sophie, already made doubtful by the efforts of his family and his own cold demeanour towards her, she'd sought love elsewhere. His Aunt Margery had been right. How could a widowed father of two children hope to compare with the handsome, dashing heir to a baronetcy.

He felt a prickle of tears against his eyelids, and recognised in horror, he wasn't as sober as he'd imagined but was on the verge of maudlin tears. The mere suggestion did much to sober him. He opened the heavy gates and turned his steps towards the church. There was nothing like a brisk walk to clear the head. ❧

Chapter Two

The bright sun and bird song awoke Sophie. For a few seconds she couldn't think where she was, and then the misery descended like a cloud.

She sat up, surprised that she was still abed alone. Surely at some point most bridegrooms shared the nuptial couch, however drunk they might be. Gervase, in spite of all her pleas, had been very drunk indeed. Disgustingly drunk, so that two of his groomsmen, only slightly more stable, had been needed to help him to his chair amidst the ribald remarks of the equally inebriated guests. This was not the bridal night she'd expected, but only Cordelia Sandys had looked dismayed, all the other females, daughter of Gervase's kin and friends, had accepted it as normal.

Her gaze travelled to where her bridegroom lay sprawled in the chair, still fully clothed. He was to all intents dead to the world. Was this the wedding night most women expected? The females of the Westwood family, although too modest to indulge in any of the raucous comments she'd heard last night, had hinted at something different. Indeed, Bess's tale of a clandestine marriage, at a ruinous castle in the dead of winter, had all the flavour of high romance, which she'd found impossible to match with the dour manners of her co-guardian, Justin Danvers.

Now why had she remembered that, for it brought Hal to mind and that was fatal. It was only by putting him totally from her mind that she'd been able to go ahead with this marriage. Tears welled in her eyes and trembled on her cheeks. Was ever a maid so undone? Why did Hal Westwood never react as expected? She'd contracted a betrothal with Gervase Harcourt purely to frighten Hal Westwood into declaring himself and what had he done?

Nothing. Whatever he felt, it showed all the signs of a huge sigh of relief, as he had set about arranging a marriage as swiftly as possible. Before she'd known it, the date had been set and the wedding clothes ordered. It seemed to her he'd not been able to be shot of her quick enough, and she had fallen into the grave error of quarrelling with him, so that there was no way back. She'd found herself suddenly caught up in the machinery of a betrothal and wedding to a man of fortune for whom she cared nothing.

What was a female to do? She'd tried talking to any of her guardian's family who'd listen, but all had been only too conscious of their earlier unkindness and were at great pains to reassure the nervous bride. It was often so, Aunt Kate had explained. After all, she was taking a big step. She remembered her own wedding to her own Henry, Hal's uncle. How nervous she'd been, how inadequate she'd felt, how she'd been certain Margery, his sister, would despise her! But once the ceremony had been over and she'd been in her dear Henry's arms, everything had come right. Indeed, had she and Margery not been the best of friends all these years?

Aunt Margery, when appealed to, had shown even less understanding. Sophia was merely indulging in a bout of the fidgets. Did she not comprehend the enormous amount of effort which had gone into the arrangements for this wedding? It had been no easy task to convince Gervase's parents that all the talk and scandal surrounding Sophia had no foundation in fact. Indeed, it had taken every penny of her fortune to gild the bitter pill of her hoydenish behaviour. And if Sophie should commit the folly of breaking the contract at such a late date, she, Margery, couldn't be responsible for the consequences.

As for Hal himself, far from throwing himself at her feet, from the moment of her announcing the betrothal he seemed to have withdrawn behind a thin veneer of glass ice, so that there was no touching him, mentally nor physically. He'd listened politely to her stumbling explanation, shrugged his elegant shoulders and re-marked blandly that such doubts were commonplace shortly before a wedding, and that if heeded by all, he doubted any would indeed make a nuptial tie.

Only Cordelia, dear sweet Cordelia, fighting her own battle not to be married to her kinsman Jack Hollings-head, had truly understood. Cordelia was every bit as fettered as Sophie was, just another of Hal Westwood's wards to be married off as quickly as possible.

A tear splashed down her nose and landed on her lace-edged and beribboned nightgown. Now what did she do? She felt a compete fool. A wife, but yet a virgin. Was she so unattractive that her husband must be dead drunk to even think of his duty? Should she remain where she was and wait for him to awaken and take his pleasure of her, or should she rouse him from his slumber? Or, better yet, should she rise up herself, and take out her own sweet mare, which Hal and Justin had brought with them yesterday?

Decisively she threw back the thin sheet. Better to do anything than wait here. She crossed the chamber to her mirror and took up her brush, tugging it ruthlessly through her tumbled curls. Her eyes travelled to her husband's form reflected in the mirror. Her hand stilled and a frown came to her face. How oddly he sleeps, she thought, puzzled. So upright, but with his head dropped forward. He'll awake with a dreadful crick in his neck. She half turned and had put out a hand to rouse him when eyes saw and made sense of the blood.

Through his modish laced coat it had soaked, a great red stain on the yellow silk, even now darkening at the edges where it was drying. In the centre of the stain was a slender dagger, which had struck through his heart. It looked as if he was pinned to the chair, like a moth to a board. Shock held her motionless, although she felt her legs begin to tremble, and suddenly she was aware of a voice coming from a long way away, screaming, scream-ing, screaming... ❧

Chapter Three

It was the screams that woke Justin out of his heavy sleep. Again and again without cease, echoing about his pain-filled head. He leapt to his feet and was out of the door in response. He raced along the upper hallway as the volume of the screams increased until he burst open a door, realising at the same moment what had brought him with such urgency to Sophie's aid.

"What in Hell's name..." his gaze followed her terror-stricken eyes and he turned to see what caused her horror. "Oh dear God!" he cried.

"What is it! What is amiss!" The door was suddenly crowded with half-clad people, none of whom he recognised. Then, as Sir Edgar pushed his way into the room, his voice rose over Sophia's screams. "What ails her? What—what—Gerry? Gerry! What has happ..." he stammered.

"Sir Edgar, your son appears to be dead," said Justin, as the older man stood with his mouth opening and shutting, all colour fading from his face, leaving it suddenly grey.

"Stop her, make her stop!" he gasped, his hand going to his chest, as he staggered to a chair.

Justin crossed to Sophie, who had continued to scream almost mechanically. He took her by the arm, shaking her. "Sophie stop it! Stop the noise, Sophie, have done!" She paid him no heed, indeed she didn't acknowledge his words or his touch, her eyes being blank, but continued to scream. In desperation, as he heard the sound of Gervase's mother's voice, he swung his hand and slapped her fully across the face.

The screams stopped abruptly, and she stared at him as if astounded, her eyes filling with tears. "Why—oh, Justin! Oh, Justin!" He received her into his arms as she became hysterical.

At the same moment, Lady Harcourt entered the chamber and a fresh bout of screaming broke out. "God in Heaven!" Justin cried, "Is there none to aid me? Oh for Aunt Margery—anyone with sense!"

"I am here, Mr Danvers." Her cheeks blanched, Cordelia, a wrap thrown over her nightgown, pushed her way through the bridegroom's relatives, the female half of whom seemed to be wailing, and came to his side.

"Cordelia! Thank God, somebody sane!" he exclaimed. "Here, take Sophie, try to calm her." He turned to the people clustered in the doorway. "One of you men, send somebody for a doctor! And is there a female not in hysterics who could assist Lady Harcourt?"

A small dark woman pushed her way through the throng. "I am Jane Selby," she said simply, "I'll help." She turned to her kin. "One of you go for some feathers quickly."

"Thank you, mistress," Justin said, recollecting that she was Sir Edgar's married daughter as she came to clasp the shoulders of her half-fainting mother.

"Sir, are you ill?" Justin, meantime, had turned his attention to Sir Edgar, whose colour was still ghastly, as he sat staring at his dead son, his hand clutched his chest. "Pain!" he muttered thickly. "Heart!"

"Does any of you know anything?" cried Justin, turning in exasperation on the assembled relations. "For God's sake, pull yourselves together and help! Where is Hal? That I should live to regret the lack of that French physician."

"He—he has a cordial," said Lady Harcourt faintly. "Kate, run and fetch your father's cordial. He suffers from cramps of the heart, sir."

Justin, who was kneeling at Sir Edgar's side with his fingers on the man's fluttering pulse, could well believe this. "Has someone summoned a physician?" he demanded. "It is imperative—Oh Hal! Thank God you are come! Where the Devil have you been?"

"Out walking. Good God! Sophie—Jesus!" This last came as Hal saw the bridegroom dead in the chair. Sophie, trembling and weeping, ran into his arms. Resting her golden head on his chest, his hand came out to clutch Cordelia's arm in sympathy. "What in God's name has gone on here?"

"The groom is dead," said Justin tersely. "Every petticoat is in hysterics and Sir Edgar isn't—Oh dear God, give me a hand Hal!" This last as the old gentleman gave a groan and slumped forward.

Hal thrust Sophie back to Cordelia and went to assist Justin, who had leapt to Sir Edgar's side with another young man. Between them, they got the ailing gentleman into the bed Sophie had only recently vacated. They piled pillows behind him to assist his breathing, and held the cordial to his lips. "I think we must clear the chamber," said Hal in an undertone, his thoughts racing. He turned to the people now crowded into one corner of the handsome chamber. "Sir Edgar is very ill. It is essential that he has air and peace. Will all those not directly involved please leave this chamber. I don't know if any has summoned a physician?"

"I've just sent a stable lad, Sir Henry." The man who had assisted them with Sir Edgar was now looking very grave. "I greatly fear it won't be an easy task to locate him if he should be from home, for his is a far-flung practice, but we must not give up hope."

"So the Bible teaches us," agreed Hal. "And you are?"

"Southgate, Endurance Southgate," the man replied. "A distant cousin. Sir Edgar employs me as his agent, we did meet briefly yesterday. I apologise for not coming to your aid earlier, I was in the stables when a servant came running with the message."

"Oh, Dury!" cried the girl called Kate, addressing Endurance Southgate with tears streaming down her cheeks. "What can have happened?"

"Now Kate," he said firmly. "Control your tears. Your brother is dead and your father is gravely ill. Your mother needs you to be strong. Come, help me get everyone back to their chambers."

"Cordelia, take Sophie to the chamber Justin and I are in, and wait there for us. Mr Southgate, who is the local Justice of the Peace?"

"Sir Charles Wicliffe," replied Mr Southgate, frowning in concern as he viewed the ill man.

"Sir Charles?" said Hal quickly. "Did Sir Edgar not introduce us to Sir Charles yesterday?"

"Possibly. We met so many yesterday," replied Justin. "At least it isn't Sir Edgar, which is probably a mercy."

"No, Sir Edgar, indeed most people in these parts were for Parliament, Mr Danvers," Mr Southgate added. "Honours come thin on the ground. Sir Henry is correct, Sir Charles was indeed a guest, but he left the stables some twenty minutes since, at first light."

"Did he?" Justin nodded. "As for being for Parliament, I'm surprised to hear you own it. I was beginning to think my father the only man in England who sided with Noll Cromwell."

The other man half smiled. "You are in Cromwell country, Mr Danvers," he said. "If you'll excuse me, I'm sure I'll be of more use if I try to expedite the arrival of the physician by sending more men in search of him."

"Can you send a groom to overtake Sir Charles?" asked Hal, who'd been wiping the patient's brow. "And the local officer of the law as well."

"You mean the Sheriff?" Mr Southgate stopped in the now-crowded doorway and turned to Hal.

"Young Mr Harcourt did not die naturally, Mr Southgate, the authorities must be informed," said Hal in answer to his unspoken question.

"Oh…Yes, of course, I remember now. Mistress Redcroft told us how you tracked down the murderer of her former guardian." His glance strayed to the still figure in the chair and he shuddered. "You think this is… other than an accident?"

"What sort of accident could stab a man in a chair like that?" asked Hal quietly.

"Yes," Mr Southgate agreed, his gaze sweeping to the bed where Lady Harcourt and her daughter now sat either side of Sir Edgar, Jane Selby hovering in attendance. "I'll go about my duties and see everything settled, then I'll return to your assistance."

"Is this all the immediate family?" asked Justin.

"No, there is Sir Edgar's younger son. He is—" Dury Southgate hesitated. "He is abroad. He and Sir Edgar don't see eye to eye."

"A message should be dispatched to him," said Hal. "He'll be needed here."

"Yes…"again, Dury hesitated, then shrugged his shoulders and hastened from the room.

"Have you looked at the corpse, Hal?" muttered Justin, noting that the women were talking softly together.

"No," replied Hal equally quietly.

"He's been dead some hours," Justin continued. "The blood on his waistcoat is dried at the edges and he's stiff."

"Not much blood either," agreed Hal. "He died quite quickly."

"Within minutes," said Justin. "Yet I wonder he did not cry out for help?"

"Too drunk?" suggested Hal. "'Tis only just after dawn and few sought their beds before three."

Justin nodded. "Aye, but one other matter, Hal. The dagger. Do you know whose it is?"

"No. The murderer's?" he suggested.

"Sophie's," supplied Justin crisply. "Bess has one she uses to open letters. Sophie liked it, so Bess made her a gift of one as a wedding present."

Hal look horrified and bent to examine the slender silver dagger which jutted from the man's chest. Hal's hand rose to remove it.

"What are you doing?" hissed Justin. "That is evidence!"

"I know," Hal replied calmly. He pulled the knife free, and wrapped it in his handkerchief before slipping it in his pocket. "And once I've found the murderer, I'll hand it over."

"Hal!" Justin exclaimed, horrified he should act so unlawfully.

"Well, and what if I leave it?" Hal demanded in a hasty undertone. "You know only too well what will happen. A nosy jade will identify it as Sophie's and then there will be hell to pay."

"But it's evidence!" Justin cried, his legal mind dismayed. "You know nothing should be touched."

"Until the arrival of another Dogberry, who'll promptly accuse Sophie," Hal returned.

"She had doubts about the marriage," said Justin pointedly.

Hal stared. "What, you think she killed him!"

Justin shrugged. "'Tis possible," he said harshly. "She has a ruthless streak and a will of iron."

"She'd need an arm of iron to sink that into his chest," Hal replied, gently pulling the body forward to examine the bloodstained chair behind.

Low-toned voices in the corridor outside heralded the arrival of the physician and the return of Endurance

Southgate. Lady Harcourt gave a cry of relief as the physician went to the bed. Mr Southgate approached with a linen sheet which Hal assisted him in draping over the corpse.

"There, that will be less harrowing for my Lady and Sir Edgar," Endurance Southgate remarked quietly. "Ah, I see you've removed that gory dagger. Thank heavens, it looked so awful. I've penned a note to Sir Charles and summoned the Sheriff." He glanced for guidance to the other men. "I don't know what more we can do."

"We should lock this chamber and summon the Coroner," replied Justin. "The Sheriff will probably want it locked. Although, I doubt it will be possible to remove Sir Edgar from here."

"I'm away to see how the bride does," said Hal, striding towards the door. "You might call me when either Sir Charles or the Sheriff arrives, if you please."

"I'll come with you Hal," called Justin, adding to the other man, "It is essential that as little as possible is disturbed in this chamber, Mr Southgate."

"I'll see to it personally, Mr Danvers," he assured him.

"Wait, Hal! Wait!" cried Justin, hurrying after him. "What do you intend?" ❧

Chapter Four

Hal halted, his eyes bright and hard as he looked his brother-in-law over with contempt. "What do I intend?" he hissed in an undertone. "Why, what any guardian should intend, to look to Sophie's best interests."

"But Hal!" Justin shook his head as if in disbelief. "To extract evidence from the scene of the crime in that manner!"

"I do not further intend to let Sophie be caught up in all this whilst we stand idly by with clean hands," said Hal through clenched teeth.

"But to tamper with evidence—it goes against all basic tenets, you know that!" He expostulated.

"I know you hate Sophie," Hal replied. "That, in spite of everything you say, you still hold her responsible for Libby's death and you'd not be adverse to seeing her suffer."

"Indeed, I do not hate her," he replied, suddenly pale. "Nor do I want her to suffer. I owe her my life and my happiness."

"Aye, and that sticks in your throat every time you are forced to remember it," snapped Hal going on his way.

Justin stood still, counted to ten, and then hurried after him so that they arrived at the door to their chamber together. Hal wasn't sure what he expected to encounter, hysteria perhaps, tears certainly. Instead, he walked into the chamber, as quiet as a church with both young women kneeling in prayer.

"Good G—" Justin stopped dead behind him and then both entered softly shutting the door. Hal sank to a chair to wait. Justin picked up his discarded shoes and waistcoat and put them on, darting a frowning glance at the young ladies.

Sophie finished her prayers first and stood up, going to sit on the fashionable sofa with which the room was furnished. She directed a watery smile at Hal and waited calmly.

Cordelia who, until six months ago, had spent her life at a nunnery in France, finished her devotions and came to join Sophie. "We were praying for Gervase's soul," she explained quietly, meeting Hal's eyes.

"I wasn't," said Sophie. "I was thanking God for answering my prayers."

"You prayed for your bridegroom to be killed?" asked Cordelia in horror.

"No, naturally not," Sophie cried in dismay. "I prayed to be released from the dreadful situation I found myself in."

"I think it would be best if you could restrain your more candid instincts, Sophie," said Justin dryly.

"What do you mean?" demanded Hal of Sophie, ignoring Justin.

"That, as I told you all repeatedly last month, I knew I was making a big mistake! The more I got to know Gervase, the more uneasy I was at marrying him. I became convinced that he only wanted my money."

"Don't be foolish, he has enough wealth of his own," said Justin, annoyed to think that in pursuit of a good match they had ignored her doubt.

"Indeed he doesn't! He has—had—but the allowance his father made him. He has debts everywhere. I can't tell you what he owes his tailor and the wine merchants in Croyland, aye, and gaming debts," she cried indignantly.

Both Hal and Justin looked shocked. "No, you can't be right," said Justin dismissively. "Everyone speaks well of the family."

"Never mind that," said Hal impatiently as Sophie began to argue this hotly. "We can dispute the matter at some other time. What I want to know, and quickly, is what exactly happened, Sophie?"

She bit her plump lip to still its trembling. "I don't know," she said. Then, as they both stared, she added: "Truly."

"Let us begin at the beginning," said Hal sharply. "The ceremony of putting the bride and groom to bed."

"You weren't there," said Sophie quickly, darting him a look from beneath her lashes.

"No, I went to speak to my groom," Hal said evenly. "No, but you were, Justin?"

"No, I was watching a game of dice between two of the groom's boon companions. The stakes made it unmissable," he replied, unconsciously giving credit to Sophie's earlier claim.

"Cordelia?" said Hal, turning to her.

"Yes, I assisted Sophie to change into her nightclothes and then accompanied her to the bridal chamber, not forgetting the posy of herbs, as instructed by Aunt Kate and Aunt Margery," she replied dutifully.

"It was nice to have one of my 'family' with me," observed Sophie tartly.

"I beg pardon," said Hal as Justin began to quibble. "You are quite right, you were shamefully neglected. As your guardians, we should have been there."

Sophie sighed. "It might have made it easier to bear," she said dispassionately. "As it was…"

"What?" asked Hal sharply as she hesitated.

"Everybody was drunk, very, very drunk," said Cordelia uneasily as Sophie began to tremble and tears filled her eyes again. "I don't mean drunk in a funny way either, as Mr Armstrong is occasionally. No, it was unpleasantly so," she stumbled over the words and colour filled her pale cheeks as she recalled the events of the previous evening. "It made us blush to hear the things being said."

Hal reddened too and looked angry. "I beg your pardon again," he said stiffly. "In neglecting my duty I allowed you both to be open to abuse. I am sorry for it."

"It was horrid, Hal." whispered Sophie, unable to look at him. She shuddered. "Oh God, I was so afraid!"

Hal briefly shut his eyes to blot out the mental picture. "Is that what happened?" he asked, and his lips were suddenly stiff with fear too. "Did you panic, Sophie, and threaten him with the knife, killing him by accident in the struggle?"

Sophie stated at him in blank surprise, her mouth dropped open in dismay. "Is...is that what you think?" she whispered numbly, tears sliding down her ashen cheeks as her voice seemed to come from a great distance.

"If it was an accident," began Justin, "if we can prove no evil intent, and, *ipso facto*, you having just gone through a ceremony of marriage—"

"Do you believe I killed him, Hal?" Sophie asked quietly, interrupting Justin.

"Did you, Sophie?" Hal replied, his eyes keen. "You tell me what I may believe."

"On my word of honour, I did not kill him," she replied with patent honesty.

"Oh, thank God!" cried Hal devoutly.

"It's no good thanking God, as if that is the end of it," snapped Justin. "What of the knife?"

"What knife?" asked Cordelia in confusion.

"The knife which killed Gervase Harcourt," said Justin crisply. "The knife Bess gave Sophie is a wedding gift."

"She didn't give it to me, I had to pay her a penny for it," said Sophie, tears falling faster now. "Otherwise, you cut the love which ties you. Why? What of my knife, you say it was used to kill Gervase?"

"Did you not notice?" asked Hal sharply. "It was sticking from his chest."

Sophie shuddered uncontrollably, shaking her head. "I got from bed and went to my table to brush my hair," she said, her voice trembling with concert with her body. "I was piqued by Gervase." She stopped, biting her trembling lips, as colour flooded her face again. "When he arrived last night with his groomsmen, Gervase was so drunk, he couldn't stand. He fell over, so his friends sat him in that chair, and there he remained," her voice trailed off into a whisper.

"He was so very drunk?" asked Hal blankly.

"Everyone was," said Cordelia helplessly. "Almost everyone except the other bridesmaid, Kate, Gervase's sister, and Mistress Selby."

"Mistress Selby?" replied Hal. "Who is Mistress Selby?"

"Sir Edgar's daughter from his first marriage," said Sophie. "The small nondescript female with her hair scraped back like a Puritan."

"Oh yes, I remember her, she just aided us," said Justin. "I didn't realise she was Sir Edgar's elder daughter." He frowned. "I have a feeling there is some scandal about her."

"She ran off when she was a girl with a distant cousin. Sir Edgar was away fighting in Ireland and she eloped with, and later married, a farmer," said Sophie, still shaking. "My lady said Sir Edgar has never forgiven her."

Hal nodded impatiently. "So, she, and Kate Harcourt were probably the only other people at the putting to bed that weren't drunk. Is that what you are saying, Sophie?"

"Yes," said Cordelia, "although she hardly helped in that she brought the loving cup for the bride and groom."

"It was a handsome cup, too, which she'd had made for the occasion," interrupted Sophie, tears filling her eyes again. "It had both my and Gervase's initials on it and the date of our marriage," she broke off, her tears overflowing down her cheeks as her recollection of the events took over and she began to sob and shudder.

After some minutes of weeping and being soothed by Cordelia, order was restored and Hal could continue with his questions. "I am sorry, Sophie," he said kindly. "But we do have to know more. So what happened to the loving cup? Did you drink it?"

"Yes, Jane presented it to me and I sipped it," she replied. "It was pretty strong as I remember, a sweet sack, with perhaps brandy and herbs. Anyway, by this time I was so terrified, I took a long drink, hoping to dull the coming occasion."

Hal frowned. "So you drank how much? Perhaps half?"

"Oh no, no, it was a big cup, not a quarter of it," she replied.

"And then?"

"Mistress Selby carried it to Mr Harcourt, who was, by this time, sprawled in the chair, as Sophie said, singing a disgusting ditty," replied Cordelia austerely. "He took it from her as Sophie got into bed. I then sprinkled herbs in the four corners of the bed as instructed by Aunt Kate and Aunt Margery."

Sophie nodded, her face suddenly flooded with colour again at the recollection. "Gervase drank the remainder down, encouraged by his companions, who were making such a fearful row as to bring my Lady Harcourt to the chamber."

"She'd been delayed," explained Cordelia. "Her arrival did calm things a little, but even so, she was…" the girl hesitated. "Unusually mellow," she added in explanation. "She began to clear the chamber, sending the young men about their business. She explained that supper was laid out for any who felt the need, and some began to move away so that we could see Mr Harcourt more clearly. He drank the dregs from the loving cup and threw it at the hearth where it shattered."

"Mistress Selby was not pleased," said Sophie. "She turned to Gervace with such a venomous look, but she is not a rich woman and I guess it upset her to see her gift destroyed by a drunkard."

"Indeed," said Cordelia. "She went at once and gathered up all the pieces into her skirt, but I think it was beyond any repair. Such a pity, it was a pretty thought."

"In the circumstances, however, it would have been a macabre reminder," said Justin. "So maybe it is just as well it is destroyed. What happened next?"

"Well, finally all the gentlemen went, leaving my Lady, Sir Edgar, Endurance Southgate, Kate and myself," said Cordelia. "I heard Sir Edgar mutter something about letting Mr Harcoat sleep the worst of it off in the chair and my Lady agreed, so I kissed Sophie and we all went out leaving her alone."

"What happened next, Sophie?" Hal asked gently. "I'm sorry but we do have to know."

"Once they'd all gone, Gervase did make an attempt to get out of the chair, indeed he nearly turned it over, crying out that his legs wouldn't move." There was a painful pause, then Sophie continued slowly. "He cursed and swore at me, he commanded me to come to his assistance but I—I..." she took a deep breath and added in a rush, "I said that if he were so drunk he needed assistance to share my bed, he could remain where he was for all I cared."

"And did he?" asked Hal gently.

"The whole night through!" she cried, as tears streamed down her face. "I awoke at dawn and I was so angry! After all that I endured, all the fear and the dread—I was—I was still—oh! So I thought, 'I'm not waiting here on his pleasure, like a Christmas goose dressed for the table!', so I got up and went to brush my hair. I looked in the mirror and I thought how still Gervase was. He wasn't even snoring like a pig, as he had been earlier, and I looked again in the mirror and I saw...I saw..."

"I don't think you should make her talk of it," said

Cordelia, putting her arm about the shuddering Sophie.

"She must talk," said Hal sharply. "She is the only witness. I'm sorry, Sophie, if this is distressing for you, but we must be sure of all the facts! As the matter stands, you and your bridegroom were put to bed last night and this morning the groom is dead by your dagger."

"You mean they'll assume I did it?" Sophie asked, still shaking piteously. "Oh Hal, shall I be arrested and cast into prison?"

"Not if we have any say in it," he assured her. "But we must continue to question you."

"I understand," she bit her lip and clasped her hands together tightly as if to still her shaking by sheer force of will.

"You mentioned Gervase snoring. When was this?" asked Justin. He'd been taking notes and his eyes were sharp as he put the question. "At what time would you say that was?"

Sophie looked bewildered. "I don't know. I was very sleepy. I suppose it was reaction to the events of the day. We were awake early, weren't we, Cordelia?" She frowned. "Gervase ranted at me for some minutes after I refused to help him to bed. He called me foul names and said he'd make sure I was an obedient wife in future. That he'd do his schooling with a stick and that I'd soon learn I was his property now, me, and my money." She shook her head, her tears showering Cordelia who pressed her hand in comfort. "I don't know, it seemed to go on forever, then suddenly he was snoring. Great loud snores! I wanted to laugh, yet I didn't dare, lest I woke him and he'd recovered enough to come to beat me."

"Did you sleep?" asked Justin with a sigh.

"Thought I'd never dare, but I must have done, for I awoke to find the candles guttered and birds singing," she replied, frowning in bewilderment.

"The windows were open?" asked Hal sharply, suddenly remembering how the casements had been thrown wide to let in the summer morning.

"Cordelia and I opened them last evening. The chamber faces west and was insufferably hot when we arrived last night. Wasn't it, Cordelia?"

"Yes," agreed the other girl. "Sophie told the servant to open them, but the maid said Lady Harcourt didn't hold with night air, that night air was a killer."

Sophie gave a hysterical laugh. "Lady Harcourt will be so pleased she wasn't wrong. It killed Gervase, didn't it?"

"Try to remain calm, Sophie," said Hal in soothing tones. "Let me think, yes, this is the west facade, isn't it? The one with the creeper over it?"

"Yes, it is, Sir Henry," agreed Cordelia. "How clever of you to remember. It is to my mind the most pleasing aspect of the house."

"It has very thick branches, too," Hal continued. "Thick enough to support the weight of an intruder, I'd say."

"You'll need more than that, Hal," said Justin. "I'll agree, it's possible, but what motive would there be? Where is proof of an intruder?"

"That is what you and I must find out," said Hal, as a knock came at the door. "Yes? Who is it?" ❖

Chapter Five

Justin went to the door to find Mr Southgate standing there. "Sir Henry wished me to tell him when Sir Charles and the Sheriff arrived," he said simply.

"What, are they come already!" said Hal in dismay, coming to join him.

"Sir Charles, you'll remember, was one of the guests last evening and had but left at dawn," explained the man. "The groom was able to overtake him just outside the village and he turned his coach about. The Sheriff was in the village itself. One of the wenches there had hung herself from the oak tree on the green yesterday. The Sheriff stayed over at the inn last night, it being too late and him being too drunk, I suspect, to go home. He's brought the Constable with him and sent for the Coroner.

"Thank you, Mr Southgate. I'll be with them within ten minutes. How goes Sir Edgar?"

Endurance grimaced. "It doesn't look good," he said quietly. "The physician is most concerned, he is cupping him now."

"An apoplexy?" asked Justin.

"He had had one before," agreed the agent. "It isn't likely he'll survive this one."

"Not if the physician has any say in it," murmured Justin.

"Where will the Sheriff and Sir Charles be?" Hal asked.

"Sir Charles is with Sir Edgar, as you know they are friends. The Sheriff awaits in the hall." He hesitated. "My Lady has a dislike of him, he was for the King, you understand, and made life very difficult for her when Sir Edgar was away fighting." He shrugged. "I know that is some years ago now but we have long memories in this part of the country."

"In our part, too," agreed Hal evenly. "Pray present my compliments to the Sheriff and tell him I'll join him almost immediately."

"Why do we delay, Hal?" Justin asked as the agent went on his way and they turned back into the room.

"We need to know more," he replied sharply. "Sophie, where was this knife?" He unwrapped the handkerchief to reveal the blade.

She looked up, her eyes widening in horror as she saw its bloodied state. "Oh! Is that the one all covered over with... Oh! Oh, yes it is mine."

"We know it to be yours Sophie, that's why I removed it from the body," said Hal in the same sharp tones. "Answer my question, where was it?"

Tears filled her eyes at his sharpness. "I...I do not remember," she said helplessly.

"For Heaven's sake, girl, use the wits God gave you!" he cried, exasperated. "Do you not comprehend the danger in which you stand? You are like to be taken up for the murder of your husband and all you can do is weep!"

"Hal, a little more gently if you please," said Justin, catching his arm. "Sophie, none have yet leveled an accusation at you, but this knife is damning! Once they understand it to be yours, they'll look about for a reason for you wishing to be rid of your husband. I pray you, tell me you've not confided your doubts to any of them!"

"Only...only to...my Lady," she whispered, tears

falling all the more rapidly as he groaned. Then, as Hal smacked his palm again his forehead in further exasperation, she recollected something. "The…the dagger…I remember now, it was on my toilet table," she stammered. "I used it to open Aunt Margery's homily. The letter she sent to me by you. I opened it and read it shortly before the ceremony. You remember, Cordelia?"

"Yes," cried Cordelia. "Yes, that's right, I do! You laughed over it, saying that if it was your only guidance as to what to do with a man, you'd be lost…" Her voice faltered and died away as Hal looked thunderous.

"Do neither of you understand how we are situated here!" he cried furiously. "I have no power, most of these people were for Cromwell, they'll be against us from the beginning. Unless we can prove you as an innocent child, Sophie, you are indeed lost!"

"I was under the impression she was an innocent maid," said Justin, his eyes narrowing at Hal. "You have been at pains to tell me so."

Hal cast him a look of mingled fury and contempt. "Sophie, heed me well, and you,too, Cordelia, for you will be summoned as a witness! You must not only be known as an innocent maid, but you must be perceived as such. An innocent maid, a shocked bride, a distraught widow. This is what they'll expect, so this you must be, is that clear? No levity, no foolish honestly. Show shock, show grief, become what they expect! I cannot linger now but must attend the Sheriff. I'll try to get him to delay sending for you, but if he does, remember my words, your life might depend upon it!"

Justin followed him from the chamber. "I am not happy at this," he said. "We should stick to the truth. Truth will out!"

"Did you learn nothing from the events of the winter?" snapped Hal. "How happy would you be if we'd stuck to the truth when you were accused of murdering your mistress? Truth will out? Did it?"

"Eventually, yes," he said white-faced, anger coming to him at Hal's reminder.

"Only after more deaths! Only because of Sophie's interfering. Not from anything clever you or I did!" They reached the head of the grand staircase as he finished speaking and could hear voices in the hall below. Hal shushed his reply and hastened downstairs.

"Sir Henry," Endurance Southgate was there, he had been engaged in stilted conversation with two men. "Please allow me to introduce the Sheriff for the county, Mr Swarby and the local Constable, Jem Styles."

"Mr Swarby, Mr Styles, Sir Henry Westwood," said Hal shaking hands with the Sheriff and nodding to the Constable. "And this is my brother-in-law, Mr Danvers. Mr Danvers is a man of law and I am a Justice in my own county."

"Sir Henry," said the Sheriff. He was a stocky middle-aged man with the pale face and pained expression of one suffering from a surfeit of ale the previous night. "I'm pleased to make your acquaintance, Mr Danvers, sir." He bowed at both men and then looked as if he wished he hadn't.

"I understand we owe your prompt arrival to your being called to the village yesterday," observed Justin.

"Yes, a matter of suicide," he replied, pulling down his lips in disapproval. "A foolish wench in the village had taken her own life."

"Stay," said Hal. "Sir, you have no refreshment! Mr Southgate, a mug of ale for these gentlemen will not be amiss I am sure." He waited until the agent had disappeared before adding: "What have you been told of this terrible business?"

"Sam Kent did come rampaging into the inn first off this morn," said the Constable at a nod from his superior. "With a tale of bloody murder been done overnight.

He said as how young Mr Harcourt be dead, stabbed through the heart, while his bride lay sleeping. And, that Sir Edgar be taken with the apoplexy and is like to die, too."

"A very accurate and succinct account," said Hal, breathing a little easier. "Forgive me, but my brother-in-law and I have had some experience in these matters."

"Aye, so Mr Southgate were saying," said the Constable, not entirely won over by this fulsome praise.

"As the erstwhile guardians of Mistress Redcroft–or Harcourt–as I suppose we must call her now," continued Hal, "I'm sure you'll appreciate our concern and desire to see the malefactor brought to book. Have you seen the body?"

"No, it still being in the chamber where it would appear Sir Edgar is even now breathing his last," said the Sheriff with a faint air of resentment.

"Then, I have to tell you the report you received was quite correct. Mr Harcourt was stabbed through the chest with this silver letter opener, taken, it would seem, from his bride's toilet table."

The Sheriff took the bloodied knife that Hal handed him gingerly. "And this was where?" he asked, frowning.

"Almost pinning the body to the back of the chair," said Hal shortly.

"Who removed it?" demanded the man, raising his brows.

"I did," replied Hal. "Sir Edgar was taken with a seizure, the bride screaming, Lady Harcourt—indeed the entire female population—appeared to be in hysterics. I judged it best to remove the dagger and have the body shrouded with a sheet so as to ease their sensibilities. We can put the dagger back when you see the body."

"Aye, when," growled the Sheriff, handing the weapon to the Constable.

"Ah, Mr Southgate, is there nothing can be done to expedite Mr Swarby's investigation?" asked Hal as the agent returned.

He shook his head. "There is no question of moving Sir Edgar," he said simply. "Not without occasioning a great botheration, but if I might suggest, we could move the body, if necessary, in the chair itself?"

"Rather macabre, one feels," said Hal pulling a face.

"I was thinking of poor Lady Southgate," explained the agent. "She is not a young woman, and these shocks…"

"It certainly is a puzzle as to what to do for the best,"

agreed Justin, as he didn't complete the sentence.

"Perhaps, in this matter, we might be guided by Sir Charles Wicliffe," said Hal, who'd had long experience of having to deal with both arms of the law, often, as in this case, at loggerheads over divided loyalties of the war. "He being, as I understand the matter, a close friend of the Harcourts."

"They both led regiments for Oliver Cromwell," said the Sheriff woodenly.

"Ah, then we'll leave it to Mr Southgate to make the suggestion," replied Hal. "For I, although too young to fight, spent my youth in France with my father."

The agent glanced to Hal. "What makes you assume I was not for the King?" he asked bluntly.

"Your name," replied Hal, surprised. "Endurance surely is one of those abstract virtues so beloved of the Puritans."

"Aye, given me by my mother, whose father was, as you suggest, a Puritan. My father was of a strong Royalist family. I, being but little older than yourself, perhaps, didn't fight, but it didn't stop one having strongly partisan feelings. Especially when loved ones die, as my father did in my infancy and, of course, most especially, when one lost everything as a result of it."

"I see," said Hal. "Then I am in error and I apologise for it, but I assumed as you are employed by the Harcourts, you shared their loyalties."

"Kin of my mother," he said briefly. "I am, indeed, barely acknowledged on account of my parentage and lack of fortune. Here comes Sir Charles now, I do believe."

Hal glanced to the stairs as a middle-aged man came into view. Short and stout, with bristling moustaches, his arrogant stare took in the whole party. "Ah, Southgate, there you are. You'd best send for young Anthony if you've not already done it. He'll be needed now."

"Sir Edgar?" said the agent quickly.

"Died a few moments ago, rest his soul," he replied. "The females are taking it hard, even Mistress Selby."

"Indeed, she is his daughter, sir."

"Aye, aye, and there's another misalliance if you like. Thank Heavens that misbegotten fellow perished before he brought further trouble."

"A thought that must be a constant comfort to her, sir," agreed Endurance with irony. "Meanwhile, let me make you known to those gentlemen. This is Sir Henry Westwood and Mr Danvers, Mistress Redcroft's guardians."

"I met them yesterday at the wedding," Sir Charles replied, according them each a brusque nod. "Swarby, I see you are come already, and the Constable, good. For this matter needs immediate attention."

"Sir Charles," the Sheriff bowed punctiliously. "When may I see the body? I am most anxious to establish this is a murder."

"It can hardly be anything else," said Sir Charles shortly. "The poor fellow was stabbed through the heart! As for seeing the body, my Lady Harcourt is still with her husband. She'll need a little time to compose herself. I understand from Jane Selby that you two gentlemen were first on the scene and took control."

"I most certainly was," agreed Justin. "Mistress Redcroft's screams roused me."

"Poor wench," sighed Sir Charles. The old soldier accepted the cup of wine Hal poured for him. "Not too pleasant a sight for a bride, eh? Such a pretty little thing too! What does she say?"

"My brother-in-law and I questioned her briefly," said Hal quickly. "But as you may imagine, she is shocked and hysterical and could only outline the bare facts. We've left her with my ward, Mistress Sandys, to try to calm her. We were indeed lamenting the lack of my

Aunt, Kate Westwood, who was, until a few days ago with them, but has been called to the side of her own betrothed husband, who has been taken with a fever. The steadiness of an older woman is invaluable at such times."

"Quite so, quite so," Sir Charles grunted. "Alas, Lady Harcourt is quite distracted herself, and I am a widower, Sir Henry."

"I also," Hal replied. "Which is why I rely so heavily upon my dear aunts. My sister has but recently been brought to bed of a child." He paused, glancing to Justin. "Perhaps we should send for Mary or Jane?"

"'Tis a three day journey," said Justin with a grimace. "Would Mistress Hollingshead not be a better person to apply to?"

"Indeed," nodded Hal. "In fact if we trespass upon Lady Harcourt's hospitality, perhaps we could all beg lodgings with Cordelia's kinsfolk."

"Do not feel obliged to leave on Lady Harcourt's account," said Endurance. "She said everyone must remain until Gervase's funeral…both funerals, now I imagine."

"Poor woman!" said Sir Charles. "Hers is a heavy burden and only that scamp Anthony to turn to. You'll have to assist her, Southgate."

"As is my inclination, sir," he replied. "I owe much to Sir Edgar and his Lady."

"Indeed, and you are a good fellow," he replied mildly. "I'm sure she couldn't put her trust in better. So, Sir Henry, Mr Danvers, what sort of tale did you get from the little widow, anything of use?"

"Not a vast deal, merely that she awoke at dawn and wondered why her husband hadn't come to bed," said Hal.

"Not bedded her!" exclaimed Sir Charles. "Good God, are you sure?"

"We are," said Justin. "It would appear Mr Harcourt was too drunk to stand last night and that his groomsmen, in a like state themselves, deposited him in a chair to sober up."

Sir Charles made a face. "This is bad news," he said. "Then if he didn't bed her, there is no marriage at all!"

"Precisely," said Justin. "A difficult legal tangle, but a matter for another day."

"On getting from her bed, Sophie went to see what had prevented her new husband from coming to her, only to find him stabbed through the heart with a paper knife."

"A paper knife?" exclaimed Sir Charles.

"A wedding gift which she says she thinks was on her toilet table in the window alcove," said Hal.

"And the window was open," continued Justin. "For Sophie opened it herself."

"Indeed, the heat was intolerable last night," agreed Sir Charles. "So, what think you Swarby? A simple case of theft?"

"Until we can ascertain if anything has been stolen, Sir Charles, I could not say," he replied woodenly. "Although, I would suggest that if it were a simple case of felony, surely, Mr Harcourt would have put up a struggle, which would have awoken his bride."

"Unless he was still too drunk," said Sir Charles shrewdly.

"In which case, why kill him? And if the man panicked and wanted to be sure, why not kill Mistress Harcourt also?" countered the Sheriff who, in spite of his aching head, could clearly think logically.

"Having examined the body," said Justin. "Which my brother-in-law and I did, when we removed the dagger—"

"You removed the dagger?" said Sir Charles sharply.

"Indeed. We wished to relieve some of the distressing circumstances for Lady Harcourt and her daughters. The body of her son with a dagger through his heart could hardly be an edifying sight for her. Or for Sir Edgar, indeed this could almost be cited as a double murder, for it was the sight of his son dead that brought on Sir Edgar's apoplexy," said Hal.

"I agree with you, Sir Henry," said Sir Charles, his thoughts diverted to his friend's fate. "I have no doubt in my mind that is exactly the case!"

"In the course of removing the dagger, Sir Henry and I noticed several things," said Justin firmly. "Firstly, that the blood had stopped flowing fairly swiftly. We therefore concluded that he died at once. Secondly, that the blood was drying on his shirt, and from that we are inclined to believe that he'd been dead some hours."

"Which would make sense, for, if he were very drunk he'd probably not awaken on hearing someone entering the chamber," said the Sheriff. "Can we safely assume he was indeed very drunk?"

"I think we can," said Sir Charles. "If he couldn't walk from a chair to bed one of the sweetest brides I've seen in a long time, he must have been out on his feet."

"Is it not strange though, that Mistress Harcourt— the new bride I mean—is it not strange that she slept through the attack?" asked Endurance Southgate.

"Not given that she was up at dawn yesterday preparing for her wedding, and that she danced the night away. Indeed, it must have been close on one o'clock when the couple were put to bed," said Justin swiftly.

"Did neither of you gentlemen observe the groom's demeanour?" asked the Sheriff.

"We greatly regret we did not attend the ceremony of bedding the bride," said Justin. "I was watching a game of dice with a thousand guineas on the fall, and Sir Henry had gone to speak to his groom."

"To speak to his groom?" said Sir Charles, frowning and darting a glance at Hal.

"Rather too much of Sir Edgar's excellent claret, Sir Charles," replied Hal with a grimace. "My head felt light, and in such circumstances, I invariably find if I take myself off for a short walk it improves my head. And, I had some concern about my horse."

"I find the night air usually finishes me off!" said Sir Charles with a short laugh. "But I'll plead my advancing years! So Swarby, you'd better begin your investigation at once. Have you any suspects in mind?"

"I usually start with finding out who bears a grudge against the murdered man," said the Sheriff. "Styles, you'll have some idea of that, I imagine."

"Bear a grudge?" repeated the Constable with disastrous candour. "Why, that would be half the County, your honour!"

"Oh, come, man!" said Sir Charles testily. "Young Gerry may have been a bit of a rip, but that's going too far!"

"Not by what I've heard, begging your pardon, my lord," he replied stoutly.

"Well, I always think it's best to ask oneself who benefits in this situation," said Sir Charles. "'*Quo bono*', don't you know."

"We, in our previous investigations, have usually started at that point," agreed Justin.

"When one knows the why and how, and the when, one invariably can discover the who," said Hal.

"Well, its plain we'd best waste no more time, gentlemen," said Sir Charles. "I suggest we all pursue our own thoughts and return here on the morrow to share them." ❖

Chapter Six

By the time Hal and Justin had eaten a belated breakfast and talked again with Sophie and Cordelia, the afternoon was well advanced. Sophie, who showed signs of weeping when further questioned, was soon dispatched to bed to rest the headache which she'd developed, with Cordelia in attendance. Meanwhile, Hal and Justin parted company to talk to as many other people as possible.

Whilst Justin went to question the servants, Hal went on his way to find some of Gervase Harcourt's companions. Hal was, he had to admit, extremely concerned, not only to hear of Sophie's opinion of her new husband but the constable's, too. He greatly feared that in the Westwood's haste to get Sophie settled, they'd overlooked obvious flaws. Yet, the Harcourt family came with good credentials. They were kin to the Hollingsheads, who were kin to Cordelia and to the Kingscotts. They were also distantly related to the gentleman who Aunt Kate was betrothed to. It was all very confusing. Hal blamed himself. He should have met the Harcourts before this, and not left it to his aunts to arrange the marriage.

"Good evening," said Hal, as he approached a young man with a simple, good-natured expression sitting on the top step leading down to the gardens. "May I join you there?"

"Yes," he replied blankly. "It's Sir Henry Westwood, isn't it? The guardian of poor Gerry's bride? I'm Christopher Withiam, mostly called Kit.

"Yes, I am Sir Henry," he agreed. "Although, friends call me Hal. How is it you are not with your friends?" he continued, indicating a small group of furtive young men, who sat beneath them at the edge of the canal watching one of their number idly casting dice, one hand against the other. "I understand I missed an epic game last evening."

Kit grimaced wryly. "Oh well, I don't know…I can't help think…it's not quite the thing, you know. Well, that is to say, my father wouldn't have cared for it…and then, I am quite done up until Quarter Day," he added frankly. "And the Devil seems to be in the bones these days, too. I don't recall having such ill luck in many a month."

"I commiserate with you," said Hal pleasantly. "Although, I am given to understand you are possessed of a considerable fortune."

"Aye," he agreed glumly. "But the devil of it is my father left all my money tied up. I have a trustee of my estate until I am five and twenty. I can't touch a penny of my capital."

"Indeed, but who would want to?" replied Hal. "That's the surest way to end in ruin, to make inroads on your capital."

"You sound like old Jenks, my man of law," the young man observed gloomily. "He is always wittering about capital."

"Dear me, how very tedious," Hal grinned sympathetically. "I do beg pardon. I, too, had a guardian until I was of age. He was an excellent fellow with a very sound head. I miss his advice sorely. He died just about a year ago," he added, half to himself.

"I'm sorry to hear it," remarked Kit Withiam amiably.

"Life is a very unchancey thing," observed Hal, recollecting his errand. "Who'd have thought your good

friend Mr Harcourt and his father Sir Edgar would
have gone as they did? Why, I confidently expected to
return here to celebrate Gervase's son's christening next
year and then that son's wedding some years hence."

"Aye, it's a shocking thing," he agreed ingeniously.
"Poor old Gerry! As you say, he looked fit for another
fifty years. The old fellow was a bit shaky of course."

"So I understand. Wasn't that the reason for an early
marriage?" asked Hal.

"Aye. Gerry didn't like the idea above half, you know,"
he confided. "Well, he was one who liked to sow his
oats broadcast, so to speak, but like me, Sir Edgar had
him over a barrel."

"Oh?" Hal frowned. "I had understood that young
Mr Harcourt enjoyed a considerable income from property settled upon him by his maternal grandfather."

"Mortgaged, d'ye see?" replied the young man suc-
cinctly. He glanced about. "Between you and me, Gerry was in deep with the money lenders. He'd had the
most cursed bad luck lately, too, and as I say, Sir Edgar
had lost all patience with him. Indeed, Gerry said only
at Christmas if something didn't turn up, he'd be forced
to finish off his father himself."

Hal offered this dubious jest a half-smile. "Christmas, you say? So, something did turn up, in the form of an heiress."

"That's the idea," the young man agreed, pleased that Hal followed his thoughts so readily. "I tell you, Gerry wouldn't have considered it unless he were truly desperate."

"Indeed?" Hal replied, his voice echoing his astonishment. "Yet Mistress Redcroft is reckoned a great beauty."

"Oh, aye, she's lovely!" he agreed quickly, recollecting that he was speaking to the beauty's guardian. "But Gerry wasn't a great fellow for the ladies, you know. He said he like his females simple. He said Sophie Redcroft had far too many brains and about twice as much spirit as he cared for. But needs must when the Devil drives, they say!"

"I see, and the Devil drove, did he?" asked Hal, rather appalled to think that for all their care, the young bridegroom's true character had remained a closed book to him and Justin.

"Completely cast away. And the creditors were getting restless," admitted the young man. "Gerry said he needed half of Sophie Redcroft's fortune immediately to satisfy his most urgent needs."

"Half!" cried Hal in dismay, for nothing of this had reached their ears.

"Oh, aye, and wasn't he furious when that lawyer fellow of yours—the sour-faced one—tied everything up so tight. The deal was not worth a candle, he'd said. He'd barely get clear and then have the trouble of keeping a wife, who if she wasn't a shrew, his name was Simon Peter."

"Mr Danvers is also my brother-in-law, and a good fellow," said Hal mildly. "Don't let that lawyer's expression of caution mislead you, he's very sound and has an excellent understanding."

"Aye?" replied Mr Witham surprised. "Truth to tell, you clever folk frighten me!" Then, as Hal smiled he added: "No, but you do, you know. You speak a different language it seems to me! Once a couple of you get together I can never follow a word you say."

"I'm sure you don't do yourself justice, Mr Witham," replied Hal. "Why, we have been discoursing for this last twenty minutes with no adverse effect."

"Aye," Kit agreed. "There's something about you I can follow, but I sat listening to your brother-in-law and Dury Southgate yesterday and couldn't understand one word in three."

"Then they must have been expressing themselves very badly," replied Hal. "Tell me, how do you view the murder of your friend Gervase Harcourt?"

"Why, it's a damned shame," he replied. "Poor old Gerry, he never did anybody much harm."

"I fear for him to have been killed in the manner he was. He must have done some harm," responded Hal coolly. "But you'd like to see the culprit caught and punished?"

"Aye, I would!" he cried, flushing with anger. "Indeed, I'd like to deal with the fellow myself!"

"Better to leave it to the law," soothed Hal. "But, my brother-in-law and myself are trying to find the murderer. Would you care to assist us?"

"Me? Help you?" he cried astonished. "But, I mean—I'm not clever you know. In fact, I'm known to be stupid!"

Hal laughed. "You are most certainly not conceited, that I'll grant. My dear sir, you are merely young and untried, I suspect, and not used to employing your brain."

"My tutor used to say I hadn't one," Kit observed dispassionately. "Do you truly think I can help?"

"Indeed. As a person with local knowledge you'll be

invaluable, and if I may be permitted to say so, one with your reputation is also useful. People don't care what they say in front of those they designate fools, and so often give away more than they would to someone like myself."

Comprehension dawned on Kit's amiable face. "You mean I should listen and tell you what is said?" he asked.

"If you'll not find the office distasteful?" asked Hal. "Also, being known as a fool, you can ask foolish questions and observe the effects of the questions on various others."

A flicker of something appeared in the young man's eyes and the amiability of his face sharpened. "Do you think I could do that?" he asked simply.

"I am sure of it," Hal replied, pleased to see he'd not been wrong in his estimation of the young man's character.

Kit paused, thinking about the proposal, then nodded. "I'd like to do it," he said. "Yes, I'd like to think I could have a hand in catching the fellow that spitted Gerry that like, if you'll tell me what I must do."

"Good," said Hal. "As for what to do, mostly I want you to listen, as I said, and ask some questions. We need to know who wanted to see Mr Harcourt worsted.

Who hated him enough to kill him?"

"That will be a tidy few," said Kit Withiam, pulling a face. "Not the most popular of people, Gerry! Had a bit of a nasty temper on him at times, especially if he wasn't sober! He'd offended quite a lot of folk one way and another."

Hal nodded. "Aye, so the constable said, that's what made me think of asking for your help. You must have the same circle of friends. Talk to them if you will. Find out who bore a grudge against Gerry—not just an idle grudge, but real rancour."

"Hey—but I say—well friends, don't you know! Could be damned difficult," he said looking alarmed.

"We are looking for someone who is a murderer, Mr Withiam," said Hal patiently. "If they are truly friends of yourself and Mr Harcourt, they'll not mind your questions. Remember, the dagger was plunged into Gerry's heart so hard as to nearly pin him to the chair. That is not the action of a friend."

"No," agreed Mr Withiam faintly, looking a little greenish. "No indeed, I'll...I'll do my best anyway."

"I couldn't ask for better," said Hal. "Ah, here is my brother-in-law. No doubt you'll like to make your escape before he starts prosing on."

Hal smiled as the young man promptly disappeared and he greeted Justin as he came up. "Hal," Justin replied briefly. "I've been talking to Thomas, the man-servant, and I've found out that those young men who were involved in that scuffle outside the churchyard yesterday were the brothers Skirbeck: Gabriel, Raphael and Michael."

"Good Heavens!" said Hal appropriately.

"They farm on the far side of the village, prosperous yeomen, it would seem, respectable and well-liked."

"Why the scuffle in the churchyard, then?" asked Hal.

"The village girl who hung herself yesterday was be-trothed to Gabriel, the elder of the brothers," replied Justin, his brows raised.

"Indeed," said Hal looking grave.

"I thought you might like to walk with me to their farm. They might have some answers to your 'Why'."

"I think they might," agreed Hal. "Having got the 'How' and 'When' so easily, I don't suppose the 'Why' will be there for the taking, but it can only help."

✤

They left immediately, walking through the heat of the day to the farm, which was off a dusty track just past the churchyard. It being the mid-afternoon, the farmer and his brothers were partaking of their main meal of the day.

Hal and Justin joined them at the big, square, scrubbed table in the kitchen, accepting a mug of ale and bread and cheese. They declined the roast beef, dripping blood and thick gravy, that the brothers were ladling over their trenchers of bread.

"Well now," said the middle brother, Raphael, eyeing them narrowly. "What would you be wanting to know why we were in the churchyard for, anyway?"

"Aye, and by what right do you come here demanding answers?" added Michael the youngest, pugnaciously.

Hal glanced at all three in turn. Named for angels they might well be, but there was nothing angelic in their looks. The epitome of yeomen they were, with their hair clubbed short to their jaws and their faces scrubbed by wind and rain to a rosy polish. Plain men, honest men.

"We have no rights at all," agreed Hal mildly. "Merely an interest, in that our joint ward was yesterday married to Gervase Harcourt, and is today a widow."

"Aye, and a him good riddance to him," muttered Raphael.

"Better off without him, she be," said the youngest. "At least he didn't have time to ruin her, as he did poor Molly."

"Molly?" asked Hal, although Justin pricked up his ears at once.

"Molly Brewer," said Gabriel in his deep voice. "Most folk called her Molly. It were a name as suited her. 'Merry Molly!' we used to cry out as little 'uns."

"Merry?" said Justin sharply. "Not so merry yesterday when she took her own life."

"Aye, rest her soul," said Raphael bitterly.

"Her soul won't rest!" Michael cried bitterly. "She's a suicide. Aye, and a murderer, too! They'll bury her at the crossroads on the moor and her ghost'll haunt us all! You know it will."

"Hush now, Mike!" said Gabriel calmly. "Be still, be calm."

"What mean you—murderer?" queried Justin. "Gervase Harcourt was still alive at one o' the clock this morning. Molly Brewer died at dawn the previous day."

"Aye, we knows it," said Raphael. "'Twas Mike here

as found her, swinging from the oak on the green."

"I mean, as how she took the life of her baby!" cried Michael, his face suddenly flushed and looking close to tears.

"She didn't need to do that! Gabriel had told her not to fret, that he'd marry her anyway and bring the brat up as his own."

"I see, she was to have a child," Hall nodding his understanding. "And the father was?"

"Not Gabriel for sure," snapped Raphael as Hal's eyes strayed to his face. "Even though they'd been betrothed these last two summers."

"Aye, and were to wed at Michaelmas," said Michael, tears now running either side of his nose. "Such a dainty little maid she were, until yesterday, when she hung there…her tongue all swollen and her face blue."

"Mike, Mike!" Gabriel's massive hand clutched the younger man's shoulder. "Don't take on so, lad." He glanced to Hal and Justin, his own eyes dull with pain. "'Twas no pretty sight," he said laconically. "And here's the Rector saying she can't have a Christian burial. It do play upon our minds it do."

"If I'd had more sense, happen I could have cut her down," his younger brother cried, sobs beginning to rack his massive chest. "Pretended it were an accident somehow. But no, I runs screaming, like a green-sick wench, and now we can't even see her laid to rest in the churchyard, decent, like a Christian."

"The Rector being one of the old sort, who rode with Sir Edgar and Noll Cromwell a-praying," said Raphael, contempt in his voice.

"Has none any influence with him?" asked Hal with compassion. "Could he not be persuaded, perhaps, to allow her burial in a quiet corner of the churchyard?"

"My Lady Harcourt might command him," said Raphael.

"Nay, Raff! She is too taken up herself, poor lady," said Gabriel. "Why, to lose her son and her husband, too..." he shook his head in disbelief.

Hal nodded his agreement. "I'll try for the opportunity to speak to her," he said. "Lady Harcourt, although distressed, will be aware of her obligations, even in her grief."

"Would you, Sir Henry?" asked Gabriel pitifully. "Why, we'd be mightily obliged. 'Tis the thought of the moor which do hurt us, and having no marker, nor a Christian word said over her."

"I'll do my best," said Hal. "As for no marker, or no Christian word...even if we can't achieve the churchyard, both of those are within our power. A simple marker, and the words of those that love her, are as powerful as any prayer from a bishop."

"'Tis true," agreed Gabriel, some of the pain easing from his face. "Thankee, Sir Henry, thankee."

"What do Sir Henry want in return?" asked Raphael, his eyes flickering from Hal to Justin's face. "It ain't to bring comfort to strangers, that he comes to our table."

"No," agreed Hal placidly. "I came to see what manner of men would think to start a fight with a wedding party. Good honest yeomen, I was told. Solid, reliable farmers all three, yet I saw you manhandled by Gervase Harcourt's friends."

"'Tis my blame, Sir Henry," said Gabriel. "I were angered at Molly's end, aye, and raw with pain. We walked to the green about this time yesterday to say a prayer, and saw the wedding going forward, and all at once I were filled with such wrath, that I determined to tell her, his bride, to stop her from making a terrible mistake!"

"First we knew of it, Gabriel gave a bellow of fury, and set off across the grass," said Raphael. "'Twas all I and Mike could do to keep up with him!"

"Aye, and then those damned fops started," cried Michael. "Grabbed him, they did, six of them, 'tweren't even a fair fight! Laid into him, they did, hauling him away as if he'd been a servant or a criminal! Him a free-born Englishman, which is more than some of them can say!"

"Yeates is Irish and Bennington is part French," explained Gabriel as Hal looked mystified. "And a sad lot of rackety young fellows they be."

"They are young, and unfortunately, without any responsibility," agreed Hal pacifically. "There is, I find, no worse master than idleness for a young man. All would be better for being tied to the soil as you are, making your own way in life."

"Aye," agreed Raphael. "But, what with prices as they be, the farm can't support us all. We were forced to draw lots to see who was to be the one to take a wife."

Hal nodded as a gloom seemed to settle over them all. "Aye, this war with the Dutch hasn't helped," he agreed.

"Well, the problem is solved now," said Gabriel stoically. "If Molly be dead, I don't care to take a wife. You and Mike can draw straws to see which of you can go a-wooing."

"I guess neither of us is that fussed anymore," said

Raphael, glancing to his younger brother. "Happen we'll wait until next spring sowing is over."

"Aye, like as not that were for the best," nodded the eldest brother. His glance strayed to their guests. "If there be nothing else you be wanting, your honour…"

"Just one question I shall be asking almost everybody over the next few days," said Justin swiftly. "I imagine you keep early hours, but have any of you proof of where you were at two o' the clock this morning?"

"We were out in the barn, helping deliver Deliah's calf," said Raphael quickly. "All night long! Come with the sun, he did, so we called him Sunup."

"He were coming tail first, and that do be tricky," agreed Gabriel. "I thought we were like to lose 'em both along o' midnight, but Raff here is wonderful with beasts."

"Aye, a fine young bullock for Michaelmas fair," said Raphael. "As for Mike, he were sound asleep. We sent him off to bed at midnight. Why, I had to turn his bed up to rouse him, same as ever, at dawn for the milking."

Justin nodded as he made a note of these facts in his book, watched intently by all three brothers.

❧

Hal and Justin took their leave shortly after. "It's all very well," said Justin. "But there's no real proof of anything at all. Like as not, they'd lie to save their own. Although, the calf they took us to see was newborn."

Hal nodded. "Newborn indeed; Now, I think perhaps I'll go to inspect that creeper which grows up the side of the house. Do you come with me?"

"Aye, although I hope you'll not be long, this heat is parching my throat."

"I rather think it was the wine you drank last night which is affecting your throat," retorted Hal. "But no, I shall not be long, we merely need to see if there are any physical signs of someone attempting to make an entry. Leaves torn off, or the branches scraped, that sort of thing."

"Well, with the house at sixes and sevens, no gardener will have tidied up as yet," remarked Justin as he followed Hal around to the west side of the house.

The inspection was, as Hal suggested, the work of moments. There were no handy footprints leading to the creeper beneath the window, no torn or broken leaves, no scraping of the lower branches such as might be made by a heavy boot.

"Well, that's conclusive," said Justin, glancing about him to observe the lawns sweeping away to the river. "There is no sign of anyone trying to climb this creeper, therefore, unless they had wings, none made an entry through the open window in my opinion."

"Which means the murderer was inside the house or had entry to it," agreed Hal. "Which rather rules out our farmer friends. I'd guess I can't see Michael making his way unchallenged to the upper floor, can you?"

"Not unheard, if he was wearing the same boots as he was today," replied Justin. "Oh, well, we must look further. I did have the feeling they'd been chosen as convenient scapegoats when the constable suggested it." He shrugged. "I'm for a drink of ale with Dury Southgate to see if he has any ideas. Will you ensure Sophie and Cordelia are safe?"

Hal assented, but on arriving in the chamber, to his dismay, he found it empty of both young women. The bed on which Sophie had been sleeping was neatly made and the clothes which had been scattered about the chamber had been tidied away, but evidence of his wards there was none. Panic assailed him. Where was Sophie, and much more to the point, what mischief was she up to? ❧

Chapter Seven

Hal hastily clattered down the stairs and into the main hall, the servant Thomas was there, clearing away the furniture from the previous night's feast. He glanced up as Hal reached the bottom of the stairs, enquiry on his face.

"Have you seen either of my wards?" Hal asked, trying not to invest any anxiety into his tone.

"The young ladies, Sir Henry? No, I've not," he replied. "But then, I've only just started in here myself. Everything as all awry today, I fear. What Sir Edgar would make of it, I dread to think." He shook his head, looking confused. "They've but recently carried Sir Edgar and Mr Gervase to the chapel, perhaps the young ladies have gone to pay their respects?"

"Possibly," Hal nodded, thinking that Cordelia may have considered that a good idea. "Most certainly I must do so, perhaps I'll find them there."

"Most likely, Sir Henry," Thomas agreed. "You know where the chapel is, of course?"

"Thank you, yes." Hal quickly went through the front door and turned into the pleasure garden. The chapel was across the lawn beyond the flower garden. As he made his way there, he caught a glimpse of a female figure turning into the yew walk and hurried after her.

"Sophie?" Hal called in an undertone as he caught up with the lone figure. "Sophie, what in God's name are you doing?"

Sophie turned at the sound of his voice, her wan face lighting up. "Oh Hal, I was praying I'd meet up with you," she said, holding out her hands to him.

"What are you doing here?" he repeated, ignoring her.

"Walking," she replied blankly. "I needed some air and to talk to you, so I came here to walk."

"Your husband is not twelve hours dead and you are talking the air," he said coldly. "Are you mad?"

"Why should I not walk?" she asked, bewildered. "I feel I must suffocate in that house! It is so hot and airless."

"True," he agreed, glancing to the sun, which even

as it dipped westward still burned like a brazen image in the sky. "It is so still, it can but be the calm before a storm."

"I do hope so," she replied, as he fell into step beside her and she tucked her hand into his arm. "This feeling of something coming is dreadful."

"Mmm," he paused to pat her hand, aware of her with every fibre of his being, but deliberately holding himself in check. "I suppose there can be nothing wrong in you walking quietly here."

"Even widows must take exercise, surely," she observed. "Although, Justin says I am not a widow, but a *virgo intacto*, or some such thing. In the eyes of the law, I must never call myself a widow if I don't want the Harcourts claiming my fortune."

"It is a damned tricky situation," he agreed. "I don't know what's to be done for the best."

"Don't fret," she replied cheerfully. "I'm sure everything will work out for the best. When I got over the shock of seeing Gervase, I knew it."

"I'm glad one of us can be so sanguine," he replied sourly. "To my mind, we are in one hell of a fix, and if we can get out of it without a lot of trouble and your fortune intact, we shall be very lucky indeed."

"You have got the glooms," she teased. "You must have more faith in Fate than this! I must confess, when you agreed to this marriage I was in flat despair, thinking we should never be together, but see how Fate has intervened!"

He stared at her, shocked as ever by her single-mindedness and her lack of delicacy. "You seem to forget, I am still a widower," he said coldly. "Neither do I see the hand of Fate in this business, more like the machinations of the Devil. If you have any sense, or a grain of maidenly modesty, you'll keep such thoughts to yourself."

Tears filled her eyes at this unkind rebuke, but she glared at him. "No, I am not a meek goodwife like your precious Libby. Plainly you have forgotten how tiresome her eternal goodness was. If I see what I want, I say so and reach out for it, and if that means I'm not meek, then I am glad of it."

"You are, as ever, and ill-bred hoyden, and I vow I am weary of your childish behaviour. Put a guard on that tongue of yours before it brings us all to grief," he snapped, stung by the truth of her observations.

Tears trickled over and slid down beside her nose. "God alone knows why my heart leaps so at the sight of you," she wept stormily. "You bring me no comfort in my fears, but like a father, continue to upbraid me for my conduct."

"A father!" he cried, indignant that he could be considered so old. Then, as her tears flowed again, his compassion was stirred and he took her into his arms, ignoring his common sense and giving way to the desire to hold her. "Nay, 'tis true, I forget the events of the day, the shock you have suffered. Hush now, hush, don't weep, you'll spoil your lovely eyes. Hush now, my darling." He broke off in dismay as a figure rounded the far end of the walk, and espying them, came toward them hurriedly.

"Oh! Mistress Selby," he said, giving Sophie a warning shake. "Is ought amiss?"

"My Lady was wondering where Sophie was," she replied, giving the girl a curious look.

Hal patted her shoulder in what he hoped was a paternal fashion, although his own senses were swimming at the closeness of her. "She thought to take a walk to cure her head ache," he replied glibly. "But, as I surmised, it really is too much for her in her present state of distress."

Sophie presented her tear-stained face to the young

woman. "My dear guardian was, as ever, scolding me for my behaviour," she said, attempting a wobbly smile. "It seems it doesn't suit his sense of the fitness of things that I should require fresh air."

Jane Selby smiled, in part reassured by her words, although the shock of seeing her dead kinsman's bride in the arms of a man who none could deny was very attractive, was still there. "Indeed, who does not require air on a day such as this? The yew walk does at least provide shade. If you wish, I could bear you company that you might continue your walk, or would you rather I made you a brew for your headache?"

"No indeed, I thank you, but Sir Henry wishes my return and my Lady waits upon it, it would seem. I bow to the decree of Fate," sighed Sophie.

"And in doing so, are rewarded, for that is thunder in the distance," observed Hal. "The storm is at hand."

"My lady only wishes to consult you as to the arrangements for poor Gervase's funeral," said the young woman as they turned about and began to walk back towards the house.

"The funeral?" said Sophie, looking surprised. "But what have I…" She stopped, feeling Hal's eyes on her face. "I mean I hardly knew…that is to say…"

"My ward, as so recent a bride, and neither wife nor widow," said Hal, stepping into the breach, "feels that her wishes can be of little moment compared to those of the bridegroom's mother. She, in her grief, must be afforded every observance, naturally. Whatever her wishes are, we shall be happy to comply."

Mistress Selby raised her brows a little at this, her ready wit comprehending the stand. "My lady views Sophie as her daughter-in-law and expects her as a widow to wish to share her grief," she said bluntly.

"As, indeed, she does, to a certain extent," agreed Hal amicably. "But, the grief of a devoted mother cannot be compared to that of a bride of a few hours. Especially one who was not a wife and cannot therefore cannot be a widow."

"My Lady doesn't see it like that," Jane replied, her glance straying to his handsome face with some admiration, for it wasn't often she met with a wit equal to her own.

"Where has been the time or occasion on such a terrible day for her to assimilate the information presented to her?" he replied, with his usual gentle courtesy. "But, when explained to her by her man of law—she does, I assume, have a legal advisor? For if there is none to hand, my brother-in-law, Justin Danvers, will be glad to explain any matters to her that she holds in doubt."

"Dury Southgate usually deals with anything legal," she replied. "Although, I'd think this tangle outside his experience."

"Outside the experience of most of us, I fear, Mistress Selby," he replied, smiling ruefully. "Who'd have thought to have witnessed such a tragic occurrence?" "Indeed," she agreed, returning his smile and recollecting his pleasant company at the feast the previous day. "I'm sure we are all knocked asunder by it."

"Yes, and you, younger, more gentle ladies must be in greater shock," he said smoothly. "If only one could delay any decisions until we all had time to recover. Alas, life must go on, come what may, and decisions must be taken. Sophie, my dear," he continued, as they paused in the dim porch. "Do you feel equal to attending Lady Harcourt, or shall I tender your apologies and see her in your stead, whilst you take to your bed with a potion for the headache?"

"If you but will go with me, Sir Henry, and my Lady will forgive me if I am lacking in any way, I will attend her now. For I would not add one iota to the poor lady's grief by any weakness of mine," she replied dutifully.

"The ache in my head is severe, but nothing to the ache in poor Lady Harcourt's heart."

Hal's eyes brightened at her cleverness, and his smile of approbation was warm enough to make Jane Selby not only wonder a little, but feel stirrings of envy.

⚜

Half an hour later, Sophie's headache was no longer assumed as the thunder rolled ominously around the house, and the atmosphere in the parlour became equally threatening.

"I must be very foolish, Sir Henry, but I fail to understand your point," said Lady Harcourt, all traces of grief vanished and her haughty face etched pale with anger.

"Your pardon, my Lady," he replied. "I think perhaps your excellent kinsman, Mr Southgate, found the topic so delicate to discuss before ladies, that he has couched his advice in rather an obscure fashion. To be blunt, madam, our ward is yet a virgin, your son failing his conjugal duty because he was too drunk. The marriage was therefore never consummated and Sophie cannot be a widow, as she was never a wife."

"You have proof of this, I assume," snapped Lady Harcourt ominously.

"We have Sophie's word for it," he replied evenly, "and the evidence of your son fully-clothed in the chair he was left in by his groomsmen."

Her eyes swept over him. "Plainly, your experience of men is different to mine, Sir Henry," she replied tartly. "I have known maids taken by men booted and spurred, as well as drunk."

"But, presumably possessed of some power of loco-motion, madam," he replied swiftly.

Jane Selby, her cheeks pink from the pictures these words conveyed, bowed her head to hide them and a small smile. This was a man uncowed by her kinswoman's tongue and haughty stare, ready with a reply, but one in which delicacy was preserved even though the point was never lost. He was also very comely looking and his smile…

"Of that one thing I can be sure, my Lady," his voice sharpened. "Our ward, Mistress Redcroft, never lies."

"Mistress Harcourt," snapped Lady Harcourt.

"A courtesy title only until an annulment is obtained," said Hal calmly.

"You seem mighty quick to be releasing her from vows taken not a day ago," she observed grimly. "I can but wonder if the rumours I've heard don't hold an element of truth."

"Rumours, my Lady, are usually sourced by gossip and ill-intent," replied Hal evenly, although his heart sank.

"Aye, and scandal. And the scandal I've heard is that she is damaged goods," Lady Harcourt snapped. "That she's been your mistress this past year, aye, and borne you a brat into the bargain. What have you to say to that, Sir Henry Westwood?"

"That the rumour is entirely untrue, my Lady," he replied, though his lips thinned a little, and his eyes began to glitter dangerously.

"If Lady Harcourt had heard this rumour so damaging to her son's future and given any credence to it, surely she would have conveyed her doubt to Sir Edgar, who would have stopped the wedding," suggested Justin blandly from across the vast chamber.

"Aye, you'd claim it untrue, naturally, but can you deny that you've taken a boy child into your house?" she cried, angry at Justin's common sense.

"I won't deny the existence of a young half-brother born the Christmas before last," Hal replied, his eyes flashing. "Indeed, I went to France personally to find my father's last child and bring him home to his family."

Incensed, the older woman waved this aside. "I begin to think, Sir Henry, that we need not look much further for my son's assassin," she cried wildly, losing grip on reality and giving way to her anger and grief. "I am told it is common knowledge that you are besotted with this pretty face and wonder that, stricken by jealousy, you killed my son before he could share the woman you lust after."

As Hal stammered with rage at such outlandish accusations, Justin's calm, logical, voice cut across the angry words. "As the guardian of Sophie Redcroft, why then, would Sir Henry have given his consent to her marriage if that were the case?" he asked. "If she were his mistress, as you claim, and mother to his child, why would he even consider her marriage to another man, when he is, as you claim, so besotted with her?"

"To cover the scandal, of course!" she snapped, rounding on him in her fury. "Do you think I don't know how his wife, your sister, died of grief over the whole affair? How his name was so blackened through six counties, how she's become a byword for a hoyden?"

"My sister died from a long and painful illness," said Justin, white to the lips now. "Her widower husband has indeed had much calumny heaped on him by unpleasant rumour, but if this were so, if it were believed by you, my Lady, I find it hard to imagine why you'd countenance the match going ahead."

"Because her son needed the money to pay his gambling debts, one assumes," snapped Hal, fury making him foolhardy.

"My Lady, I think you must withdraw your accusation against my brother-in-law, or we shall be obliged to seek legal redress," continued Justin in measured tones, totally disregarding Hal's hot words. "Much as we sympathise with the trials which beset you and the tragedy of your double loss this day, and understand how your head must be spinning with despair and dismay, such a wild and patently unlikely accusation must be rescinded at once."

"Never!" she cried dramatically. "I stand by my accusation! Let him prove himself innocent. If he has nothing to hide, he has nothing to fear. Ha! Why, my kinswoman saw them not half an hour since in each other's arms!"

"I was seeking to comfort my ward in her not unnatural distress," cried Hal tartly, turning a reproachful glance upon Jane Selby.

"What distress?" cried Lady Harcourt. "With her

own lips not three days ago, she told me she had no love for my son and didn't want to marry him."

"I meant the natural distress of the circumstances of waking to find a man she assumed she'd spend the rest of her life with stabbed by a dagger!" cried Hal. These graphic words seemed to bring home to them all the full impact of the day's events. They hung on the air between them and they all seemed to see again that stark picture. Sophie gasped and tears inadvertently filled her eyes, whilst Lady Harcourt blinked rapidly, her high-colour fading, leaving her looking strained and old.

"Sir Henry!" protested Dury Southgate, looking shocked. "Your pardon, but I must beg you regard the feelings of a fond mother, aye, and indeed, a new bride."

"'Tis a picture I feel I'll never get from my memory," whispered Sophie, as she turned to him in appeal, tears sliding down her nose. "Oh why, why did it happen Hal? Who has done this wicked thing?"

"I know not, Sophie," he gently replied. "But we shall discover him, rest assured Madam," he turned haughtily and addressed Lady Harcourt. "You have seen fit to level various accusations at me which I demand are rescinded. I am not an impatient man nor am I unaware of the distress you suffer at your double loss, but such wild accusations cannot be allowed to stand unchallenged."

"Sir, my Lady meant no harm," Dury stepped in hastily. "She…she is mad with grief, beside herself at so grievous a loss. In short, sir, she spoke wildly with no thought to her words. Naturally, she doesn't think you have anything…"

"I do, and I stand by it!" cried Lady Harcourt. "Either he or that trollop of his, has murdered my son. Where was he last night? By his own admission he was out walking. Where was she? In the same chamber. It would be the work of a moment to grant him entrance, to assist him to kill my son."

"Madam, to what end?" asked Dury blankly. "Look at the sweet lady, see her tears. If she'd not wanted to marry Gerry, she'd have said so yesterday when the minister asked her."

The older woman turned her eyes in the direction of his out flung hand and seemed at once to understand the full import of her words. Her high colour faded again and she visibly sagged. "For—forgive me…" she said, in broken tones. "My dear Sophie, forgive me, I don't know what I am saying. I cannot believe—and Edgar, too…" To the amazement and dismay of all present, her voice cracked and tears began to fall. Jane Selby went hastily to her and led her blindly from the room.

"Sir Henry, Mr Danvers, your pardon," exclaimed Dury, looking after the women in astonishment. "She cannot have…you've seen how she is…in short, she is beside herself."

"We observed," said Justin dryly. "However, Mr Southgate, sympathetic though my brother-in-law and I are, Lady Harcourt cannot be allowed to continue hurling insults and accusations about in such a manner."

"Indeed no; Be assured, gentlemen, I shall attend to the matter. I'll explain the situation, why it is impossible that she continue."

"Let her be, poor lady," said Hal, whose temper had cooled. "She has lost those most dear to her."

"Sir Henry, you are too good, too kind," the other man cried warmly. "You speak the truth. This will be the end of my Lady. 'Tis a blow she'll not recover from, I fear. Gentlemen, let me tell you, until this day, I had never in all the years I have lived in this house seen that dear Lady shed a tear."

"I fear she'll more than make up for that in the next

few days," said Hal with a sigh. "For Sophie, however, you must agree, it is a different matter. Although she'd taken her marriage vows, the marriage was not consummated, therefore she wasn't a wife and cannot be a widow."

"I see your point, Sir Henry, but it is a legal one, and I doubt Lady Harcourt's man of law will agree."

"'Tis not only a legal point, although I agree that it is important, but also one of degree. Sophie had not the time to become attached to her bridegroom. She cannot be expected to display the same depth of grief as if she had."

"Who can say how deep another's grief is," said Justin somberly. "We have had our fair share, Hal, these past few years, yet I'd not presume to judge another."

"Indeed," Hal agreed. "But, we mustn't detain Mr Southgate, he must have a hundred tasks at hand. I will merely add that we will remove ourselves from this house as soon as is possible. That we should intrude upon Lady Harcourt no longer."

"No!" Dury Southgate cried sharply. "My lady wishes all to remain. I beg you won't think of removing yourselves."

"Naturally, we shall remain for the funerals and to

support Sophie, but once both the gentlemen are laid to rest, we shall all, including Sophie, return to Westwood Hall until such time as this dilemma can be resolved. In the meantime, we have taken the liberty of moving Sophie into the chamber my brother-in-law and I were occupying, and asking my ward Cordelia Sandys to remain with her. For, I fear for her reason if she had to return to the bridal chamber."

"Oh indeed, poor, sweet lady," Dury Southgate replied with ready sympathy. "I trust you'll not object, sir, to the offer of my own chamber for your good selves? It is small and some distance away, but I'd be honoured if you'd accept it."

"You are too good, sir," said Hal. "We shall gladly accept, if it doesn't greatly inconvenience you."

"Indeed no, I can find another lodging elsewhere. It will be finding the time to sleep that I will have difficulty with," he replied with a sigh.

"If either I or Sir Henry can be of any assistance, we are not without expertise in legal matters," said Justin, with the idea that he might more readily elicit information from keeping the man's company. "You have but to say the word."

"Mr Danvers, Sir Henry, once again, I give thanks,"

Dury replied. "You cannot appreciate how grateful I am for your support, you calm common sense, in a world upturned by mayhem. In short, sirs, I am obliged to you both." ⚜

Chapter Eight

"So," said Hal later that evening as he and Justin settled into the cramped chamber which belonged to Dury Southgate. "What should we do next?"

"We must think," replied Justin, testing the mattress on the narrow bed and deciding on the truckle bed Dury had brought along earlier. "Think, and think again. The answer is there somewhere."

"So, who are the obvious suspects?" asked Hal, frowning. "Who benefits?"

"According to Lady Harcourt, you and Sophie," said Justin, making a wry face. "We must address that at some time, Hal."

"I don't think we should make too much of it," he replied acidly. "Once she has had time to consider, she'll realise her error."

"Well, I'm still not entirely sure about the Skirbeck

brothers," remarked Justin, stuffing his bags under the bed in the hope that they'd help with comfort.

"I, personally, believed them," sighed Hal. "I thought they had an innate honesty and we had more or less ruled them out."

"Possibly, although I'd not like to stand up with such a thin plea before you," replied Justin rolling his travelling cloak to form a pillow. "Their alibis work for each other, you know."

"I'll grant you they are three angry men." Hal nodded and stretched at full length on the bed. "Justifiably so, in my opinion. But I can't see any of them gaining entrance to this house to creep along the corridors and stab a man. If they'd killed Gervase, it would have been out there, in that churchyard yesterday before all his kinsfolk, the result of an unlucky blow. They were all three hot at hand yesterday, 'tis true, and spoiling for a fight—but honest men at heart."

"Mmm." Justin nodded in agreement, but still frowned. "I can't deny you are probably right, but they'll be the people the Constable and Sheriff produce, like as not."

"Yes," Hal nodded gloomily. "Their minds won't go much further than them causing a scene and having reason, therefore they must be guilty. By God this is an uncomfortable bed!" He added suddenly. "How does poor Southgate get any sleep at all?"

"Probably he is so exhausted he passes out," replied Justin dispassionately. "So, '*Quo Bono*', as Sir Charles suggested. Who benefits? Certainly not his debtors. So, I suppose, the next brother?"

"Ah, yes, Anthony Harcourt. Something of a black sheep, one gathers."

"And that amongst pretty dingy sheep anyway," agreed Justin. "I thought Dury Southgate was magnificent in his reticence, didn't you?"

"Incredibly so," said Hal. "Fortunately the servants are not quite so coy. One of the grooms has told Lawrence that the younger brother made the elder brother look an angel."

"That doesn't make for good hearing," said Justin with a grimace. "Though why you should trust that Lawrence fellow of yours, Hal, I don't know! I'd not give a groat for any fellow who'd turn King's evidence on his cronies."

"That fellow is but sixteen…" replied Hal.

"He looks twenty and is at least fifty in equity," interrupted Justin.

"He is but sixteen and was forced to work with a gang of footpads since he was ten," continued Hal imperturbably. "With his evidence, I was able to break up what amounted to an armed rabble in Rushington Wood and ensure that travellers through our district now go unmolested."

"It is popularly supposed he'd do murder for you," said Justin idly. "Personally, I'd be afraid to expose my back to him too often."

"Provided you don't irk me, you are safe enough," returned Hal dryly. "And you can't deny he has access to the sort of information which invariably eludes us."

"No, I can't deny that," Justin agreed. "I can and do deny its usefulness—but that is another story."

"So from whom would you have obtained your information of Anthony Harcourt? His mother? His sister?"

"I'd have talked to Dury Southgate. Indeed, I will still do so, for a probably more balanced view of this matter."

"And from whom would you have learned that Dury Southgate to enamoured of Mistress Kate Harcourt, and she of him?"

Justin's brows rose a little. "I did not know it was so, but I can readily imagine it is. I wish them joy."

"Don't do that," said Hal, "for there is none for them. Sir Edgar forbade his daughter to even look her lover's way, and Gervase reckoned to horsewhip Dury before a stable yard full of servants."

"Ah." Justin pulled a face. "Not pleasant, Hal, but recollect your father treated me in such a manner. I didn't kill him!"

"No," Hal agreed sombrely. "I did that."

Justin shied away from the subject. "What I mean is, yes, it smarts. Yes, one is filled with anger, fury even, but mostly that is because it's the truth! Dury Southgate is better connected than I was, but neither of us are truly gentlemen. Your father was right, I am the son of a tradesman, and having had to sacrifice his son to the daughter of a tradesman, he saw no reason to repeat the procedure."

"You are a gentleman by education and manners," said Hal firmly. "Both of which are better than my father's. Even Aunt Margery admits that."

Justin laughed. "That's only because your Aunt Margery still disliked your father even more than she does me."

Hal grinned. "Aye, but it's a close-run thing."

"What I'm trying to explain," continued Justin,

echoing his grin wryly, "is that I can understand Dury Southgate's feelings. I love Bess every bit as much as he does young Kate Harcourt. I know the despair which fills his soul, but I don't think he'd consider murdering her brother to achieve his aim, do you?"

"I don't think it likely," agreed Hal. "Any more than he could have guaranteed Sir Edgar dying as he did. But, in truth, Justin, someone murdered Gervase Harcourt. And, even if one has a sneaking sympathy for the person, it is against the law. We require proof. If Anthony Harcourt is still abroad, then although he sounds the most likely suspect, it can't be he. So we are left with the other obvious solutions."

"You mean, as long as it's not Sophie, you don't greatly care who it is," said Justin shrewdly.

"No," said Hal firmly. "I am, I hope, still on the side of justice. I know Sophie couldn't have killed him."

"I wish I had your confidence," murmured Justin. "No, don't eat me, I'll agree it's unlikely…but not impossible, Hal. You must admit that, and that she had the most cogent reasons for wishing him dead."

"Don't even speak of it!" snapped Hal. "There must be no word of it. No doubts between us! If we ever admit a doubt, they'll happily fix upon her. As we've said many a time before, we must eliminate all the possible and what is left, however impossible, must be the truth!"

Justin shrugged. "So we must talk to everyone. I'll start with Dury Southgate tomorrow."

"I need to speak to him also. I doubt very much I have any influence with Lady Harcourt, but he may be able to persuade her to speak to the minister about that poor village wench."

In this, Hal was only partially successful. Dury Southgate, when hearing of his errand next morning, raised his eyes to Heaven and held out little hope. But, in the event, he fared better than he and Hal had expected. Lady Harcourt would not deign to speak or write to the Reverend Berwick, but relayed a message via the agent to the affect that she left it entirely in his hands and that she had no objection to the foolish wench being laid to rest in a deserted corner of the churchyard if he thought fit. With this, Hal had to be content, well aware that the character of the minister, as appeared at the wedding, did not lead him to suppose he was possessed of a generous heart.

He was about to set out for his errands the next morning when he was delayed by the arrival of Cordelia's kinsfolk. Jack Hollingshead and his mother were accompanied by his own kinsman Thomas Kingscott, all brought hither by the news of the tragedy. After condolences had been properly expressed, and the matter thrashed out to their satisfaction, Hal mentioned his task at hand and presently left the house in company with Tom Kingscott and Madelaine Hollingshead, both of whom had volunteered their assistance, professing to have some influence with the minister.

Tom Kingscott was a cousin of Hal's. His Aunt Margery had been married to Tom's father, and in spite of their difference in age and outlook, they had an easy relationship which hovered on the edges of friendship without quite achieving it.

Mistress Hollingshead was a different matter. Their acquaintance was but of a few months, and the circumstances difficult. Hal had found Cordelia Sandys in a convent in France whilst searching for his stepmother and her child. Cordelia had been abandoned there some sixteen years before by her father, a Royalist, who been killed shortly thereafter. In returning her to England and seeking out her kin, Hal had caused Jack

Hollingshead to lose his property, which was, by rights, Cordelia's. And, what was in Jack's and his mother's eyes worse, he gave little encouragement to Jack's pursuit of his kinswoman as he tried to regain his lost acres.

The distance from Harcourt Hall to the Vicarage was short, and in no time they were received by the minister, a spare man with the unbending stance and fierce eyes of a zealot.

"Mr Berwick," Mistress Hollingshead took the initiative. "You see us come on an errand of mercy."

"Indeed," he replied, his cold eyes flicking from one to the other in some surprise, as he bade them be seated.

They complied and allowed her to enter into a lengthy discussion as to the horror which had overtaken the family at the Hall. And then, only when all had expressed themselves very properly, did Mistress Hollingshead broach the real reason for Hal's errand. "And the tragedy not only confined to the great," she said, shaking her head. "No, it seems to dog the village also. A young woman dead, too, so I understand!"

"A village wench, a shameless jade of no account. Don't give her a thought, Mistress Hollingshead," replied the man dismissively.

"Not a thought? Why, sir, that is rather hard," said

Tom Kingscott in his usual kindly fashion. "Molly Brewer was a sweet lass. Her father had worked for me on and off for thirty years, until he was taken last winter. I don't know his equal as a hay trusser. Aye, and he laid a good hedge. No beast ever broke out after he'd hedged and ditched a field."

"Many a good honest son of the soil breeds up a Jezebel," replied the Minister coldly. "A fallen woman was Molly Brewer. Drowned in the sin of Eve, and as if that wasn't enough, she took her own life. She'll burn in the fires of Hell for all eternity. It is a blessing her father and mother weren't alive to see it."

"If, perhaps, her parents had lived, she would still be alive, too," said Hal sharply. "Perhaps it was the lack of someone to turn to in her hour of need that drove her to her dreadful end."

"Perhaps," he agreed. "Although, where such a female could expect to find help, I do not know."

"Surely at the door of any good Christian?" replied Hal. "Most certainly at the Lord's own House."

"She had sinned!" snapped the Minister. "If she had sought succour here, she'd have been sent forth with curses and lamentations, as the Good Book says!"

"Is there no forgiveness, then, in your house for the

repentant sinner?" asked Hal, contempt sounding in his tones.

"Not without penance," replied the man harshly.

"The young woman has, by this time, faced her Maker and surely been forgiven," soothed Mistress Hollingshead. "As I understand the matter, the poor wench was much wronged. Aye, and by one who shall, even as we speak, surely be called to answer."

"You mustn't give credence to all you hear ma'am," the Minister replied. "The young hussy wasn't above leveling her finger at her betters in the hope of escaping the retribution which awaits her."

"It is a matter of some dispute, as we are given to understand," said Hal. "But I put it to you, sir, that if you are prepared to give Mr Gervase Harcourt a Christian burial, can you, in all honesty, deny one to his mistress and her unborn child?"

"His mistress, you say!" cried the man. "A self-confessed harlot and an unborn bastard? You expect them treated with the equality of one of Sir Edgar's sons?"

"Are we not promised that in Heaven the first shall be last and the last first?" asked Hal pointedly.

"You seem to assume, Sir Henry, this drab will take her place amongst the elect!" he cried angrily. "I take leave to doubt it."

"But she was a young woman, scarcely more than a child, and more sinned against than sinning!" protested Hal.

"That is why we are enjoined to keep a guard upon ourselves, Sir Henry. The Devil lays snares for the unwary," the Minister replied coldly.

"Yet, you'll bury the Devils tool," remarked Tom Kingscott impatiently. "My kinsman is correct to talk of double standards."

Mr Berwick coloured a dull red. "I do not excuse Mr Harcourt, Mr Kingscott!" he stammered, thrown off balance by this condemnation from one of the local gentry. "But you, sir, will comprehend that in such tragic circumstances and with no proof, merely this wench's claim…"

"You do not care to disoblige your sponsor!" said Mistress Hollingshead bluntly.

"Alas, we are all of this world, ma'am," he replied with a smile of a crocodile. "My personal feelings of sympathy must be put aside, not only in deference to my betters, but also that the message which goes out to my flock should not be misunderstood. The wages of sin is death, Sir Henry."

"Indeed, and the young woman is dead," he agreed.

"She has her wages, as has her supposed lover. Both are dead. In death there is equality. It is the great leveller."

The Minister looked harassed. "You make out a case I cannot deny, sir," he agreed, "if only I did not have to offend…"

"Lady Harcourt?" interrupted Hal. "Take heart, my friend, I bring you word she leaves it all to your discretion. Provided you can find a deserted corner of the churchyard, she says she has no objection to Molly Brewer being laid to rest with her kinfolk. You see, even she tacitly acknowledges her son's fault in her desire not to see this poor wench ill-treated."

The Minister closed his lips over a hasty reply, only saying after a pause: "It is against canonical law to do so."

"Indeed," agreed Hal. "But I do not believe any will raise a word of protest if you close your eyes on this occasion. The poor young woman was clearly demented, and are we not bidden to give a special care to those of unsound mind?"

"Precisely, Sir Henry," said Mistress Hollingshead. "After all, Mr Berwick, none can be so sure of the future, that we know what will come of us. The poor soul who was minister here in my husband's father's time went quite mad, you know. Yes, his wife and children, all six of them, were taken in the space of ten days by the sweating sickness. He was never the same again. He had to be locked up for his own good, and even then, he died sometime later in odd circumstances."

"There is nothing odd in these circumstances. Molly Brewer hanged herself," protested the Minister sullenly.

"Ah, but who can say what was in her heart?" said Hal. "The poor wretch may have decided to climb the tree, for who knows what reason, and slipped to her death."

"And the rope about her neck? No, don't trouble to think of a reason, Sir Henry, I can see you are set upon the matter and have engaged some formidable assistants. I merely ask why?"

"What can I say? We came here for a wedding and are surrounded by death. Must we add to the misery? I merely think to speak up for Gabriel Skirbeck, who is so distressed by this tragedy."

"The Skirbeck brothers are good Christians all," agreed Tom Kingscott. "They must be very concerned for the fate of one who they knew so well. Indeed, I understand all of the villagers are."

"Molly was to wed Gabriel in the autumn, I believe,"

said Mistress Hollingshead, nodding. "One feels for his grief, poor man."

"I see I must bow to the pressure put upon me," said the Minister with a bitter smile. "If you should see Gabriel Skirbeck again, Sir Henry, perhaps you could acquaint him with the glad tidings. Although, I'll beg you'll stress that it must be a very secluded corner of the churchyard that receives the body of this sinner!"

"I will take care to do so," Hal replied, picking up his hat and getting to his feet. "I thank you, Mr Berwick, for your generosity of heart.

"Nay sir, 'tis nothing beside your own, which is so dis-interested, too," he replied sarcastically as he escorted them to the door.

"He has a point, Hal," said Tom Kingscott, as they re-traced their steps across the green opposite the church, and paused by the stocks to look up at the tree in ques-tion. "Why are you so determined to see the wench laid to rest in hallowed ground?"

"I feel few of us are so very wicked that we can't be laid amongst our brethren," he replied. "And I wished to oblige the Skirbeck brothers. They are the salt of the earth, the backbone of this land of ours. Without such men as these, we'd struggle to maintain our positions, Tom."

"True, they are good fellows," he agreed. "Indeed, I thought Gabriel had run mad in offering to wed young Molly. I can't see him wedding at all now, he was powerfully set upon her."

"I think she'd have been trouble for sure," agreed Mistress Hollingshead. "Very flighty, was Molly, although good enough at heart. Well, Sir Henry, where is our next errand? Who else must we interview to convince them that black is white?"

Hal smiled. "Why ma'am, I am done for this morning, and you surely must be after collecting your son and making your way home."

"Oh, I am quite ready to leave Jack where he is," she replied. "I hope he is perfectly content, and it must be a weight off your mind to know your ward and the poor little widow are attended by a man of character."

Hal, who'd been puzzled by her help, now understood and nodded with some resignation. "Indeed, madam," he agreed.

"I am only sorry you can't return to my home," she continued. "But, I understand Lady Harcourt not wanting Sophie to leave and, of course, your determination to stand by Sophie."

"And to find her bridegroom's killer, ma'am," he replied.

"However, once the funeral is over, perhaps then you and your brother-in-law will come and stay with us," she added in a determined manner.

"Alas, ma'am, Sir Henry is promised to me these past two months," said Tom Kingscott. "It is a longstanding agreement at least five years old, so I don't feel inclined to give it up, having finally got him to this part of the world."

"Indeed, Tom, I shall not fail," said Hal with a smile, "if you don't mind the scandal we bring."

"Perhaps then, Sir Henry, when you have finished your visit with Mr Kingscott?" said Mistress Hollingshead, not to be put off.

"You are too kind, ma'am," Hal said uncomfortably, "but, I do feel I must return home. My children, ma'am, are motherless and will miss my presence, and as Justice I must be there for the Sessions, my leave cannot be indefinite."

With this, Mistress Hollingshead had to be content and presently they parted company in the garden, Hal to go in search of Justin. He was found, however, by Jane Selby, who came hurrying after him, having seen him from the house. "Sir Henry," she called as he entered the Yew Walk.

"Ma'am," he turned about and surveyed her gravely.

"Sir Henry, I'd not want you to think…" she broke off and stood before him, the picture of confusion. "That is to say…Sir Henry, I did not mean to tell Lady Harcourt. I did not think she would use the information as she did. I merely mentioned in passing yesterday that Sophie and you had been walking together, and that you appeared to exhibit a great deal of affection for each other." She stammered over the last, and seeing the look on his face, added desperately: "Which isn't, indeed, surprising. Sophie is a very affectionate young woman. Even in the few months we've known her we've come to understand that, and the…well… the hero-worship she has for you. She is full of tales of your cleverness! Indeed, she kept us spellbound for the best part of a week with tales of your adventures and your skill at unravelling events and murders! Tell me, sir, but…oh, I am talking too much. I always do when I am embarrassed." Her hands fluttered over her face as she smiled up at him with a guileless air.

"So I observe, ma'am," he replied with a twinkle coming to his eyes.

"Are you still angry with me?" she asked, biting her lip. "I can fully understand how you may be."

"I was somewhat annoyed," he agreed as they continued the walk. "But that was yesterday. Today I am no longer so."

"You looked absolutely furious," she said bluntly. "I felt my knees must knock together from the look you gave me!"

Hal blinked. "I beg your pardon, it was not meant so. My fury was for your step-mother, although, as you suggest, I was irritated by your seeming to run to her with a tale she had delighted in misconstruing."

"Yes," she replied doubtfully. "I fear my Lady does tend to jump to conclusions in a rather disconcerting manner.

"Indeed," he agreed, "I imagine she has often been a source of difficulty for you."

She smiled in a troubled way. "My marriage was not approved of by either Lady Harcourt or my father," she confided.

"But surely, your father had the arranging of it?" he asked in some surprise.

"No sir, I fear my marriage was somewhat scandalous, a runaway match. My father went to Ireland with Mr Cromwell, taking both my brothers with him to learn warfare, for his was to be a long stay. As you observe,

Lady Harcourt and I are not on good terms. I had a cousin from my mother's side of the family, Roger Selby, for whom I had a fondness. Only, my Lady forbade him my company, saying that he was not my equal."

"When was this?" asked Hal in surprise. "Good God, Oliver Cromwell has been dead these past seven years, surely?"

"Not quite, sir, but I confess I was but a child when I eloped with my cousin."

"Then how long have you been a wife—a widow?" he asked in astonishment.

"I was but sixteen. A bare sixteen," she explained, "when I gave birth to my son and have been widowed these past eight years."

"You have a child?" he asked blankly. "But I have not observed him."

"My Lady does not permit his presence," she replied bitterly. "Or, indeed, mine. But for Gervase's wedding, I would not be in this house, only my father willed it so. Harry and I have a cottage in the village next to the church."

"He is called Harry?" Hal asked. "I have a son called Harry. Do you have but the one child? I have two sons: Harry, who is five years old and the baby, Francis."

"My husband died within days of Harry's birth," she replied sadly. "So many years ago now. But your wife died quite recently, I do believe?"

"In November," he agreed bleakly. "Unfortunately, I was in France at the time and failed to comprehend how ill she was."

"I never understood, being so young, that Roger was sick unto death," she confided. "I thought his cough would mend and grew angered with him that he seemed so sickly and couldn't help more."

"Did not your family assist you?" he asked.

"No, we lived on Roger's farm, which was a distance away and quite run down. Once I left, my Lady wouldn't see me, and my father had not yet returned. Only when I grew sick after Roger's death did Gervase come, and he insisted on bringing me back to Harcourt."

"That is the best report I've had of the young man since his death," said Hal. "I am glad he had some finer feelings."

"Gervase could have been a good man, but he was weak," she replied earnestly. "A strong wife—Sophie— would have been the making of him. Drunk, he was a bully of a man, who gambled away his fortune. I had hoped Sophie would have set him to rights. It was my father's greatest wish."

Hal pressed her hand as her tears began to fall. "Your pardon, my dear, I forget your grief for your father."

"I would that we had had time to heal our differences," she wept. "That he could have seen and accepted his grandson! You see, he never truly forgave me for my marriage, and my step-mother encouraged him in his anger!"

"Oh, surely not!" Hal cried, a little dismayed at her sudden show of emotion.

"She did. She is a vile and wicked woman, and now she is well paid out for her evil ways!" she cried wildly. Then, seeing his face, she took hold of herself. "I beg pardon, I forget myself." She looked up at him meekly.

"No, no, don't trouble yourself," he replied smoothly, squeezing her trembling hands. "It is of no matter, I mind well how you, too, must be mad with grief."

"Only, I am not allowed to show it," she cried, sobbing all the more. "My Lady, she can be prostrate. Kate, she is treated as ever, like a petted child. Whilst I, well… Jane will do this, Jane can fetch that, Jane will undertake every disagreeable task to save others the trouble."

He nodded. "'Tis often so in a family, I notice," he agreed soberly. "My sister Mary has a fiery temper, Bess always seems to excite sympathy, and Hetta is our little pet. Whilst Jane, yes, she shares your name, Jane uncomplainingly undertakes the dull and the dirty, the tasks we all would rather forget about."

She glanced up, diverted, and wiped away her tears. "You have sisters, sir?"

"Indeed, and a brother, Ned," he said thankfully, handing her a handkerchief.

"But apart from Mary, they are, like your brothers, born of a different mother."

"One whom you dislike?" she asked quickly.

"No, indeed no," he replied swiftly. "My mother died at my birth. The only woman I called by that name was my father's second wife, a good and gentle lady who treated me as if I were her own until her death."

Jane sighed as she wiped away the last of her tears. "I shouldn't have spoken of my Lady in that manner," she admitted reluctantly. "I know she has troubles with her sons, but you see, the money was my mother's." She glanced up to him again, her reddened eyes filled with resentment and bitterness. "Sir Edgar married an heiress. My grandfather was like your brother-in-law, a member of the legal system, and my mother his only child. It was her fortune which made all this possible."

"Indeed?" said Hal frowning. "I thought this was Sir Edgar's family home."

"It was, until he came near to losing it by unlucky investments. My mother's fortune set it all right again and bought property through the war. I am left penniless, but for my ruined farm."

"What became of your dowry?" he asked, shocked.

"I never had it because I married against father's will. And now, it is gambled away, like Kate's," she said bitterly. "It's all gone to give Gervase an hour's entertainment, but I shouldn't say so. I must be grateful that he had enough goodness of heart to seek me out in my despair all those years ago and persuade my father to give me a pittance."

Hal nodded again. He was disturbed by the abrupt changes in her moods, then he recollected her grief and remembered how it felt to be newly bereaved. "How often after a death one feels remorse for things unsaid, for hasty words or actions," Hal said more kindly. "I, too, wish oh so much that I had not gone away. That I'd returned home sooner to be with my wife. The thought of Libby, so good, so gentle, dying alone and in pain will haunt me forever."

She glanced up to him, her cheek still red with emotion, and returned the pressure of his fingers. "Oh, Sir Henry, you should never reproach yourself. I am certain your excellent wife would have understood! By all that I've heard, she was a sweet creature and adored you. Her only thought would have been for you. She'd have known naught but the direst necessity would have kept you from her side."

"Indeed, you attribute me with too much…" he began, but broke off, the words dying on his lips as Sophie suddenly flounced into his vision and strode across the lawn in a most unbecoming manner, seeming to emit sparks as she walked.

"There you are, Hal!" she cried, her eyes shooting daggers as she saw their clasped hands. "I have been searching for you all over the house and garden. Sir Charles Wycliffe is come. No doubt you have been too agreeably engaged to notice, but he awaits you by appointment."

Hal met her flaming eyes, reproof in his own. "Indeed, is it yet that hour? I have been to the village in company with others to beg the minister that Molly Brewer be given a decent Christian burial," he replied, his measured tones at variance to her emotional ones.

"Oh, was she a pretty wench?" snapped Sophie, trembling with fury.

"Not in death," he replied coldly. "She'd hanged herself.

"Poor Molly," said Jane with a sigh, as Hal loosed her hand. "I knew her well, for she often helped me in the cottage. Indeed, I greatly fear it was in my home that Gervase first met her."

"Ha! So you admit you run a bawdy house, Mistress!" cried Sophie, beside herself with rage. "Mayhap this is the attraction for my guardian?"

"Sophie! You forget your manners," said Hal sharply, anger hardening his voice. "Make your apology to Mistress Selby and be gone until you can better command your temper."

Sophie gave a gasp and, having cast the startled Jane Selby a horrified look, turned on her heel and ran off to the house.

"I do most sincerely beg your pardon, Mistress Selby," said Hal, his voice echoing his displeasure. "Indeed, I hope, to one as understanding as yourself, I need hardly explain. But I cannot deny the disgust..."

"No, indeed, Sir Henry, I too was at fault," she replied quickly. "I'd forgotten Sophie is Gervase's widow. They were only wed yesterday, for me to mention a mistress in her hearing was unforgiveable."

"I doubt me Sophie would have minded that," he replied, some of the disgust leaving his face. "She was not a wife of any long standing, to be hurt by his actions, but pray forgive me, I must go. Sir Charles awaits me. I must attend him immediately. Mayhap we can continue our conversation on another occasion."

"I am always yours to command, Sir Henry," she replied, curtsying in return for his formal bow. ⚜

Chapter Nine

Hal hastened into the house, well aware that he'd been gone a good while. He expected everyone gathered, awaiting his pleasure, but found instead Sir Charles, still talking to Lady Harcourt and Endurance Southgate. At that moment, Justin entered the Hall from the nether regions.

"Sir Henry, well met," said the Justice. "I see you and your brother are both prompt, although our local men are not governed by such courtesy."

"The Constable and Mr Swarby are at this moment in the stable yard," said Endurance. "I do believe they have been talking to one of Gervases's men. My Lady, by your leave, I've ordered wine and ale to attend upon us."

"Well done, Dury," she replied mildly. "Thank you for your care. Now if you'll forgive me gentlemen, I will retire, alas, I have the headache."

"I'll send Kate to you, my Lady," replied the agent. "Sir Charles, Sir Henry, Mr Danvers, if you'll begin your discussion, I'll send a servant to find Mistress Harcourt and fetch Mr Swarby and his man."

"Well, Sir Henry, how have your investigations gone?" asked Sir Charles. "I'll not conceal from you, I've learnt precious little, other than the shocking news that Gerry was loaded with debt."

"So we understood from local gossip yesterday," said Hal. "You have proof of this Sir Charles?"

"To my grief, I have," he replied. "I've been with Sir Edgar's man of law. My Lady gave me leave to speak to him. He made no bones about it. Sir Edgar had forced his son into this marriage by threatening to disinherit him if he didn't go through with it. It seems the scamp had gambled away all of his maternal grandfather's money and Sir Edgar had no intention of letting him get hold of the estate." He sighed. "Poor Edgar, he hinted that he had a few problems—but by Heaven! I thought them nothing compared to this!"

"He certainly kept them well hid," agreed Justin coldly. "Indeed, his smoke screen was most effective. We would never have allowed our ward to be allied to such a rackety young man had we known."

Sir Charles smiled thinly. "You must be doubly glad, Mr Danvers, that you tied Mistress Redcroft's money up so tight. Gerry couldn't get his hands on it!"

"Indeed," agreed Hal. "But 'tis the character of Mr Harcourt that most disturbs us. His gambling and profligate ways were totally concealed."

"Oh come, come, gentlemen, you surely weren't so green!" replied the Justice testily. "It isn't as if you weren't offering damaged goods yourselves. Edgar thought them well-matched...a rake and a hoyden, if not worse, he said!"

Hal went white. "Our ward is not damaged goods!" he snapped. "And were Sir Edgar alive today, I'd call him to book for those words."

"Hmm...so the rumours are true then," he remarked, eyeing Hal's face. "Happen my Lady wasn't so far out in her accusations."

"Do you care to repeat them, Sir Charles?" asked Justin, his eyes narrowed.

"So you can sue me for slander? Not I!" Sir Charles chuckled. "Sir Henry's private affairs are his business. I am sure he'll be able to provide a convincing explanation for his absence from the house at the time of Gervase's death."

"You know I cannot, Sir Charles," said Hal shortly. "I was out walking to clear my head and I met nobody."

"What was your destination?" asked Sir Charles. "Did you perhaps have an assignation in mind?"

"I had neither an assignation nor a destination," snapped Hal misliking his air of tolerant amusement. "I walked to the end of the lime walk—then through the pleasure garden, until I came to the canal. I walked about that several times, as I recollect, and then as the birds began to sing in the tree tops, I realised how late or—rather how early—it was. I retraced my steps to be met in the stables with news of a catastrophe and hurried to see what was toward."

"He arrived at the house some five, ten minutes after Sophie started screaming," said Justin.

"Time enough for him to have climbed in through the window, killed Gervase, climbed out and hurried around to enter the house and come upon the scene," Sir Charles observed.

"Mr Harcourt was killed long before dawn," said Justin. "I believe I've already said the blood on his waistcoat was drying and there was a stiffening of the body."

"Yes, the Coroner who came last evening said the stiffening had gone off completely," agreed Sir Charles.

"But it is still a thin tale, Sir Henry."

"Is your alibi any better, Sir Charles?" returned Hal. "You were fleeing the house when the murder was discovered."

"Fleeing? I was returning home!" he cried indignantly, then catching sight of Hal's face, comprehended his point. "Aye…well, happen you are right, Sir Henry, like as not none of us has that good an alibi."

"Dury Southgate does," said Justin.

"Indeed, I wasn't aware he was a suspect," said the Justice, raising his brows.

"We were working on the theory of those having a grudge against Mr Harcourt," explained Hal. "Other, of course, than his numerous creditors."

"Oh, aye, Dury had a grudge against Gerry sure enough!" agreed Sir Charles. "He never let an opportunity pass to bait the poor fellow."

"And of late, we were given to understand there was more heartfelt reason for the enmity?" suggested Justin.

"What? You mean his infernal impertinence in wanting young Katherine?" he replied. "I don't know about enmity, as I recollect the matter, Edgar told him pretty smartly to put the idea from his mind. To my knowledge, he has done so. He values his position too highly to jeopardise it."

"You know nothing, then, of Mr Harcourt threatening to horsewhip him in the stable yard over it?" asked Hal.

"No, I'd not heard of that…steward's room gossip, by the sound of it, although Gerry could be very hot at hand if the need arose."

"Well, as I say, Mr Southgate appears to be in the clear," said Justin. "He drank a cup of wine with me and we retired to bed. The head groom confirms Dury was off at first light to visit a sick beast."

"Indeed, 'tis so," agreed Sir Charles. "I took my leave of him in the yard as he arrived back. He came from the east whilst I took the south road."

"Hal and I have been to see the farmers who caused the furore in the churchyard at the wedding," continued Justin, consulting his notes.

"Gabriel Skirbeck and his brothers? I know them moderately well," said Sir Charles thoughtfully. "Good fellows, all of them. Gabriel, the eldest, was with Sir Edgar and I at Worcester you know. Aye, Edgar had recently returned from Ireland, bringing back his two lads, and my boy was alive then, too."

"I am sorry to hear he didn't survive, sir," said Hal.

"Oh, he didn't die at the Battle of Worcester," replied Sir Charles. "No, he took a fall out hunting, what, six years ago now? Luckily, he'd married early and his wife had born him twins. So now I've a grandson and daughter. I miss Jamie though."

"All three vouch for each other," said Justin. "At least Raphael and Gabriel do, and they say Michael was abed, as ever."

"Aye, like as not...indeed, I can't think them guilty, not over Molly Brewer."

"They are deeply grieved," said Hal.

"Aye, I expect they were," he replied. "She was their companion from their earliest days, but you know, I rather think in the weeks to come they'll find their grief tempered by relief. A troublesome wench was Molly."

"Then we are left with Anthony Harcourt, and he, it would seem, is abroad."

"A good thing for him that he is," said Sir Charles. "A very rackety young man is Anthony! I'd not put anything past him...not even fratricide."

"Then you are back to your first suspect, Sir Charles," said Hal tartly. "Me. For naturally one doesn't consider his bride."

"Indeed, no," he agreed. "Pretty little thing like that,

where would be the need to kill her husband? If she didn't care for him, she had only to say no earlier."

"Exactly," said Hal, relieved the Justice saw it in the way he wanted.

"As for yourself, Sir Henry, I was only poking fun at you. I can no more imagine you could scale the creeper than I could! No, we must think again, gentlemen. The answer must be there somewhere. In the meantime, I will take leave of my Lady and pursue further questions about Anthony Southgate."

"It might be as well to find out where Sir Anthony is," said Justin thoughtfully. "'Abroad' can cover many lands."

"Aye, it is no more than a few hours' crossing from the Low Countries," agreed Sir Charles. "That's where he is supposed to be…in Flanders. So it's not impossible that he could be in the country, indeed, I was surprised he wasn't at the wedding. A good time to make up quarrels, a wedding. I'll ask Dury Southgate if he has any ideas."

"So," said Justin, who had been taking notes, "we're ruling out the Skirbeck brothers?"

"Well, I don't feel any inclination to proceed against them," said Hal. "I can't imagine any of them coming to this house uninvited and trying to gain entry. And as for the creeper on the side of the house we've examined it, Sir Charles, there is no sign of anyone having been anywhere near it."

"Now that is very true," agreed Sir Charles. "They stood out like sore thumbs yesterday in the churchyard. Had they tried to enter the house, they must have been even more obvious."

"So it must be someone who'd fit in," said Justin. "Mr Southgate fits in, none would question where he went, or when."

"I wonder the sweet little bride didn't waken," said Sir Charles. "But then, as you say, it had been a long day, young people seem to slumber so well." He sighed. "I don't know, gentlemen, we don't seem to be getting any further forward do we?"

"No," said Hal in a dissatisfied tone. "There doesn't seem to be any way to grasp hold of this murder. We must be missing some clues. I'm going to see if I can find out anything more from Kit Withiam, one of Gervase's friends."

"I doubt me he'll have any useful information," smiled Sir Charles. "But you are right, Sir Henry, we must dig deep. The answer is there somewhere."

❧

Taking his leave of Hal and Justin, the Justice disappeared in the wake of a servant. Justin decided to go and further interrogate Dury Southgate, and Hal went out into the garden in search of Kit Withiam. He found instead Jane Selby in the herb garden, carefully laying herbs out to dry in the sun. He paused, watching her for some moments, reminded even more of Libby in her methodical neatness. She suddenly became aware of his scrutiny and hastily crossed to where he stood in the gateway of the walled enclosure.

"Sir Henry, did you want me to assist you in any way?" she asked, looking flustered. "I came to collect some herbs for Lady Harcourt, I'm afraid the ravages of the last few hours have used up many of our simples and I must brew some more."

"My wife always brewed our potions," said Hal with a slight smile. "If I ever couldn't find her with the children, she'd be in the herb garden, especially this time of day when the sun is baking the beds, or in the early morning, if she needed the dew on them. My Aunt Margery taught Libby the rudiments, and a local wise woman taught her more, but she had a natural talent for it."

"You must miss her very much, you talk of her with great fondness," she replied, veiling her eyes. "I'm sure my potions don't compare. Indeed, Sophie made one only the other week for poor Kate, who had taken a head cold. She said it worked so well. Sophie said it was your wife's recipe."

"Yes, Libby taught Sophie briefly," he replied. "Luckily she kept a book, too, so we can still make up the mixtures as required."

"Can I assist you, sir?" she repeated, as he stood looking into the past.

"No, no, I thank you, I am in search of Mr Witham, who I have persuaded to assist me," he replied. "I thought I might find him in the garden."

"Some young men are on the terrace playing quoits," she replied. "My Lady forbade them dice. They are very bored, I think, and will be glad to be gone tomorrow after the funeral."

"I'm sure they will," he agreed. "I'll seek them out and see if Kit is of their number. Thank you, Mistress Selby." ❧

Chapter Ten

Hal surveyed the young men clustered on the terrace about a game of quoits but could see no sign of Kit Withiam. A trickle of unease ran down his spine. Perhaps he shouldn't have involved the young man, he was curiously vulnerable. Hal hesitated and then walked on to the stables. His young groom, the ubiquitous Lawrence, always seemed to know where anyone was to be found. He didn't, however, need Lawrence's assistance, for he found Kit there with another young man. They were looking at a showy chestnut gelding. Hal crossed to join them, intrigued as to what was going forward.

"Sir Henry," Kit hailed him pleasantly. "See, here is Beniston trying to sell me his five year old. He's just what I need for hunting next season, he insists."

Hal smiled. "He's a handsome beast," he agreed amicably. "A little light for your weight," he added to the other young man. "But, he would probably suit Mr Witham well. Has he the stamina for a day's hunting? He looks a little fine to me."

"He's wiry, don't you know," replied Beniston. "He looks like a breath of air would blow him away, but by God, he's a stayer, as long as the ground isn't too heavy."

Kit made a face. "I tend to hunt over heavy ground in Cambridgeshire," he said doubtfully. "I think I should probably get my groom to give him a look over before I decide. He's been with me since I was a lad, and you know how these servants are who've been with you forever. However, I sent him home this morning to warn my mother I've been delayed. Perhaps I could try him out tomorrow, Beniston?"

The other young man nodded glumly and slouched off across the yard. "I think you may have done me a service, Sir Henry," Kit said. "I don't think I care for that horse at all, but didn't know how to say so."

Hal smiled. "Good nature does need an armour, I find, so many are ready to take advantage of it. You must remind yourself every time you are in a like situation, that you are in no hurry. Indeed, use the character that you are known for, cultivate indecision as a shield."

"Why, that's an excellent thought," the young man

agreed. "They'd just accept that, wouldn't they?"

"Possibly," ageed Hal, thinking how badly this young man needed someone to protect him. "Do you have any information for me?"

Kit, who had been plainly considering new aspects of duplicitous behaviour, looked blank. "In form—oh, aye, well…no, not yet. But I am to share a few bottles of wine with one of Gerry's friends later, and I am hopeful of the outcome."

Hal's heart sank but he made an effort. "That is splendid news, but if I could suggest you drink but the one glass?"

Kit stared at him for a few seconds, bemused. "Oh I see, get him drunk, you mean? But remain sober myself."

"I find it helps to retain the information," explain Hal apologetically.

"But won't the fellow smell a rat?"

"Feign slight drunkenness to begin," said Hal. "Be clumsy, upturn your own goblet, be ready to refill his at every opportunity. Pretty soon, he won't notice you aren't drinking…and my last thought…"

"Yes?" said Kit, frowning over the task set him.

"A very drunk man will say anything, so know when

to stop plying the wine."

"There's more to this business than meets the eye, isn't there?" said the young man thoughtfully. "Yes, right, I think I understand."

"Do your best, I'm sure that will be good enough… yes?" Hal turned as a servant from the house approached.

"Mr Southgate was asking after you, Sir Henry," said the man.

"Dury? Yes, I'll be there," he replied, turning back to Kit. "Do take care, Mr Withiam, and I'll meet up with you later.

❧

Hal retraced his steps to the house, pausing to frown at the sight of a horse outside the entrance hall, sweating, with the look of having been ridden hard. He entered the lofty hall to hear voices raised and stopped short at the sight of a dusty and travel-stained young man, who was shouting after Lady Harcourt's retreating figure.

"Aye, and I am master now Gerry is dead! You'd do well to remem…" He stopped as Hal's steps sounded on the marble of the hallway. "Who the devil are you? No, don't tell me! You must be the bride's guardian. Sir Henry Westwood, is it?"

"Indeed, and you must be Sir Anthony Harcourt," observed Hal, thinking privately that the newcomer was even more rackety than he'd expected. "You have my condolences, sir, on your double tragic loss."

"Eh? Oh, my father and Gerry, you mean!" he replied, shrugging. "Oh aye…them. Well, 'tis an ill wind, Sir Henry, and in truth, there was little love lost between any of us!" He glanced at Hal's face, which aptly mirrored his distaste, and added roughly: "I'm not one of your smooth-tongued snakes like Gerry. My father cordially hated me and I returned the civility. No more had I any time for Gerry's lies and flattery. A simple solider, me, with no fancy airs and graces about me!"

"Yes, I understood you had been in Ireland," Hal replied, somewhat at a loss at this blunt revelation of his feelings.

"In Ireland? Not these past ten years!" he said. "I was but a lad of fifteen when I was last in Ireland! A country of thieving cutthroats they are, too. No, I've been in the Low Countries, selling my sword to keep a coat on my back. Ah, here is my loving mother, come to bring me succour."

Lady Harcourt, her face like thunder, entered, followed by her manservant and his maids bearing refreshment. "Sustenance will be laid out for you, Anthony, in the dining parlour," she announced in Arctic tones. But you will recollect this is a house of mourning and refrain from drunken carousals."

"*MY* house of mourning," he responded. "And if I want to drink myself senseless, I shall! Thomas, bring me that wine…Sir Henry, you'll take a cup?"

"I…erm, yes, thank you, I will," Hal replied, not really caring for the company, but determined to discover what he could from this loose-tongued fellow. Hal accepted the goblet of wine and took a seat, as indicated by the new knight. Sir Anthony tugged off his sword belt and threw it into the corner with a clatter, before sprawling over a settle. "So, the old man is finally dead, hey?" he said, addressing his mother, who signed for Thomas to remove the sword. "And dear Gerry too! Well, well, who'd have thought it?"

"Your father died of an apoplexy yesterday. The direct result of your brother's murder," said Lady Harcourt, coming to take a seat beside the empty hearth.

"Gerry was murdered? I'm not surprised! I always said he'd go in a drunken brawl," said his brother with an air of unconcern.

"Indeed?" said Hal politely. "Your brother was, in

point of fact, stabbed as he lay sleeping."

Sir Antony opened his eyes wide. "Gerry? Stabbed? Sleeping? I don't believe it. He wasn't the sharpest of fellows in a fight, but neither was he a complete novice."

"Sir Henry seeks to spare our blushes. Your brother was in a drunken stupor," snapped Lady Harcourt, impatient with the pretence.

"Tut, tut, and on his wedding night, too," gibed her son. "Poor Gerry."

"I think perhaps your mother is one to be pitied," said Hal pointedly. "To lose both a husband and a son within hours of each other."

"She's still got a son, but not her precious Gerry. He was her golden-haired boy, wasn't he, ma'am? Oh no, Gerry could do no wrong. Come what may, I always took the blame for ought that went amiss!"

"You, neither of you are...or, were, but a candle to the sun of your father," she replied coldly. "I'll not see his like again."

"Amen to that and praise the Lord!" he replied, raising his glass.

"You forget yourself!" she cried, anger rising in her voice.

"I don't forget the beatings as a child," he returned

swiftly. "Aye, nor the jibes as a man."

"Talking with you serves no purpose," she replied, getting to her feet wearily. "Spare the rod and spoil the child! 'Tis plain we did so. The funeral is tomorrow. Until the funeral, I insist you behave with decency and decorum. Your father and brother will have the respect they are due. I shall not return to this house from the church. After that time, you may go to the Devil as you chose."

"Twenty-four hours isn't long to get the Dower House ready," he remarked blandly. "But at least you'll be closer to your grandchild! Will you be taking Dury Southgate with you?"

"Endurance will do as he is bid," she replied. "You'd be a fool to get rid of him. He has served your father well."

"Aye, and himself," he retorted. "I don't want him about me. I care too greatly for my skin!" Then, as both turned to look at him, he laughed. "What? Do you not even consider him as your murderer? My, he has worked well on your affections."

"Endurance? Kill your brother? Nonsense!" said Lady Harcourt contemptuously. "He hasn't a wicked bone in his body."

"No? Yet, I swear I saw murder in his eyes when Gerry took that horsewhip to him last summer!" Anthony jibed. "Aye, and Dury hated my father, too, on account of his father losing his land. No, Sir Henry, if you are looking for a murderer, look no further than Dury Southgate!"

Hal glanced to the young man with dislike. "If you have a formal charge to bring, Sir Anthony, I suggest you present yourself and your proof to Sir Charles Wicliffe tomorrow afternoon. For, make no mistake, proof will be required, not just hearsay and spite. Now, if you'll excuse me, I must seek out my wards and discuss matters with them."

Hal hastened away, a little dismayed to find the heir to Sir Edgar's estate was so unpleasant a man. They would have trouble, he could foresee, in getting Sophie free from the tangle of this marriage. He guessed that not only the dowry, but the bride herself, would be powerful lures to Sir Anthony Harcourt. He hesitated outside the door to his chamber. He knew he must take Sophie to task for her behaviour, yet in some ways he felt it would be unwise to be too harsh with her. This was no normal situation they faced. The last thing they needed was to be quarrelling. Sophie, too, had undergone a traumatic experience and some leeway could be made for her tantrums, but this notwithstanding, she must apologise to Mistress Selby for her bad manners. On this hopeful thought, he knocked upon the door.

Hal entered to find Cordelia reading a book of devotions and Sophie sitting at the open window, staring into space. She neither moved nor spoke on his entry, although Cordelia politely put aside her book and gave him her dutiful attention.

"Good evening," he said, feeling rather awkward and not wanting to start with a lecture. "How are you managing? I beg pardon that I didn't get to come to you earlier."

"We are managing well enough," replied Cordelia with her tentative smile. "Mostly, we are left to ourselves, which suits us very well. Mistress Selby comes to enquire regularly as to our comfort and bears messages from Lady Harcourt."

"Snooping busybody," muttered Sophie crossly over her shoulder.

"And in yourselves?" said Hal, letting this go. "Your spirits are bearing up?"

"The atmosphere is a little lowering," agreed Cordelia, "with everything being placed so oddly, but we try to keep cheerful." She glanced doubtfully to the girl at the window. "We understand Sir Anthony has arrived already?"

"Yes," agreed Hal. "This half hour past. He seems a devil-may-care sort of young man, but perhaps he improves upon acquaintance." He hesitated, then, as Sophie made no move to join the conversation, he added with some difficulty: "Cordelia, I am concerned that you have been kept cooped up best part of the day. It is bad enough that poor Sophie must be so immured. I beg you will go down to the gardens and take a walk now, as it is a little cooler."

Cordelia looked surprised. "I am quite contented here, Sir Henry. I've not been sitting so very long. Recollect, I spend some hours in my cousin's company in the garden whilst Sophie slept this afternoon."

"I...I would speak to Sophie privately," he said hastily. "I will be but a few minutes. A brisk walk will save your eyes straining over your book all evening."

She smiled and rose gracefully to her feet. "You are too kind, Sir Henry. In truth, the Sisters used to chide me for reading too long, telling me I'd ruin my eyes."

"I don't think you could spoil something so pretty, but you'll give yourself the headache," he replied, opening the door for her.

"Are you always so ready with the pretty compliment, Sir Henry?" snapped Sophie as he closed the door.

He stood for some seconds, debating, and then advanced to sit beside her in the window. "You know well that I'll invariably use a soft word rather than a blow," he said blandly.

"Aye, I know well," she cried, rounding on him. "A soft word! I'll warrant it was more than soft words Jane Selby had from you this afternoon!"

"I gave her the limited comfort one can take from a comparative stranger," he agreed in the same even tones. "That's to say, I sympathised with her plight and extended my condolences."

"Condolences!" she spat. "What had she to be condoled upon?"

He looked a reproof. "The death of a beloved father with whom she'd been at odds for some years," he replied coldly.

"Oh, Sir Edgar! Oh, I beg her pardon..." Sophie blushed and looked close to tears. "I'd forgotten Sir Edgar."

"Because Mistress Selby doesn't indulge in hysterics, she has no less feeling than another?" he reproved her. "She had an affection for her brother, too."

"For Gervase?" she cried in disbelief.

"Because one's sibling does not become a perfect adult, it doesn't mean one loves them less. Indeed, one can mourn the loss of all the potential which Mistress Selby insists could have been realised by marriage to a sensible, strong-minded wife."

Sophie stared in disbelief. "A sensible, strong-minded wife?" she repeated. "I don't believe it."

"No more do I," he agreed. "But then, recollect Jane Selby doesn't know you!"

She glared at him, annoyed by his quicker wit, yet at a loss to explain herself. "I mean that I don't believe Gervase could have been saved by anybody—certainly not by me!"

He frowned. "When did you become so convinced, Sophie?" he asked. "When did you decide against this marriage? You cannot always have thought so badly of him."

"No," she sighed, and seemed to put aside her irritation. "No, 'tis true I was taken in...I liked him well enough at first. Indeed, it was only when I saw him drunk that I began to have doubts, and the more often he got drunk, the more my doubts grew."

"I am grieved that we paid little heed to you," he said. "That you could have ended up in the hands of one who wouldn't have valued you as he should."

"Yes," she retorted with a return of her sharpness. "In your haste to be rid of an embarrassing encumbrance, you were prepared to see me wed to almost anyone!"

"No!" he replied firmly. "Not to anyone. I'd have been happy to see you wed Adam Blackwell, 'tis true, had he been to your liking, but you declined. I was under the impression Gervase Harcourt was your choice."

"You know my choice!" she snapped.

"Of those available to you," he said, almost as quickly.

She reddened and looked away, tears stinging her lids. "Was it only to lecture me again that you sought me out?" she asked in martyred tones.

"No, indeed. Until now I haven't lectured you, although you know I have cause to reprimand you for your behaviour towards Mistress Selby. Not to mention the danger of your position," he said evenly.

"You are no longer my guardian," she replied pettishly, "so you cannot reprimand me. As to the danger of my position, I am a widow. I don't see any danger."

"I don't suppose you do," he said grimly. "Very well, if that is to be the tone you wish to take, I'll remove myself from your presence. But, if you imagine that a nineteen year old widow will be allowed to arrange her own affairs, you'll find you are sadly mistaken. Justin and I, concerned for your welfare and your fortune, have sought to keep you under our protection, but if this is not to your taste, then we'll depart and you can manage things as you see fit."

"I have not said I wish you to abandon me to these people," she cried, dismayed, "merely that my status means I am not subject to your authority now."

"If you are not a wife and under the charge of your husband, then you must still be a maid, and therefore under our care. You can't have it both ways, Sophie," he said irritably. "I suggest you make up your mind, and do so swiftly, before one or the other of us comes to grief."

She stared at him rebelliously, wishing just occasionally he wasn't always so right. "Does it matter either way to you?" she asked piteously.

Hal sighed and sought to stop the coming furore. "Pray, do not enact me a tragedy at this moment in time, Sophie. I have neither the patience nor the time for it."

"Then I think I'd best remain here," she muttered, blinking away tears. "If I am to live amongst strangers, 'tis probably better I do so with those who don't pretend to care for me."

"If that is your considered decision…" he began.

"Aye and you are quick to snatch at it, to be rid of me!" she cried, unable to believe he still wouldn't remonstrate with her.

"Sophie, I fail to see why I should be obliged to beg you to remain in my care, that you might continue to plague me," he replied reasonably. "If you wish to assume the status of a married woman, then you must also accept some of the responsibility. If you wish to remain in the care of an older person, you are obliged to submit to their authority."

"Oh, why must you make it sound so prosy and complicated?" she cried in exasperation.

He blinked. "Presumably because I am, as you phrase it, 'prosy' and you, by your behaviour, invariably complicate everything," he replied, with an edge to his voice.

"Do you have any feelings for me at all?" she demanded, tears spilling over.

He frowned. "You must be aware by now, Sophie, that we all hold you in affection and esteem," he said distantly.

"Affection!" she spat. "Esteem! You all? What, even Justin?"

"Indeed, Justin was saying only yesterday how much he owes you for your assistance last winter, and how he values your quick wits," responded Hal swiftly.

"Oh, hold your tongue!" Sophie cried, angry tears running down her cheeks. "I won't hear such…such nonsense! I'd sooner the truth. That it galls him past endurance that by my agency he was proved innocent."

"I didn't say it didn't!" Hal replied tartly. "There are two sides to every coin, Sophie. Justin can be galled by the knowledge he owes his life to your interfering ways, even whilst his conscience forces him to acknowledge his debt."

"And you?" she rounded on him. "Just how much affection and esteem do you hold me in?"

"What would you have me say, Sophie?" Hal returned, his face pale. "I told you I desire no tantrums."

"Then give me the truth," she cried. "Tell me what is in your heart!"

"The truth?" he snapped. "The truth is you are the very devil of a nuisance. You have been ever since I set eyes on you! You plague me past endurance, and I thought to be well rid of you into matrimony by now."

"Well rid of me?" she cried, aghast.

"Yes, well rid of you," he repeated with deliberate coldness. "You implied this marriage was what you wanted and I was forced to go along with it. There could be no possible objection in the eyes of society and I convinced myself that, if nothing else, I'd gain a measure of peace from it."

"And have you?" she gasped, horrified that his main desire was to be rid of her.

"No…because as ever, with you, there can be no peace. Even a simple thing like a wedding you complicate beyond belief. How many brides wake up to find their groom murdered, do you think?"

She shook her head numbly, her tears falling thickly. "Is this my fault?" she whispered brokenly.

His conscience smote him, for he knew well that it couldn't be, but neither could he deny Sophie attracted trouble. "Have I said it was?" he demanded, only further irked by this knowledge. "Have I come here to blame you? No, I came to warn you and as ever, we end up quarrelling! I tell you, 'tis best we part."

She bowed her head to hide her tears. "Leave me then," she commanded. "If I am such a trouble and trial to you, leave me to manage as best I can."

"No!" he snapped. "I cannot do so, I'll leave you in-

stead to Justin, he doesn't suffer so at your hands."
He stood to leave.

"I am the same with Justin as I am with you. The difference is that he doesn't care. His emotions are not involved," she observed.

He checked on his way to the door, struck by this, but carried on leaving the chamber and her tears without another word. ⚜

Chapter Eleven

Hal hastened down the stairs, intent on finding Justin and telling him he was abandoning this particular investigation, leaving him in sole charge. After all, none had thought to level a finger at Sophie, and Justin could easily settle the matter in his own time. It wasn't as if his cousin Tom Kingscott wasn't expecting him, and being at Tom's house should effectively distance him from everything and rid him of the troublesome presence of Sophie for the foreseeable future.

Unable to see Justin in any of the public rooms, he made his way to the stables. His intention was to inform his groom, Lawrence, that they should be packing to leave immediately after the funeral for his cousin's home. As he arrived, he saw Justin in conversation with Lawrence.

"Justin," he joined them, some of the irritation

smoothing from his brow. "I was in search of you. We have matters to discuss. Lawrence, my horse and baggage in readiness to leave after the funeral, if you please."

"Sir," the young groom acknowledged the order with a flicker of surprise. "If you please, Sir Henry," he added as Hal made to turn away. "That young Mr Withiam, he has been searching for you all day."

"Kit Withiam," said Hal surprised. "I've just been with him."

"No doubt he's finally discovered his wits are missing," observed Justin sarcastically. "Hal, what is this? You cannot be leaving at this stage?"

"Yes, I am," he replied. "And don't let Kit Withiam's looks confound you, he's not the fool he appears."

"Indeed, one hopes he couldn't be," agreed Justin. "But Hal, you must be in jest, you cannot be abandoning the chase?"

"Why not?" demanded Hal, his conscience touched by Justin's incredulity. "Why for must I stay? Because you tell me so?"

"No, no indeed," replied Justin, taken aback by the attack. "I merely thought that with Sophie involved…" He broke off as enlightenment dawned. "Oh, I see, she's at her tricks again is she?"

"I don't comprehend you," replied Hal with dignity. "Lawrence, when did Kit Withiam ask for me?"

"Earlier on, Sir Henry," replied the lad looking from one to the other, his sharp brain alive. "All of a dither he were, and mighty excited over summat."

"Indeed..." began Hal, but was interrupted by Justin irritably.

"For Heaven's sake, Hal, when will you achieve a sense of perspective! You cannot continue in this fashion, darting from here to there like a gad-fly! Each time we look into a murder it is the same. No method, no set procedure, merely you haring off hither and thither, until some aspect of it irks or distresses you, then everything must be forgotten or abandoned because your finer feelings are hurt," Justin stopped, aware he'd said more than he'd meant or should say before servants.

"Thank you," said Hal icily. "How kind of you to point out the faults of my character so clearly. I'm obliged to you."

"Yes, yes, I'm sorry," said Justin hastily, grabbing his sleeve and dragging him aside. "But you are enough to try the patience of a saint!"

"Pray let go my arm," snapped Hal. "I am plainly all that you say...but I see no need to manhandle me."

"No need, but much inclination to slap you!" hissed Justin through shut teeth. "Don't come the haughty 'my Lord' with me, Hal. Come off your high horse and give heed to what I say."

Hal compressed his lips over a retort. "Justin, I pray you, let me go. I have much to do," he said with studied calm. "I have my apologies to present to my Lady, my papers to put in order, and this lad to see to before I can attend my packing."

"So that's it, is it?" snapped Justin. "Sophie gets into a miff at your attendance on Mistress Selby and you're hot footing it away."

Hal who had turned away, turned back, real anger in his eyes. "Certain developments no longer require my attendance," he said dangerously.

"What, has she pierced the armour again?" Justin asked unkindly. "Got the old emotions stirring when you'd thought them frozen? Well, yes, indeed Hal, that's the ticket, you run off to your Cousin and leave me to deal with the mess here. There's only a murder to solve and three females' hearts to mend. I'll manage that standing on my head."

"I don't doubt it," Hal replied. "You are always at pains to tell me how competent you are."

"Not to deal with the petticoats!" Justin snapped. "They are your wards, not mine."

"Sophie is our joint ward, and you are my man of law," Hal retorted. "For what else do I pay you, but to settle my legal affairs?"

Justin's mouth hardened. "Indeed," he replied. "I forget my position, Sir Henry. I am yours to command, as ever."

Hal nodded and walked off, his conscience at war with his affection for his brother-in-law. Theirs had ever been a stormy relationship. Both as obstinate as mules, and, Hal had to admit it, hot at hand. He had every right to leave if he wanted, he told himself angrily. And Justin no right to protest. It was true, Justin was in his employ and it was his task to sort out the legal tangle of Sophie's marriage. Not to mention arranging an understanding with the Hollingshead family, just in case Cordelia should be persuaded to agree to her cousin's suit. Justin presumed too much upon their connection, another man in Hal's position wouldn't give such matters a second thought, and no more would he. Instead, he'd find Kit Withiam and Dury Southgate, and then continue with his plan to visit Tom Kingscott.

"Sir Henry," Jane Selby appeared before him as if

conjured up from the atmosphere. "I have been seeking you."

"Me?" he replied, a shade uneasily. "Then, Mistress I am at your service."

She smiled. "Dear Sir Henry, so kind, yet, I fear, I must appear guilty of trespassing upon your time and kindness. My Lady has sent me to ask after the health of her new daughter by marriage. For, in spite of my attempts to gain her confidence, Sophie is far from forthcoming as to her feelings."

Reflecting how fortunate for Jane Selby it was that Sophie had shown such unusual restraint, Hal, aware that he was observed from a window by the young lady in question, decided the time had come for a salutory lesson. He made his very best bow and offered the young woman his arm.

"My ward is, I fear, Mistress Selby, in a very confused state of mind," he confided, taking care to press her hand as it rested on his cuff. "I do trust you have not been subjected to any more unseemly behaviour on her part."

"More unseemly behaviour?" said Jane, her face glowing as she raised it to his. "No, indeed no. She is often, well, a little short in her replies. Curt, one might almost say. Indeed, but for Mistress Sandys' prompting, I think I might have enquired in vain, but no, she has said nothing that cannot be explained by the circumstances we find ourselves in."

He nodded. "I am relieved. Alas, such is Sophie's temperament that tantrums and sulks are almost second nature to her. If I might presume to advise?"

"Pray do, Sir Henry," she responded quickly, a slight flush mounting her cheek, as he turned his compelling gaze on her. "I know well, even after so short an acquaintance, how sound such advice is."

"Then, send a servant to further your enquiries, or get Dury Southgate to go. Or failing that, seek the opinion of Mr Danvers, but don't go yourself. To my annoyance, she appears to have taken you in dislike."

"Dislike, Sir Henry?" she cried in dismay. "But why?"

"I can only assume she is jealous of one so good, so kind and patient, so generally admired as the epitome of female virtues," he replied smoothly.

"Oh, Sir Henry," this time her blush was deep enough for Sophie, watching above, to grind her teeth in fury.

"Only look at that!" she cried to Cordelia, who had just reappeared. Cordelia obligingly approached the window and sat beside her.

"Sir Henry and…oh, Mistress Selby," she replied. "Yes I see."

"No, you don't, look at her face," cried Sophie wrathfully. Cordelia, who was short-sighted, could see little beyond blurred white discs. "Her face? Yes, she looks… she is quite pretty, don't you think? Not beautiful, like you, naturally, but when she smiles…"

"She simpers and blushes and twitters!" snarled Sophie with venom. "Like a…like a fool."

"Sir Henry appears to find her smiles to his taste," remarked Cordelia thoughtfully. "He attends her most often I notice."

"She is my Lady's messenger," snapped Sophie.

"Yes," agreed Cordelia. "But my Lady is no fool and Sir Henry a widower."

Sophie looked blank. "Surely such as she can have nothing to offer Hal," she cried, appalled at the thought.

"She is a quiet, well-bred gentlewoman," observed Cordelia dispassionately. "She plainly admires him enormously and offers him ease and companionship."

"You mean she is Libby again!" cried Sophie in sudden panic.

"Libby? Oh, Lady Westwood? Yes, I do believe I heard Mr Danvers say only yesterday Mistress Selby reminded him of his sister."

"Oh, what have I said? What have I done?" Sophie cried as Hal bent low over Jane Selby's hand again, lifting her fingers to his lips. "Dear God, have I driven him from me?"

"You do berate Sir Henry on almost every occasion you meet, Sophie," agreed Cordelia. "Did you spend the last hour quarrelling?"

"Yes...no...I don't recollect. Yes!" she cried in a panic. "Oh, what should I do? How shall I act for the best?"

"I don't know," said Cordelia. "It is so difficult with you."

"Difficult?" cried Sophie, as Jane Selby indicated the stables, and Hal set off in that direction again. "What mean you, Cordelia, difficult?"

The other girl smiled and clasped her hand. "I don't know, but as soon as you are together, you both behave differently, Sophie. He is stricter, more inclined to find fault. You, defensive and quarrelsome. With other people, he is so charming, so kind and tolerant. Look how he listens to Mistress Selby, how he spent hours this morning talking to the Rector to persuade him to let them bury that poor wretch in the churchyard. How he refused to push me into marrying my cousin, although

I know Mr Danvers wants it. Sir Henry only says it is a suitable match, if I am agreeable."

"Is it me, then?" Sophie cried, becoming more agitated. "Am I a wicked person?"

"No, of course not, Sophie," Cordelia hugged her. "You, too, are kind and charming. Look how you've helped your friends in Chawchester. How you forgave Sir Henry's sisters for their dreadful treatment of you. How little Harry and the baby love you. No, it seems to me it must be something written in the stars. You and Sir Henry are not meant to be."

"But I love him!" said Sophie, tears trickling down her cheeks. "Truly love him, Cordelia. To me, he is everything, without him my life can have no meaning. He is the reason I breathe."

Cordelia looked shocked. "Sophie, you are forgetting the Lord," she said reprovingly.

"No, no Cordelia, I am not," she returned. "Hal is my Lord, he is the sun, the moon and the stars to me. I want no other."

"Then you are wrong to set your affections on earthly things," said Cordelia, even more shocked. "Sir Henry is human, like us all. If he becomes a god to you, you will both suffer. There must be some balance, Sophie."

"You misunderstand, Cordelia," replied Sophie. "In Hal, I see all that the Lord represents. I see his goodness, his security and I love him through Hal. But I know Hal has faults, it is with the human part of him I quarrel. Oh, Cordelia, what should I do?"

Cordelia, who was frankly scandalised by Sophie's words and found, as ever, her own theology was only further confused by Sophie's, took refuge in common sense. "I'd play Mistress Selby at her own game," she astutely replied. "What does Sir Henry admire so much in her? Why, her good manners, her perfect decorum, her attention to the needs of others. In effect, you must behave as he's asked you to, like a widow. Quiet and contained. You know he loves you, Sophie, it is in his face when he looks at you, but he is afraid of that passion, too."

"You think he loves me?" Sophie cried, turning to her.

"I know he does," Cordelia answered.

"Oh, then I must go to him," she said. "I must make him understand how things are."

"No, Sophie, no!" cried Cordelia quickly. "Don't, for Heaven's sake, run after him so impetuously. Recollect my words."

Sophie frowned. "How then must I approach him?"

"Jane Selby usually comes with a message, I notice," she replied. "If you must seek him out, do so quietly and discreetly, and go with a message from someone, so as to appear obliging."

"From whom?" asked Sophie blankly.

"I don't know, make one up," said Cordelia.

Sophie got to her feet. "Yes, yes I see," she smoothed her skirt. "Do I look the part?"

Cordelia nodded. "Yes, the mourning gown you had for your guardian is quite suitable. But stay, here, put on this cap to hide your hair."

Sophie looked a little mutinous, but submitted to wearing a lace cap from the stock Aunt Margery had provided, and thus armed with Cordelia's advice, went decorously in search of her guardian in the direction of the stables. ❧

Chapter Twelve

Sophie slipped from the house and made her way sedately through the flower garden. It was here that her path crossed that of her host. He paused, his hard eyes scanning her lovely face as he made her a low bow, his earlier mood in no way improved by the vast quantity of wine he'd consumed since.

"Madam, well met. I had not looked to see you from your couch of grief. As your new brother, I must surely claim a kiss of kinship."

Sophie kept her eyes downcast but obediently extended her hand that he might salute her fingers, thus keeping him at arm's length. "Sir," she replied softly. "You'll forgive me if I do not dally, I go in search of my guardian with a message."

"Nay, how so?" he said, retaining her hand. "Your guardian? Surely that enviable position falls now to my lot. For, with Gerry and the old man gone, I am now your new head of family."

"Sir, this is not the time or place for a discussion, but in short, I am informed that as I was never a wife, I cannot be a widow and therefore not of your family," said Sophie, vainly trying to withdraw her hand.

"What, you'd have me believe you still a maid!" he cried. "Either you take me for a fool, or Gerry was one." He pulled her roughly toward him, adding impatiently: "Here now, sweetheart, give me a kiss."

Sophie, with a cry of mingled fear and annoyance, struck out with her other hand, giving him a sharp slap across his flushed cheek and followed that with a swift blow to his shin with the toe of her shoe. He gave a howl of pain and hopped off the path, unbalancing to fall on the grass in agony. "Why, you… bitch!" he cried in fury.

"You, sir, lack manners!" cried Sophie over her shoulder as she hurried on her way, her fears by no means calmed by the venomous look he sent after her. She almost ran out of the garden, afraid he might hobble after her, for the memory of Giles Durward's assault on her was ever in her mind.

The stable yard as she entered it was stifling in the

heat of the evening, even in the shade of the arch, there was no protection from the burning sun. Flies buzzed lazily about the heads of the horses, and the cat lay stretched out in the corner in the shade of the water trough. Sophie, with her ears straining for the sound of a pursuit, caught the echo of Hal's voice and ran at once in that direction. She came thankfully to his side, forgetting, in her anxiety, all that had gone before and Cordelia's instructions.

"Hal! Thank heavens I've found you!" she exclaimed.

"Sophie," he replied, his voice cold and harsh. "Why, what is amiss? Did you imagine me lost?"

"No," she replied, faltering as she met his cold stare and remembering his anger. "I came in search of you with a message, but that dreadful man, Gervase's brother, Sir Anthony, accosted me in the garden. He demanded a kiss of kinship as if I were a kitchen wench." She shuddered, much in the manner of a prudish maiden aunt.

He gave a half laugh at this. "Sir Anthony rates himself too highly to claim kinship with a kitchen wench," he remarked. "Am I to take it you declined to comply with his request?"

"Indeed!" she replied vehemently. "I boxed his ears

and kicked his shins for good measure! He'll think twice before he tries to catch me in future." Then, as she saw his groom approaching, she added: "What do you here? It wants but a few moments to supper."

His smile deepened at the visual scene she painted, but he was, in fact, still much angered and hurt by her, so he replied as coolly as possible. "I came to find Kit Withiam, who, I am informed, is looking for me. But none seems to have seen him this last hour or more. Lawrence has been to see if his groom knows his whereabouts." He paused, and mindful of his new resolution, added mildly: "Sophie, far be it from me as your former guardian to instruct you how to comport yourself, but do you honestly think such an assault will endear you to your new family?"

"Yes," she said quietly, finally recollecting Cordelia's advice on how she was to behave in a more becoming manner. "For I see now you were right, Hal. I don't want to be allied to the Harcourt family. My Lady cares for none, and Sir Anthony is next best thing to a rascal. I have, therefore, come to the conclusion I'd rather remain in your guardianship."

"Indeed," he replied sharply, with some foreboding. "Is this a matter for congratulation? I take it that you will, therefore, submit to my authority in future."

"But of course," she replied with a docile air. "Just as I have always done."

"Which is to say, not at all!" he retorted. "By the by, what was your message? Oh…what is that you say, Lawrence?" He added, as the groom suddenly called out.

"Mr Withiam's groom says he went off in the direction of Windfell Wood about an hour ago," replied the lad laconically. "But, like as not, he's back at house now, as it's suppertime."

"Most probably," agreed Hal, glancing uneasily in the direction of the woodland he indicated. "And yet, you know, I think I'll just walk that way myself. For some reason, I am uneasy in my mind."

The groom shrugged. "Will I see the Lady safely back to the house?" he suggested.

"No," said Sophie hastily, as Hal was about to agree. "I'll go with you, Hal."

"No, you shall not," he said firmly, determined, if she was to submit to his authority, she'd do so at once. "I gave instructions for you to remain in the house. Give me your message and then return there. Lawrence shall accompany you lest you should meet up with Sir Anthony again."

"What use will he be?" she demanded. "He is but a child and a servant. Sir Anthony can order him as he sees fit. I'll not go back to the house until you are there to protect me." She drew closer to him and added in an undertone: "He's a dreadful man, Hal, he truly frightens me. He's like Giles Durward…only not so handsome, of course."

The memory of her terror at the hands of the murderer Giles Durward made him warm to her a little. He nodded dismissal to his indignant groom and turned aside from the stables, taking her hand and drawing it through his arm. "Very well, I'll protect you from Sir Anthony," he agreed as they crossed a field of sheep. "But tell me, who is to protect me from you?"

She did not reply to this with anything but a look of disdain, although presently she remarked on the sorry state of the flock of sheep.

Hal grunted. "Aye, I'd not be happy with my shepherd if mine were in a like case. But, I'm pleased to see you've not wasted your time whilst with us. Plainly, you are judge of a good beast."

"Beast or man, surely it is the same thing," she replied, panting a little as the way led uphill. "One merely observes: why should Kit Withiam come here? I know he was witless, but he was hardly the sort of young man to admire nature, especially in this heat."

"Yes, my thought entirely," Hal agreed as they entered between the slim tree trunks and went under the canopy of leaves which protected them from the harsh sunlight. Hal paused to mop his brow. "How do you contrive to look so fresh and cool?" he asked, glancing to her slightly flushed face with admiration, thinking how delightful she looked.

"I'm not," she replied frankly. "I'm sweltering. Indeed, I'd like to abandon my gown and petticoats and run cool in my shift."

"I beg you will not!" he said hastily, although his heart leapt at the thought of her skipping through the wood like a nymph.

She laughed. "Oh, don't fret, I'll not put you to the blush. I know I am to play the placid widow."

"I'm pleased to see you suitably attired," he agreed. "From whom was my message?"

"Cordelia, she says she wishes to discuss her marriage with you at your soonest convenience," she said, grasping at the first thought which entered her head. "It was she who insisted I put on this gown, but it is so hot," she added as she pulled off the lace fichu Cordelia had arranged around her shoulders, revealing the lovely curve of her neck and the swelling of her breasts as she used it to fan her face. "There is so little air, and I am so tight-laced."

Hal, who'd began to feel even hotter, slipped off his silk coat and loosened his neckcloth. "Shall I spread this here for you to sit on whilst I scout round for this young fool?"

"No, I'll come with you," she replied, slipping her hand in his. "I'm still unnerved, I'll not stay alone."

"Very well," he agreed, and he could not forbear squeezing her fingers slightly. "It can't be much further now. I'll speak to Anthony Harcourt when we return to the house. It is not fit he should offer you such an insult."

"Oh, don't let him provoke you into a fight, Hal!" she cried fearfully.

"A fight?" he laughed.

"He might kill you!" she replied, clasping his arm to her.

"I am not in my dotage," he returned, with an edge to his voice. "I'll engage to take on Anthony Harcourt."

"Giles Durward nearly killed you," she reminded him.

"He caught me unarmed and half-stunned after crashing through a window!" he cried indignantly. "I'd have easily disarmed him in a fair…" His voice trailed off, as they came to a spring which leapt out from the rock between two banks, for there in a little ferny pit, was the body of Kit Withiam, fresh spring water flowing over his bloody shirt and dripping off his lifeless fingers.

"Oh…Hal…Hal!" she cried in horror and as her startled eyes took in the sword wounds and the ghastly young face with the eyes turned upwards. She felt her own senses swimming and her knees buckled under her.

"Sophie! Good God!" he caught her to him as she crumpled at his side and lowered her gently to the mossy bank, folding his coat to make a pillow for her head. Recollecting her words about tight lacing, he tugged at the ribbons of her bodice and they pulled into a knot. In desperation, he took his knife to them and cut them, releasing the bodice a little before dipping his handkerchief into the stream above the body and sprinkling the icy water over her face. The colour in her cheeks, which had drained dramatically, gradually began to return, her breathing slowed its rapid rate and, as he pressed the cold pad of handkerchief to her temples, her eyes fluttered open. "Oh…Hal…Hal," she cried, on the verge of hysteria.

"Now stop that!" he said sternly. "Close your eyes and remain perfectly still with that cold compress to your temples for a few minutes whilst I take a look at the body. No, don't disgrace us both by an attack of the vapours, if you please, but try to remain a calm and sensible woman whilst I attend to things."

Still feeling very muzzy, she obediently did as she was told, keeping her eyes firmly shut, merely muttering rebelliously: "I suppose the sainted Libby was never so foolish as to swoon at the sight of a corpse."

"On the contrary," he replied. "She fainted away when we discovered my uncle dead a few weeks after we were married, but then he'd been dead that long and the smell was indescribable. Indeed, it turned my stomach and I was violently sick myself." He added, recollecting how, in that past which now seemed so distant, his first feeling had been one of irritation with his bride, promptly followed by shame and then compassion. Today, he'd felt nothing but love and a quickly suppressed rush of desire at her nearness.

Sophie tentatively sat up, keeping her back to the corpse and laid the handkerchief on the nape of her neck. She clutched at her bodice in dismay as it gaped open. "Oh, I am undone!" she exclaimed in surprise.

"Yes," he answered absently, his attention taken with the position of the knife thrust. "I cut your laces…they were much too tight anyway."

"But they are too lose now!" she cried. "I can't go back to the house looking like a drab."

"Can't you take the bodice off and re-lace it?" he asked, grunting as he lifted the body slightly to see the exit mark of the wound. "Either that, or put my coat over you."

She cast him a sidelong glance as she removed the bodice and began, with shaking fingers, to try to re-lace the fraying ribbons.

"Can you not untie the knot?" he asked, coming with wet hands to crouch before her. "Shall I dampen down that handkerchief again?"

"Please," she stammered, weak tears filling her eyes. He did so and then returned, taking the ribbons from her and giving her the handkerchief.

"Wash your face," he suggested, his arm still sprinkled with drops where he'd splashed the reviving water over it. "I'll see if I can't release these knots. Good heavens, why do you tie it so tight?"

"To pull in my waist, of course," she replied shakily, trying to stop the tears coursing down her cheeks.

"You do not need to pull in a waist so trim," he said, intent on the knots. "You know your figure is as lovely as your face, Sophie."

"Do I?" she whispered. "None ever tells me so."

"What, not even your bridegroom?" he countered.

"My bridegroom found my person so desirable, he preferred drinking himself senseless to sharing my bed," she said, the tears falling in earnest now.

"More fool he," Hal returned. "You know how desirable you are, Sophie."

"I don't," she whispered. "Do you think I am?"

He finally released the knot and met her eyes drowned in tears. "Sophie," he said his voice husky with desire. "Don't try me too far. I am on fire for you at this very moment. If I gave way to my animal instincts, I'd take you here on this mossy bank like a brute. I struggle to remember I am a gentleman."

She smiled. "I'd sooner you forgot," she murmured provocatively, her heart singing at his defeat. "I don't mind a rustic idyll."

"Nor a corpse as an onlooker?" He suggested, handing her the ribbons. "When we meet as lovers, Sophie,

I want nothing amiss. Are your hands any steadier?"

"No," she replied, laughing ruefully and beginning to shake as reaction set in.

He took the bodice, looking puzzled. "How does it work? Oh, I see…can you stand and put it on? I'll attempt to make you look as respectable as possible… Well hold on to me! Good God, Sophie, you are enough to turn a man to drink!" She laughed up into his face, her tears like diamonds in the wavering sunlight, her lips trembling. He bent and kissed her crushing her to him feeling, as her body moulded to his, as if he had come home. "Oh God, Sophie, how I love you!" he murmured into her neck.

She gave a little cry of delight and satisfaction, and laid her head on his chest as they stood so for some minutes with birds singing all about them and the trees rustling their sweet music. Then, he shook himself and her, too. "This will not do," he said. "We cannot indulge in such joy when this poor fellow lies lifeless beside us. Come, we must go back to the house to find servants to move his body."

"Wait, Hal, wait!" she insisted. "Before we are off in a rush and this is put aside, I want an oath from you."

"An oath?" he replied in an arrested tone.

"A solemn vow," she countered. "Several times now you've held me in your arms and told me you love me."

"Five," he replied quickly. "Each occasion is carried in my heart."

"But you've not discussed marriage," she returned. "I know you are a widower but soon you will be out of mourning. I want your promise that we shall be married at that date."

He looked down into her face, his own troubled. "Not that soon, Sophie," he said slowly. "It would offend too many...and you'll not have been a widow long enough."

"I am not a widow, because I wasn't a wife," she reminded him.

"Even so, I don't think you can remarry so quickly," he said doubtfully. "Like as not, there will still be legal matters to arrange."

"If I was never bedded, I cannot possibly carry Gervase's child," she said impatiently. "That's the reason for the year of mourning, I don't see why we should have to wait."

"No, I don't suppose you do," he said sharply. "But, I'm not prepared to compromise either my good name or yours."

"A promise, Hal…to marry," she said quietly. "At a given time in the future."

He took her hand. "That I'll give right gladly," he agreed. "A promise to marry, Sophie, in the not too distant future." ⚜

Chapter Thirteen

In all the fuss and drama of getting the body of Kit Witham back to the house and all the exclamations and questions, Sophie was able to make good her escape to her chamber to sit and daydream of the future. Hal, by contrast, found himself yet again in the thick of things, and supper was well over when he heard his groom was asking for him.

"Well, Lawrence, what is it?" he asked, going to the side door nearest the stableyard.

"I wondered exactly what time you wanted me to be ready, Sir Henry," replied the boy, his eyes sharp as he viewed his master.

"Time?" repeated Hal blankly.

"You said to make ready to leave after the funerals, sir," the boy reminded him.

"Leave? No, don't be ridiculous...Kit Witham is

dead. Killed most probably as I searched for him! I cannot leave now."

"Oh," said the groom. "I didn't think that need make no difference."

"But of course it does," cried Hal crossly. "It's probably my fault he was killed! He was asking questions for me."

"Aye, Robson, the head groom, said he were poking about asking a lot of fool questions," he agreed. "Seems he found summat out, too, by what that there lad of his says."

"Kit's groom?" Hal asked quickly. "What does he say?"

"That he'll not open his mouth to you!" grinned the lad. "That he's too fond of life to be seen in your company! He is off at first light back to his old home."

"See what you can find out for me, Lawrence, before he leaves," Hal said quietly. "I'll pay, if necessary."

"Aye? Same terms as afore? I'll be keeping my ears open...and my eyes. I'd no wish to be skewered like Fool Withiam."

Hal nodded and returned to the hall where a lively discussion between Sir Charles, just arrived, Justin and Dury Southgate was in progress. He avoided Justin's glance, however, and went to join Cordelia as she sat sewing long seams, saying as he took a seat beside her: "Cordelia, I understand from Sophie you wish to discuss the matter of your marriage with me."

"Marriage?" said Cordelia blankly, for her thoughts were miles away.

"Yes," he replied with a patient air. "When Sophie sought me out earlier she brought me a message from you…did she not?"

Realising what had occurred, Cordelia felt she only had herself to blame. "Oh, yes…" she agreed faintly. "Only this last dreadful occurrence sent it from my head."

"And no wonder," he agreed. "I am greatly grieved, but that is no reason for not discussing your marriage. I must confess, I was pleased you wish to talk over the matter. I had begun to be afraid that you were avoiding the issue."

"Oh," said Cordelia in a small voice, realising this was exactly what she had been doing. "Oh, no."

"Indeed," he agreed warmly. "I need not have feared. You, I know, I can trust to do the right thing."

"Yes," she said faintly again.

"Yes," he smiled briefly at her and, detecting from

her expression that all was not as well as he wished, he added hastily: "Don't think I am not fully alive to the courage of your decision. 'Tis no mean thing to make such an alliance, believe me, I know. My own was such a marriage of convenience as the saying goes."

"Your own marriage?" said Cordelia in surprise.

"Yes, indeed," he said smiling brightly again. "I met my late wife, Libby, but a few days before our wedding. To speak plain, I married at my uncle's command, to secure the inheritance, and I'll not deny I was glad to do so. I was a penniless returned exile, heir to a ruined estate, my prospects were grim indeed. The offer my uncle made was a godsend and I never regretted taking the step which made my fortune."

"And your wife?" said Cordelia. "Did she never regret it either?"

He looked disconcerted. "She never gave me cause to believe…obviously there were times…but then, even… marriage isn't a bed of roses, but when all is said and done…"

"Yes?" she asked as he broke off, looking uncomfortable, his face pale. "I cannot speak for another," he said stiffly. "Especially one no longer with us. I only know I did my best to be a good husband, and I hope it is to my credit that mostly she was happy."

Cordelia, realising that it was not that long since his wife's death, felt guilty at causing him pain. "Indeed, so everyone says," she assured him gently.

"But, living as you have these past six months in my home and Sophie's company, you cannot fail to be aware of the true facts." He added, with the painful honestly that she found to be his most endearing trait. "I did my best, but it was not good enough. I wish you better, and I think, with your training, and your unselfish dedication to what you perceive as your duty, you'll succeed where I failed. I know that when you undertake to marry your cousin and right the injustice done to him by the turn of events, you'll not fail to live up to your vows."

"An injustice?" she faltered. "Is that how you see it?"

"Yes," he agreed decidedly. "What else can we call it? Yes, I suppose his father, your father's cousin, was looking to his own best interests when he bought up your father's estates and paid off his debts, but would any of us do any different? And at least the land stayed within the family, so to speak. Let us be thankful that they did, for they have improved it immensely, that is plain to the eye. Many a good estate has been ruined by the ill management of these fellows from Cromwell's army who had the pick of the King's land, that would indeed have been a tragedy. No, the property has been well looked after, by both father and son. For their own end, 'tis true, but there has been no nasty legal quibble. Jack Hollingshead came prepared to return it, provided we had proof of your parentage. All he has asked was the right to woo you, and you have been very properly sensible of his delicacy of feeling, which has, in the end, triumphed. It is the most sensible answer to a difficult situation and, as I said to his mother only a few days ago, I was sure, if you were not pushed into it, you'd come to it of your own accord. You are a good, sensible girl who knows not only her duty, but her own best interests."

"Yes," agreed Cordelia, numbly.

"Exactly," he said, sensing somehow she was wavering on the verge of either tears or a decision. "But see how everything is coming good."

"Good!" repeated Cordelia. "Good? When Sophie's husband has been murdered and now that poor young man has been slaughtered too!"

"Ah, now you mustn't let unrelated events cloud your judgement," he said hastily. "These things, these quite dreadful occurrences, are nothing to do with you, except that your companion is involved."

"My friend," she corrected. "Sophie is my friend. My only friend," she added mournfully.

"Indeed," he agreed. "It has been a great comfort to Mr Danvers and I that you could share this companionship at such a difficult time for you both, and I am certain your friendship with Sophie will endure for many years to come. But don't think her your only friend. I, too, would make such a claim, and my aunts and sisters. You may lack a family, in many senses, Cordelia, but we'll always stand your friends."

"Oh, indeed, and thank you, Sir Henry," she leaned forward impulsively and clasped his hand. "I didn't mean to sound ungrateful, and indeed I am not unmindful of your great generosity, your own devotion to duty. Why, many a man might have indeed have left me to my fate…"

"Now, if all you wish to do is to applaud the actions that any man would have made, then I have no compunction in interrupting you. I can't tell you how pleased I am by this affair. Why, it will go a long way to compensating us for all this botheration before us. I can't wait to see young Jack's face when he knows he's been successful."

"But you can't be thinking of saying anything, Sir Henry!" she cried in dismay.

"I was…why not?" he replied "Oh, I see! The circumstances."

"Indeed," she cried, glad to clutch at any straw, although it had not occurred to her.

"How like you, my dear, to think of another's pain," he said kindly. "For although it is plain Sophie doesn't care greatly, it is hardly the time for such an announcement as far as the Harcourt family are concerned."

"They would be very shocked, I think," she ventured. "And Jack isn't one to keep his jubilation to himself if he were told privately."

He agreed, frowning. "However, his mother is a woman of impressive discretion and one who has obliged me. A few words to her, perhaps?"

"I beg you will not, Sir Henry!" she cried earnestly, then, as his frown deepened and suspicion entered his eyes, she added: "Only, think how it should look…so thoughtless and care for nobody!"

"There is much in what you say," he agreed, thinking privately that he needed to get her wedded as quickly as possible before she could think of changing her mind.

"Very well then, we'll say nothing of it for the moment. Indeed, we'd be hard put to do so with this latest development. Ah, forgive me, Cordelia, I see my good brother-in-law beckoning to me. I must attend this council of war." He glanced to her warily. "You look fatigued, my child, you will not be missed if you seek your bed."

Cordelia needed no second bidding. Tidying away her needlework, she hastened from the chamber, merely pausing to curtsey in their general direction. Hal, having seen Cordelia depart, crossed to join the discussion going forward.

"Sir Henry." Sir Charles cast a sharp look at the younger man. "Your man of law tells me you discovered the latest corpse in company with the little widow."

Hal stiffened slightly, aware of something in the man's tone which was no longer cordial. "Yes, I came across Mistress Redcroft shortly after she'd had the pleasure of meeting Sir Anthony. It appeared a period of calm would be necessary to return her spirits to some equanimity after the encounter, so I took her with me in my search of poor Mr Withiam."

Sir Charles' eyes goggled. "He upset her?" he asked incredulously.

"Rather more than upset," replied Hal tersely. "I de-

cided a separation was necessary for all if there wasn't to
be an unseemly quarrel in a house of mourning."

Sir Charles looked mortified. "Anthony really is a
scoundrel!"

"Thank Heaven none of this came to my Lady's ears!"
cried Dury. "She has more than enough to bear."

"Yes," agreed Hal.

"What took you in search of Mr Withiam, Sir Henry?" asked Sir Charles, his eyes sharp again. "Had you
some notion he'd been harmed?"

"None," replied Hal quickly. "I had a message from
Kit via my groom, who said he'd gone in the direction
of Windfell Wood. If I'd thought he'd been harmed, I
would not have kept Mistress Redcroft with me."

"I am surprised you did anyway," said Sir Charles.
"She should have remained with the women."

"The house is like an oven," said Hal shortly. "She
wanted to walk in the shade, to come to terms with
the dreadful experiences of the last few days. I probably
should have returned her to the house and the women.
However, the prospects of doing so accompanied by
hysteria made me choose the more cowardly course, for
which I was paid out. The tears came on finding the
corpse of the young man."

"A shock for you, too, Hal?" asked Justin, his fine nose detecting something amiss.

Hal hesitated. "Rather worse than that," he replied. "I'd spoken more than once to the young man since his friend's murder. He was a good lad at heart. I feel responsible for his death, for asking for his assistance. The need is doubled now to find the monster who has caused this mayhem."

"Mayhem indeed!" agreed Sir Charles. "Who do you think we should be looking at, Sir Henry?"

Hal paused thoughtfully. "I know none of these people enough to judge, Sir Charles. Your knowledge is far deeper."

"Going back to our original conversation," said Justin quickly, "Sir Anthony benefits."

"Sir Anthony was still in the Low Countries," said Sir Charles.

"Was he?" asked Justin. "Yet he arrived here today… the day after his brother's wedding."

"He said he got drunk and missed the tides," said Dury, as if in explanation.

"I've no doubt he got drunk, but not necessarily in Flanders," said Justin. "You need to find the master of the ship who brought Sir Anthony home, Sir Charles.

I think he has been in England more than just the one day."

"Yes," agreed Sir Charles. "I'll send my man to seek him out at the port. But you, Sir Henry, who do you think the most likely candidate? I am given to understand you have experience in these matters."

"Then I am inclined to agree with my brother-in-law," said Hal. "But, we need proof, and the members of this household need protection."

"Yes, I see your point, Sir Henry. I will call for Jem Styles, the constable from the village. He can take up a position in the hall overnight. Meanwhile, gentlemen, the ladies must be reassured but told to keep each other's company at all times," concluded Sir Charles.

⚜

Cordelia, meanwhile, had discovered Sophie in their bedchamber. "Oh, Cordelia, I am glad you are come!" cried Sophie as she entered. "I vow, I am weary of these four walls! Oh, that we could pack our bags and leave! I long to be back at Westwood, to be free of these prosy people! Why…what is it?" she added, as Cordelia looked fit to cry. "Surely there was nothing wicked in what I said!"

"No...no, indeed, no," Cordelia replied, unable to stop her tears. "Yes, I'm sure you must wish to be gone from this place."

"Cordelia, what is amiss? Why do you weep!" cried Sophie, coming to her side and embracing her. "Why, I've never seen you shed a tear before, not with all that has befallen you."

"Nothing ever did befall me before," she replied though her tears. "I see that now. You said the real world was different, Sophie, and you were right!"

"But what has occurred? Oh, Cordelia, you've never fallen foul of that Anthony Harcourt!" she cried in horror, knowing her friend was in no way equipped to deal with such a man.

"Sir Anthony...no!" she replied. "Why should he be a trouble to me?"

"Because he's a...a scoundrel!" Sophie said, hesitating over what word to say. "Never be alone with him, Cordelia, he is no gentleman."

"Oh, I see," Cordelia smiled a little through her tears. "Rather like the priest at Saint Sauvy."

Now it was Sophie's turn to look shocked. "Oh! You mean that..."

"That nuns have similar problems? Yes!" she laughed,

and then began to cry anew.

"Oh, Cordelia, what is wrong?" Sophie came to clasp her hands in comfort.

"Sir Henry..." began Cordelia, choked by her tears.

"Hal!" cried Sophie, stiffening, her heart suddenly in her mouth. "Never say Hal has made advances!"

"No!" Shock now stopped Cordelia's tears. "Oh, Sophie, how can you say such a thing! Sir Henry is a gentleman. Besides he loves you, he just told me so."

"Yes, he told me so too," said Sophie with satisfaction in her voice. "Oh, Cordelia, I am so happy!"

"And I am so miserable!" she wept.

"But why?" asked Sophie in astonishment. "Never say you love him, too, Cordelia!"

"No! No, of course not," she said impatiently. "At least, not in the way you do. No...it's that I've said I'll marry Jack Hollingshead."

"Marry Jack? Why?" cried Sophie in dismay.

"Because Sir Henry seemed to think that's what I wanted to discuss with him," she replied. "He was so very good and kind, he spoke of his own marriage and said he aware of my courage and sense of duty and applauded my good manners!"

This last sent her off into a fit of weeping, whilst Sophie

sat stock still in astonishment, realising her thought-lessness had led to this catastrophe. "But Cordelia, you don't care for him, do you?" she asked tentatively.

"No!" wailed Cordelia. "I don't like him at all!"

"Then what's to be done?" asked Sophie in dismay. "Have you told Jack?"

"No...I managed to stop Sir Henry doing that. I said the circumstances were wrong."

"Oh, well done!" cried Sophie in admiration. "That was quick-witted of you. Well, it's not a problem then. We'll tell Hal you've changed your mind."

"I can't!" she wept. "I can't, Sophie, he was so pleased, so happy something was going right. He's so upset by all this trouble and now with that poor young man killed, too, I can't add to his troubles by being a silly little fool. He said I was a sensible woman and that he knew he could rely on me."

"As opposed to me, I suppose," remarked Sophie. "Yes, I can see what you say, Cordelia, but my dear, this is important. You say you don't like Jack Hollings-head...yet you think to marry him?"

"Perhaps it won't be so bad. Sir Henry said it wasn't so bad. That he only met his wife a few days before his wedding. That it was necessary to mend his fortunes. At least I'll get my home back this way," sniffed Cordelia.

"Not so bad?" echoed Sophie. "Cordelia, this is marriage...forever!" Then, as the other girl shook her head and began to mop up her streaming tears, she added: "Cordelia, have you ever kissed a man?"

"No!" she said indignantly.

"Oh, dear heavens...Cordelia, do you know what is expected of a woman in marriage?"

Cordelia blushed. "No, I know one must be his helpmeet, and companion, to take care of his body and soul..."

"And to bear a man's children," interrupted Sophie.

"Yes..." faltered Cordelia.

"Do...do...dear heavens, there is no delicate way of putting this! Cordelia, do you know what happens?"

"I...I know woman must endure much," she said, shamefaced. "That this is our punishment for the taking of the apple in the Garden of Eden."

"Oh, nonsense!" cried Sophie crossly, and in a few pithy words told the other girl exactly what marriage meant.

Cordelia turned as pale as she'd been fiery red before. "But how can...oh, dear God, Sophie, no wonder you were so afraid at your wedding!"

"Yes…exactly. Now you've agreed to do exactly the same thing, only with Jack Hollingshead, whom you cannot like."

"But I…I don't dislike him," she stammered. "And he is my kin. Sir Henry said it was a just solution to the problem of my returning to claim the estates."

"Bother the estate, Cordelia! You can't think of going ahead with it!" said Sophie. "Not when you patently don't like your cousin."

"I…I don't dislike him," she repeated miserably.

"But you still don't like him," Sophie emphasised.

"Sir Henry says love and respect come with time," she returned quickly. "Anyway, I have said I will, so I must."

"No, you must not," said Sophie with equal quickness. "Cordelia, this is very wrong! Why, what would Adam say?"

"Adam, why should he say anything?" returned Cordelia sharply. "Mr Blackwell has nothing to say about my concerns."

"Perhaps not, but he has a lot of interest…or hadn't you noticed?" Cordelia glanced away, her face taught. "Mr Blackwell is an agreeable acquaintance, I'll agree, who takes an interest in most matters."

"Oh Cordelia, he's been head over heels in love with you these past three or four months, you know he has!" said Sophie impatiently. "And I thought you felt the same about him."

Cordelia reddened slightly. "I...I have a liking for Mr Blackwell," she admitted cautiously. "His manners are such that one cannot but help but admire him."

"Indeed, I do myself," agreed Sophie. "But never, even when I thought of marrying Adam, did I jump at the sound of his voice. Nor gaze longingly at him when he visited. Nor hang on to his very words."

"I don't do that. Do I?" she cried turning in appeal to her. "Oh, pray Sophie, don't tell me I have been immodest! I would hate to think I have appeared unmaidenly."

"You are a darling!" laughed Sophie. "I know, for Adam told me so."

Cordelia blushed with pleasure. "Truly, Sophie?" she whispered.

"Truly," she replied, smiling. "Now, knowing this, do you still say you'll marry Jack Hollingshead?"

Cordelia's shoulders sagged in despair. "I must. Sir Henry expects it," she replied, looking away, tears filling her eyes.

"Cordelia!" Sophie grabbed both her wrists and made her look at her. "Cordelia, have you dreamed of Adam's embrace, his kiss?" Then, as the other girl looked away in confusion, she added brutally: "Well, think now of Jack Hollingshead's arms about you…his wet lips on yours…exactly!" she cried as she felt Cordelia shudder in horror. "That's what it will mean."

Cordelia, blinded by tears, pulled away. "Don't… don't!" she cried. "Have pity, I must marry him, I can't let Sir Henry down." Cordelia ran sobbing from the chamber.

"Bother Sir Henry!" said Sophie to herself. She sat for a space staring after her friend, wondering what to do for the best. An appeal to Hal, she hastily put aside, knowing that he'd think it none of her affair and be angered by what he deemed her interference. Then, suddenly, her brow cleared and a smile curved her lips. She nodded once or twice, and then moved across to the table set in the window on which stood Justin's pens and papers. Selecting a quill at random and a sheet of blank paper, she drew the inkwell forward and fell into a reverie as she considered what to write. ✤

Chapter Fourteen

Sophie, with a shawl cast over her bright yellow curls in the hope of disguise, glanced about the stable door as the sun rose over the yard, and caught the eye of Lawrence, Hal's young groom. "'Tis safe enough, Mistress Sophie," he said with a grin. "'Tis nobody here but me and Mr Blackwell."

"Adam!" she cried in delight. "I can't believe it! Only wrote a letter to you last evening! I am so pleased to see you! Surprised, of course, but so pleased! I was amazed when the maid gave me your note."

He took her hand in his massive fist. "I'm very sorry for your tragic loss, Mistress Harcourt," he said formally.

"Don't be," she replied candidly. "I've no doubt in my mind it was all for the best. Although it was the most dreadful shock at the time."

"It must have been," he agreed, rather taken aback as she led the way to some hay bales and sat down.

"But you don't say, what do you in this part of the world? I was so amazed to get your note. I thought you a hundred miles away."

"No, I have been visiting some distant cousins in Cambridgeshire and thought, whilst in the area, I'd ride on to visit Bickmarsh Hall and call on Mistress Sandys. But, I was told she was here for the wedding, which of course my own sense would have told me had I thought about it."

"Indeed it should," she agreed, her eyes lighting up at this evidence of his continuing interest in Cordelia, the Cambridgeshire border being some miles away. "And I am piqued that you could be in the area and not think to come to my wedding, Adam."

He looked disconcerted. "Oh, yes, well, Sophie... Mistress Harcourt, I should say, but well...I didn't think to be welcome," he said awkwardly.

She covered his hand with her own more slender one. "You would always be welcome, Adam, wherever I am," she said seriously. "Whether married or single, wife or widow, my friends are always welcome."

He smiled crookedly. "I am honoured to be viewed as

such, Mistress Harcourt."

She grimaced. "Not that odious name your lips, please Adam! Justin and Hal tell me I must revert to being Mistress Redcroft, but you call me Sophie as you've always done. Let me tell you why you are doubly welcome at this moment in time." She proceeded to outline in some detail the various problems besetting them, dwelling mostly upon Cordelia's unhappiness, and Hal's gentle pressure for her to marry her cousin.

Adam sat silent for a few moments, digesting these facts, a frown marring his brow. "You think she might marry Mr Hollingshead merely to oblige Sir Henry?" he asked in depressed tones.

"Not merely to oblige him, although I can't deny that which Cordelia perceives to be her duty does hold a great deal of sway with her, but mostly from the lack of an alternative."

"Lack of an alternative?" he repeated.

"Having refused to take the veil," said Sophie. "She is seen as desiring marriage."

"Yes," he agreed. "Yes, but she is an heiress, she can surely take her time."

"Heiresses, and I should know," said Sophie bitterly, "are never allowed to take their time. There is always somebody who knows of an excellent match for them."

He nodded gloomily. "True, but you were not pushed into this marriage, Sophie."

"No, I wasn't," she agreed. "My reasons were…are unimportant now, 'tis Cordelia I am anxious about."

"Aye, it's difficult to know what to say," he replied.

"No, Adam, it's not," she retorted impatiently. "Or are you like Hal, forever blowing hot and cold."

"What has this to do with Sir Henry, save that he is her guardian?" he asked suspiciously.

"Cordelia has nothing to do with Hal, 'tis I who… no, never mind that, Cordelia is the one we discuss. Adam, do you love Cordelia?"

He looked taken aback and, to his annoyance, found himself blushing. "I, well…that is to say, er, I was given to understand, mostly by the announcement of your betrothal, that you…no, I…that we, no not we…"

"Adam!" she laughed. "Oh Adam, I'm not hinting that you jilted me! Far from it. But I know from almost the first time you set eyes on Cordelia you were taken with her, and she you."

"Was she?" he asked quickly.

"Mistress Sandys was…impressed by you, yes," she laughed to see how eagerly he snatched at her words.

"But, recollect you were but the third man she'd ever met."

"Oh yes, of course," he said, reverting to his former depression.

"Adam, I am teasing you!" she cried. "Believe me, I'd never seen a more obvious case of love at first sight than when Cordelia set eyes upon you. Granted, she was young and impressionable...no, no, 'tis a jest."

"Pray don't, Sophie," he said grinning ruefully. "My heart is battered at the best of times and surely you shouldn't be laughing."

"No," she sighed and made a face at her gown of mourning. "Although I can't tell you of the feelings of relief I have."

"Relief?" he repeated, shocked. "But I thought the marriage was your choice, Sophie."

"Oh, it was," she agreed. "But you know what a fool I am, Adam."

"I know you can be hasty," he agreed.

"Yes," she sank her chin to her hand wearily. "I was so cross back at Christmas when Aunt Kingscott made me come here with Cordelia. I mean, I was happy enough to bear Cordelia company, but Mistress Kingscott was so blatant with her intentions to see me married, and

Hal so determined to let it happen, that I thought I'd teach them both a lesson. So, I encouraged Gervase's advances."

She looked rueful. "It worked wonderfully, Mistress Kingscott was beside herself with glee, and I thought I'd really show Hal, but I failed. He didn't care."

"So you were trapped?" said Adam with sympathy.

"Yes, and then I was really foolish. Instead of keeping my head, I decided to go on with it. I was so angry with Hal that I thought I'd be done with him. That if he cared so little for me, I may as well marry Gerry, who seemed pleasant enough."

"You'd really show Sir Henry, eh?" smiled Adam.

"Exactly," she said. "Only, once I agreed to marry him, Gerry changed, and I didn't like the change. It was as if he saw me as his possession, and I'd no intention of letting that happen."

"So didn't you tell Sir Henry or Mistress Kingscott?" he suggested.

"Yes, and didn't she fly into a rage! There wasn't one incident of our previous acquaintance she didn't rake up, examine in detail and prove that I had accomplished with the sole idea of bringing infamy and disgrace to the Westwood family."

"Oh dear," he said inadequately. "And Sir Henry?"

"He was distant," she replied, tears filling her eyes. "Distant and cold, he still is, sometimes, I never know where I am with him."

"Perhaps he felt abandoned?" Adam suggested diffidently, with some fellow feeling. "If you recollect, you had announced your intention of marrying Sir Henry, initially."

"I may have done so, but I was greeted with so little enthusiasm, that I was humiliated. And he was so pleased that I was to marry Gerry. He was plainly itching to get me off his hands."

"And now?" he asked curiously, for he'd not truly understood her attraction with the stern Justice, nor his with her.

"He's more concerned that I don't get accused of murder than anything else," she said. "Although he said we shall be married at some time in the future."

"Accuse you of murder, the bride?" he laughed.

"It was my paper knife," she rejoined. "I found Gervase dead."

"Aye, so I heard," he replied, wondering if she had any idea of the rumours which were abounding, and suddenly feeling a measure of sympathy for Mistress Kingscott.

"What was Mistress Kingscott's reaction?" he asked mischievously.

"Justin says it will probably be the death of her," she replied dully. "Indeed, she has frequently predicted I would be the death of her many times these past six months."

He smiled faintly. "And now?" he repeated.

"Now, I don't know," she sighed. "Justin—Mr Danvers—says I'm not a widow, because I was never a wife. Gervase's family insists I must be, because they want my fortune. Sir Henry says I must decide for myself, either I am to remain in his care and so submit to his authority, or give myself over to the Harcourts and obey them. I thought a widow was allowed to choose for herself!"

"My dear stepmother always insisted it was the best position for a woman," he agreed. "The dignity of marriage without the inconvenience of a husband, she always declared. Although, I notice she never remained a widow for more than a few months."

"Indeed, how is dear Mistress Blackwell? Sally Rose, the seamstress in Chaucester, hasn't mentioned her in her letters in ages," said Sophie, diverged from her main object.

"Now, that does surprise me," he replied. "I feel certain her next letter will mention Mistress Blackwell, for Susanna is to have a child."

"A baby!" cried Sophie. "Your dear stepmother?"

"Yes, she is not so very old, you know," he explained. "A little old, mayhap, for childbirth, but at thirty-six she is not too old."

Sophie nodded, thinking privately this was very old indeed. "I must write to her and wish her well, but we mustn't be diverted from our purpose like this. Time is short, at any moment someone may arrive and say I shouldn't be talking to you."

"What is our purpose, Sophie?" he asked with some foreboding.

"Why, to get you and Cordelia married at once, of course!" she replied.

"Married?" he repeated, his jaw dropping.

"Yes, you can't believe how fortuitous your arriving here like this is. Only last evening I wrote to you and got Lawrence to take it to the post house for me. Then, to hear that you were here in person, but I thought it must be a least a sen'night before you arrived." She noticed suddenly the glazed look in his eyes. "Why, what is amiss?"

"Sophie, do you have an idea of…well, of what is

being said?" he asked slowly, then, as it was her turn to stare, he answered himself: "No, of course you haven't, you are too innocent entirely. But to hear you plotting another wedding like this, well…"

"Don't worry, Cordelia won't stab you!" she replied, angry that he could think her capable of stabbing anybody. "Yes, I do know what is being said by everybody. That I am bad luck, a Siren who lures men to their death, an enchantress who has no heart. I've heard them all! You see, Mistress Kingscott isn't alone."

"Sophie, I'm sorry," he caught her hand and raised it to his lips as a tear splashed onto her gown. "I didn't mean to hurt you, but you must see how it looks." Then, as she nodded, averting her face, he continued: "Come, tell me more. Tell how I can persuade Cordelia to marry me."

"I know she wants to, Adam," she said earnestly. "Just as you want to marry her, don't you?"

"It is my heart's desire," he said simply. "The stuff of dreams."

"No, Adam, we must make it a reality," she said, her tone sharp. "Not a dream, not to be longed for, but to be accomplished."

"How?" he asked simply.

"I need action," she said. "Prompt action. You must obtain a license. I'd written all this in my letter to you, of course."

"A licence?" he repeated.

"To be married," she explained. "There is not time for banns. So you must go to a Bishop and get a licence." Then, as he stared at her agape, she added: "You do want to marry her, don't you?"

"Yes...yes indeed, I do," he said quickly. "But now? So immediately?"

"If you don't, and speedily, her cousin will!" she replied tersely. "I thought you understood this was an emergency."

"Yes," he said slowly. "Yes I can see it is, but..."

"But!" she exclaimed in disbelief.

He smiled. "Yes, yes I know, Sophie, but I'm not so quick as you. Give me a moment to think, to gather my thoughts before you go sprinting off like a hare. I am a tortoise and I need to catch up."

"We haven't got time," she said crossly. "I tell you, Cordelia has given Hal her consent to marry her cousin."

"Her consent?" he replied gravely.

"Aye, she felt obliged to," she explained, "and then

came to our chamber and wept her heart out with despair."

His face changed, although he made no remark.

Sophie sighed. "Ah well, I was wrong," she said, getting to her feet. "I thought you'd care enough to do something."

"Wait!" he commanded heavily. "I do care, you know I do!"

"Yes, but not enough to defy stuffy old notions of what is right and what is wrong," she declared, making as if to walk away.

He shook his head. "It is not that easy, Sophie," he muttered. "You are such a child in these matters."

She turned on him. "A child?" she cried, anger in her voice. "I am not a child. I am a widow, I've been married and today they bury my husband. I may not be despondent, but I am not without feelings."

"I'm sorry, I didn't think," he stammered. "I beg pardon. Only tell me what I must do."

"Go to the Bishop and get a license," she replied wearily. "Return here later today. Now I think of it, the funeral is an ideal time to accomplish the elopement. Yes," she sat in frowning concentration for a few moments and then nodded. "Yes," she repeated, "you come back later and I'll engage to have Cordelia ready and waiting for you."

He stared at her agape. "Ready for an elopement?" he asked numbly.

"Ready for a private marriage in her own home," she replied firmly.

"Without her guardian's consent!" he pointed out.

"Hal has enough trouble on his hands," she replied. "He won't make a fuss once you are married. If Justin starts to interfere, just remind him that his marriage was clandestine and unapproved both by his family and the Westwoods."

Adam's jaw dropped further and he hastily closed his mouth, unable to see himself doing any such thing. He got slowly to his feet. "I'll...I'll go to...who is the Bishop?" he asked doubtfully. "I've never met a Bishop."

"The Bishop of Lincoln," she replied. "I don't think you have to know him personally. No doubt there is a procedure. Just say that in view of the events here, you and your betrothed's guardian feel it would be better to be married quietly."

He nodded, still seeming leaden-footed. "Lincoln, then," he said as if dazed.

"Remember, you must be back for this afternoon,"

she said, following him. "Speed is essential, Adam."

He nodded and called to Lawrence to bring up his horse. "Essential," he repeated, taking the bridle.

"Lawrence will get word to us on your return," she called, viewing him with approval as he mounted his horse and raised his hand in farewell. She watched as he rode away hastily and wondered whether he would be up to scratch. Then she recollected that Adam may take some time to get going, but once set on course, he was a force to be reckoned with. ❧

Chapter Fifteen

"You look grim, what's amiss?" asked Justin, entering the cramped chamber they were sharing, having broken his fast with Dury Southgate.

"I am writing to Kit Withiam's mother," Hal replied.

Justin grunted. "Not a pleasant task," he agreed. "Has Styles come up with any idea of what happened?"

"Oh yes, he has it all quite clear," said Hal. "It seems that poor Withiam was talking to two of his friends about the arrangements for the funeral today when suddenly something seemed to occur to him. Both Beniston and Brownlow are certain of that. Apparently, he exclaimed, clapped his hand to his head in amazement, and cried that, 'That was it!'."

"'That was it'?" said Justin, puzzled.

"Not a very eloquent young man," agreed Hal. "It was his equivalent of 'Eureka' or 'I have it', etcetera.

He then announced to the whole stableyard that he'd solved the mystery and must see Sir Henry at once."

"And you were?"

"I was, by my good fortune, visiting the Rector in company with my cousin Tom and Mistress Hollingshead," replied Hal. "And by further good fortune, did not spend one moment of the entire day alone. An occurrence overlooked by the murderer, one feels."

"Mmm," agreed Justin. "Not an unduly forward-thinking fellow, certainly. Are you his target, or will any suffice?"

"Not unnaturally, I feel he has me in his eyes, but perhaps I am being a little uneasy on that head," replied Hal with a shrug.

Justin frowned and sat thinking as Hal returned to his letter. He waited patiently until Hal was heating the wax in the candle flame before remarking: "So, were you able to deduce anything from…who was it? Jamie Brownlow and Pip Beniston? Were you able to deduce anything from their conversation with Withiam?"

"No," returned Hal, dripping the wax onto the folded letter and applying his seal to it. "Strangely enough, both have declined to talk to me. Indeed, I begin to wonder at your daring."

Justin smiled thinly. "I hardly think they stand in any danger from the murderer."

"We have known murderers run amuck before," said Hal starkly. "We can never forget Chawcester where five died because of our meddling."

"Six, if you count Libby," retorted Justin. "Aye, I know we were to blame, but this occasion is different. Here, as with other occasions, we are directly involved. Or do you think of leaving Sophie to her fate?"

"I had decided on just such a course yesterday," he said wearily. "But now, that poor foolish boy has been killed I cannot do so. He must be avenged. He'd no more discovered the answer than flown, although he'd plainly remembered something."

"And is the fate of young Withiam the only thing to influence your decision?" asked Justin, casting him a sidelong glance. He was aware that more had happened to Hal, for there was a quiet satisfaction about him, an inner radiance almost.

"No," he agreed. "No, I am naturally influenced by the lad's death, but other, more important, issues hold sway. Your words were not without effect. I acknowledge some truth in them. As usual, your view is heavily biased on the side of pessimism, but there was enough truth to sting me into action. I'll not abandon this pursuit of justice, and I'll try to act in a more orderly manner." Hal paused and drew a deep breath. "I am…that is, we, Sophie and I, have reached an understanding," he said in a jerky manner. "At some time…a time mutually convenient and acceptable to all, we shall be married."

"I see," said Justin heavily.

"There is no occasion for hurry," said Hal. "But I…I have given my word to her."

"Are you expecting me to approve?" asked Justin with a curl of his lip.

"I neither want nor need your approval," returned Hal, his face pale. "It was not something I even considered," he added, prevaricating. "Although common courtesy usually admits congratulations."

"Congratulations?" repeated Justin. "In expectation of your future happiness, you mean?"

Hal frowned. "Yes, yes, I do mean that," he replied. "We have been companions now, as well as brothers though marriage, for some years. Like brothers, we have our disputes and our disagreements over matters of principle, but ultimately, surely, as brothers, even though Libby's death will always stand between us, do you not desire my future happiness?"

Justin looked taken aback. "Why, why yes," he agreed. "Yes, I must do, only…"

"Only?" prompted Hal.

"Not with her," he said quickly. "It cannot seem right that she should profit so from Libby's death."

"So, you cannot like Sophie," concluded Hal. "Even though she was instrumental in saving your—and Ned's—life, neither of you can tolerate her."

"But, don't you see, but for her, for her ill-considered actions, there never would have been the turmoil there was. Neither of us would have been in danger of our lives."

"How can you say so?" cried Hal angrily. "How did Sophie make you take a mistress who was thereafter murdered? How did she set a highwayman on Ned?"

"But it all stems from the fact that she has divided us," countered Justin. "When ever did Ned ride out alone previously? He was ever in your company. Wasn't it because of Sophie, Bess and I quarrelled so bitterly that I could even think of forsaking her for another woman?"

"You cannot attribute such decrees of fate to another," he replied. "You cannot blame Sophie for your own failings."

"Maybe not," he agreed. "Maybe Ned would have been set upon anyway…maybe Bess and I would have quarrelled as bitterly over something else, but the fact remains, Hal, Sophie is trouble! Just by being herself, things occur. She will always attract trouble. Don't expect a life of domestic bliss with Sophie, it won't happen."

Hal smiled faintly, acknowledging the truth of his words. "Untrammeled domestic bliss, no, I don't foresee that," he agreed, "but, by Heaven, I'll never be bored!" He saw Justin's face close as he took this as a criticism of Libby, and added hastily: "See here, Justin, you and Bess, you've been happy in your marriage for the most part, haven't you?"

"Indeed," he agreed. "But for those few months of my stupidity, very much so."

"Then, why would you deny me such felicity?" Hal asked. "Starting from now, and putting the past behind us, am I not allowed as much happiness as the next man?"

"I wish you all the happiness in the world, Hal," he replied earnestly.

"But?" said Hal.

"But I don't think you'll find it with her," he replied.

He was silent for a space, and then added vehemently: "Why did she have to appear in our life? We were perfectly happy before we met her! She ruined everything, nothing will ever be the same."

"Nothing ever is," replied Hal. "Everything changes all the time. And you may have been perfectly happy, but in the superior position of bliss I now occupy, I know I was just existing. I'm sorry, I don't mean to offend you, and I was fond of Libby, but the affection I had for her in no way even approaches the adoration I have for Sophie."

"And it will be your downfall," said Justin. "You are like an old man in your dotage, taken in by a pretty face! She'll bring you nothing but misery."

"You allow her no good qualities, then?" asked Hal, his face troubled. "Admire nothing in her character?"

Justin hesitated. "I can see little merit in her beyond a desire to rule you and exercise her will," he replied grimly.

"You don't see her innate honesty, her sense of justice, admire her passionate convictions?"

"The intemperance of youth," Justin replied dismissively. "I doubt many of her supposed principles will outlive the testing of them."

"I am grieved," he replied. "That a man so fine should be so marred by prejudice against another."

"I am not alone," returned Justin.

"No," agreed Hal. "I am grieved also that I am not more beloved by my kin that they might accept my bride for my sake."

"You bade us put aside such duplicity," said Justin. "The truth you've demanded of us, and so we give you."

"So, I am paid out for my youthful arrogance," he sighed.

"It is but the first payment of many," said Justin heavily. "You'll pay all your life."

"Forgive me, if I am not to cut my own throat or yours, 'tis best we part," said Hal. "I wish you good morning."

Hal went out hastily, shutting the door after him with such exact care that it was plain he was inclined to slam it. His instinct was to seek out Sophie's company, but the earliness of the hour and the knowledge that Cordelia would be keeping her company, drove him from the house. He turned toward the stableyard, hopeful that his groom would be around. In this, he was equally unlucky. Lawrence was out exercising his horse, and the stableyard was deserted.

Hal stood, looking out on the yard, feeling suddenly very much alone and longing for Sophie's company. It was not so much her arms he longed to be in, although he couldn't deny a quickening of his blood at the thought of it, so much as her quick intelligence and uncomplicated response to him he so desired. He was weary of the bonds of guilt which bound him to Justin, tired of his patent disapproval. They were like a team of ill-matched harness horses, who'd never learnt to pull successfully together. Both were constantly chafed and rubbed by the other's inability to suit. It would be better, he decided, if their union were dissolved.

The sound of footsteps jolted his consciousness and Dury Southgate appeared, trudging wearily across the yard. When the man saw him, he said in his usual placid tones: "Sir Henry, what do you here this morning?"

"I was seeking my groom, but he seems to be away. And where have you been?" replied Hal.

"I have been at the Dower House in the village since dawn," he replied. "You know my Lady is to remove there today after the funeral?"

"I have heard it was her intention," agreed Hal, falling

into step with him. "Well, needless to say, with Sir Edgar's death being so sudden, nothing is prepared. But, my Lady is adamant she'll not remain at the Park after Sir Edgar has departed it, so needs must. I launched an army of servants on it yesterday, and began removing some of my Lady's possessions there first thing. I have but to coordinate the funerals this afternoon, and hopefully, by that time, all will be complete. I have no hope of having it fit to receive my Lady or Mistress Kate, but at least they should be able to lay their heads in their own beds."

"Poor Lady, this has been a heavy sorrow," said Hal.

"Aye," he agreed morosely. "Until Sir Edgar's will is read tomorrow, she cannot know how everything is left."

"The property is entailed?" asked Hal.

"Oh aye," nodded Dury. "I remember Sir Edgar insisting the entail remained. He said neither of his sons showed a grain of sense, and he owed it to his forebears to see it wasn't squandered on a game of chance."

"And, my Lady has her jointure, obviously," said Hal.

"Aye, and the use of the Dower House for her lifetime. No, 'tis Mistress Kate who she is in a fret of anxiety over. She is concerned that Sir Anthony may get her dowry."

Hal nodded his understanding. "And how about you, Mr Southgate? How are things left for you?"

Dury shrugged as they entered the house and the agent made for a cupboard of a room where he settled the accounts. "I have no clear idea of my future," he said bleakly. "Sir Anthony dislikes me every bit as much as his elder brother did."

"Will you go with Lady Harcourt and her daughter?" suggested Hal, as the man removed his coat.

"Obviously, I am at their disposal for the near future," he replied, turning to a cupboard and bringing forth a jug of ale and two battered pewter mugs. "But my Lady's holdings are hardly of a stature to merit an agent. She will have several tenants, I imagine, and she'll deal with them herself."

"What happened to your own estate?" asked Hal bluntly, accepting the ale with a word of thanks.

"It was sold to pay my father's fines," he replied bitterly. "Sir Edgar purchased it after the war. He promised me when I came to assist him here that I should have a hand in its restoration, and that ultimately, it would be mine again someday if I worked hard."

"Mayhap he will have left it you?" suggested Hal hopefully.

"I doubt it very much. Not an overly warm man, Sir Edgar," he replied crisply. "The milk of human kindness didn't flow freely through his veins. I have little doubt it is lost to me entirely."

"You are a good fellow and deserve better," said Hal. "As a temporary measure, my ward Mistress Sandys may desire an agent for her estate."

"I thought Jack Hollingshead had the running of that," he replied.

"Indeed he does," agreed Hal. "Bickmarsh Hall belongs to Cordelia, and if she doesn't marry Jack immediately…"

"Oh, is she betrothed?" asked Dury with interest.

"Well, nothing is spoken of, naturally, but she has indicated that she'll marry him," said Hal.

Dury nodded and said: "I have to meet with the carpenter from the village, Sir Henry, to pay for a stout coffin which will carry Kit Withiam to his home. He awaits me in the chapel where the poor fellow is laid out."

"I'll go with you," said Hal, drinking off the last of his ale and then, aware of the other's curious look, he added: "My brother-in-law and I have quarrelled bitterly. There is no comfort in keeping company with one whom one is at odds with."

"I am sorry to hear you have quarrelled," Dury said as they left the room together and started toward the chapel.

"I am sorry for your predicament. What shall you do?" asked Hal.

"Look about for a permanent situation," he replied. "If you get to hear of any, Sir Henry, in your part of the world, I would be grateful."

"I cannot immediately bring any to mind, I fear," said Hal. "Surely, Lady Harcourt, knowing her husband's intention, would find you something?"

"I don't care for the crumbs from my Lady's table, Sir Henry," he replied tartly. "Neither is her jointure such as to render her a wealthy woman. I doubt she'll want for much, but 'tis my guess she and Mistress Kate will use up their income."

"I am sorry to hear you say so," Hal replied. "And, on a personal note, if my Lady leaves today, so too must we. Where is the nearest decent inn which we can remove to?"

"I thought you were to go to the Hollingsheads at Fordham Manor?" asked Dury in surprise.

"We were thinking more of my ward's property at

Bickmarsh. But, that is a good distance away. Until we have some decision on Sophie's position, we don't care to leave her alone. Especially if Lady Harcourt is to remove herself. Indeed, if she does, Sophie will have to go with us, too, for staying alone with Sir Anthony, she will not."

"No," he agreed. "Sir Anthony's character does not give one to believe that he'll run a house such as any lady of delicacy could think to live in."

"Quite," said Hal. "And in truth, she can have no claim upon Sir Anthony, her bridegroom's death coming, as it did, before Sir Edgar's."

"Yes," he agreed, opening the door to the chapel. "Ah! Miller, I see you are already busy."

"Yes, Mr Southgate." The carpenter nodded and unhurriedly continued with his nailing down of the coffin lid. "You're keeping me powerful busy, sir," he added, as an assistant came to help him hold the lid down.

"Yes," said Dury, making a face as the sweet sickly scent of decay hit their nostrils. "It has been rather an eventful few days."

"Wat, here, is going to set off with the body at once, sir," he explained, as another fellow came to help carry the coffin from its trestle to a waiting cart. "'Tis cooler now, and in this weather 'tis best we don't delay."

"Yes," agreed Dury faintly. "The Coroner has seen him, I suppose?"

"He came last evening after supper," said Hal. "Sir Charles spoke to him. They agreed that it was essential there wasn't a delay taking him to his home. The cause of death was plain to see and there are always fears of the plague, you understand," he added.

"Yes," Dury repeated blankly. "Yes, it just seems so... so final, poor lad. I had a liking for him, he was not vicious like most of Gerry's friends. Only rather young and foolish. He got in with a bad lot, and now he's dead. It isn't right."

"No, it isn't," said Hal. "And it must stop. I'll call a meeting of everyone later, after the funeral, and before Lady Harcourt finally departs. We need to thrash this out." ⚜

Chapter Sixteen

Cordelia came hurrying to the chamber she shared with Sophie. Hal had instructed her not only to pack up all of their possessions, but to ensure that Sophie was suitably attired as the grieved bride.

"Cordelia!" Sophie turned from the window, her eyes sparkling with excitement. "People are arriving for the funeral!"

"Yes, I know! Tens and tens of them, we are like to get lost in the crowd, for which we can be thankful," replied the girl. "Hal says not to forget your role, and please make sure you are gowned so as not to offend, which I can see you are. Well done, Sophie, that is exactly how you should look."

"Yes, I even had the veil, which is very useful, as is the fact that we women don't attend the service, but sit back here at the house."

"Well, you'll need something to hide your face," agreed Cordelia. "You look too happy for words."

"I am, especially now Adam has come! Adam, come and make your bow to Cordelia!"

"Adam!" Cordelia's face turned first red, and then very pale as he stepped from behind the door. "Oh! Mr Blackwell! How…how very nice of you to attend. I'm sure Sophie appreciates your support."

"He's not come here to support me, you ninny!" said Sophie scornfully, seeing that if she didn't have a care, these lovers would lose themselves in a maze of doubt and confusion. "He's come here to elope with you."

"Elope!" cried Cordelia in horror.

"Nay, then, Sophie," cried Adam, seeing Cordelia's face and getting rather embarrassed himself. "I've come to…to help all I can. Not…not to push Mistress Sandys into…into…"

"Oh, dear Heavens, was anyone ever so cursed with star-crossed lovers?" cried Sophie in exasperation. "Cordelia, do you love that pompous fool Jack Hollingshead?"

"Sophie, you know I've given Sir Henry my…"

"Forget Hal!" she commanded. "He'll not be having your cousin in his bed. Don't tell me you are truly going to spend your life ministering to Jack Hollingshead's wants, listening to him prosing on, fetching this for his comfort and that for his pain, for he's the sort that will ever have something amiss."

"Oh, Sophie!" Cordelia laughed guiltily, for Jack's trifling ailments were already a thing of amusement.

"Well, answer, Cordelia. Adam stands here, wondering if he's travelled night and day on a fool's errand. Do you love Jack Hollingshead?"

"Indeed, Mr Blackwell, you must be dreadfully tired," said Cordelia, looking concerned. "Alas, we have no place we can offer you to rest, although Dury Southgate speaks well of the inn at…"

"Cordelia!" cried Sophie, as Adam began tentatively to express his thanks. "Stop that and tell Adam how much you love him."

"Sophie!" she cried, her cheeks afire, not daring to meet the young man's guileless eyes.

"Sophie!" Adam's voice broke across Sophie scolding tones. "Don't bully Mistress Sandys. I am here at her disposal. If she wishes, I can escort her wherever she wants to go. Or, I can speak to Sir Henry for her." He smiled, his eyes filled with love. "I am yours to command, Mistress Sandys. Your happiness is of paramount importance to me."

"Is it?" she asked breathlessly.

"Indeed it is," he replied. "Sophie will have told you, even if you won't trust the evidence of your own eyes, how much I love and esteem you."

"There, Cordelia, you can't marry Jack after that!" cried Sophie.

"Nay, Sophie," he replied sharply. "If Mistress Sandys feels she must marry Mr Hollingshead, that she has given her word to Sir Henry and cannot go back on it, then I'll not dispute with her." He smiled crookedly, "Cost me as dearly as it will."

"You'll not!" said Cordelia, a little dismayed.

"No, I'll not force you to do anything you consider wrong or underhand, my dear," he said simply. "But if you are, as Sophie insists, desperately unhappy, then I'll try my best to help you in any way I can."

"Oh, thank you, Mr Blackwell!" she cried in heartfelt tones. "Sophie is right! I am quite, quite desperately unhappy, but I can't let Sir Henry down. I've given him my word, do you see?"

"I do," he replied. "And Sir Henry is such a grand fellow, you'd not want to disappoint him. I understand he has enough of that with Sophie." He smiled as Sophie protested. "But do try to look at it more widely, my dear. Sir Henry brought you from the convent in France out of concern for your welfare, did he not, to his own personal cost?"

"Oh yes, and you see it's his great kindness that makes me so obliged to him," she replied, her tones earnest.

"Yes, he is very kind," agreed Adam. "A good man, and the very last thing he'd want is to force you into a marriage where you'd be unhappy. Of that, I'm certain."

"Yes, but even so, you must understand his sense of justice and fair play means that he feels for Jack Hollingshead. For all the work he's put into my property these past years."

"Any man would agree with him, but it doesn't require that you sacrifice your life to Jack Hollingshead to make Sir Henry feel justice has been done," Adam replied, equally earnestly. "All we need to do is pay the fellow off."

"Alas, I have no money," she replied. "It would cost a great deal to recompense the Hollingsheads for all their time and money they've put into Bickmarsh. I feel that I cannot ask Sir Henry to advance me that sort of sum, knowing that I'd have to mortgage the house to do it. And even if I were to take such steps, I have no idea of how to run such a place, even if I could do all these other things."

"Why not leave all that to a husband?" he asked gently. "I am selling the Old Manor House to Ned Westwood, he's long wanted it. I can pay off the Hollingsheads with that money. I also know how to run a reasonable property, and I'm sure we can hire someone to assist us in the short term at Bickmarsh."

"Oh, Mr Blackwell, you would do that for me? You'd sell your home?" she cried, on the verge of tears.

"It's not my home," he said. "Elmley Park was my home and I lost that, but we can regain Bickmarsh, if you are willing, if you can put your trust in me to do so."

"Oh Adam!" she cried. "If only we could."

"Well, of course you can!" cried Sophie impatiently. "For Heaven's sake, Cordelia, tell the poor man you love him! He's laid everything he has at your feet, and you've only just remembered his name."

Adam smiled as Cordelia looked shy and confused. "Sophie, I beg you will desist. This is a delicate wooing, and not to your taste, 'tis plain. But some are not so precipitate."

"I tell you, if Hal and I held back and hesitated as you

two do, we'd never have settled anything," she cried. "You've not even kissed her yet, Adam, nor told her how much you love her."

"Cordelia knows how much I adore her," he said, his voice unsteady. "And if, or when, we do reach that blessed felicity of a kiss, it will be an occasion of great moment not to be overlooked by the likes of you, Sophie Redcroft."

"Oh, what shall I do?" cried Cordelia, tears welling in her eyes at this sincere avowal, as Sophie reminded Adam she was a married woman. "I don't know how to act for the best. I don't want to disappoint Sir Henry… but I do dislike Jack Hollingshead."

"And love Adam," prompted Sophie.

"Sophie," said Adam sharply. "None of that if Cordelia wants only my help. I'll not have her bullied into professing love in the mistaken thought it's the only way to procure it."

"Oh Adam, you are so good, so kind and gentle, how could I help but love you?" said Cordelia, clasping his massive hands.

He swallowed and raised her hand to his lips. "Sweetheart, you've made me the happiest of men," he said simply.

"But Adam, much as I love you, I don't see a way out of this tangle that doesn't involve pain and disappointment, fuss and turmoil. I know it's cowardly, but I shrink from all that and wonder if it's not my wicked pride tempting me away. Perhaps it is ordained I should follow the path Sir Henry decrees."

Sophie sighed. "Yes, that's where your upbringing leads you astray. You see what you long for and immediately think it must be a sin to possess it."

"The road to Hell is a primrose path, Sophie," she cried, shocked. "That to Heaven strewn with rocks and troubles."

"Indeed it is, my darling," agreed Adam, keeping a firm grip on her hand. "That's why the Lord sends us a helpmeet, a companion to help scale it."

"Do you truly think so, Adam?" she cried hopefully.

"I know it, my love," he replied stoutly. "With a loved one at one's side, even the steepest path can be tackled. But alone, one must often despair and fall at the wayside."

"Oh Adam, how tempting it sounds," she said. "If only I could be sure it's not the Devil at work."

"How would Adam have anything to do with the Devil?" cried Sophie in exasperation. "Oh Cordelia, do have done with your doubts, or you'll not get away in time."

"Get away? Oh no, I cannot possibly elope!" she cried. "What can you be thinking of, Sophie? Why, everyone would be so shocked and angry!"

"So they'll be shocked and angry, they'll get over it, and you and Adam will be married. They can do nothing about it," said Sophie. "What is more, it cuts out all the fuss and turmoil you dread."

"Oh Sophie, those are the words of the Devil!" Cordelia cried. "If one hasn't the courage to stand up and fight for one's convictions, then one doesn't deserve the prize. It would be cowardly to run off to be married, don't you think so, Adam?"

He smiled. "If you think it is so, Cordelia, then we will not do so. But I'll not deny I have a license in my baggage and have made arrangements for a priest to meet us in the chapel at your house later today."

"Adam!" she cried. "I cannot believe this of you. Do you not believe we should face up to all this trouble?"

"Oh yes," he agreed. "But we'll do it better from a position of strength, my dear. Once the knot is tried, they'll find it a devil to untie. And look at it rationally, today is the funeral of Sophie's bridegroom and his father. As I understand it, later you all move to an inn, and thence to your home. When can we think to put all this to Sir Henry? Not today, nor yet tomorrow, and then he is still troubled by these murders. I can see it will be weeks and weeks before we'll have time to discuss it all. And, in the meantime, Jack Hollingshead is pushing for the marriage."

"Yes, and we'll be closer to the Hollingsheads. They'll be forever at Bickmarsh, Cordelia. Whereas, if you marry Adam, they'll be so offended they'll not come near nor by," suggested Sophie.

"That, I shouldn't like, for they are Cordelia's kin," said Adam. "But, sweetheart, if only you'll put your trust in me, I'll deal with all this for you. As your husband, it is my right to make sure none ever bother you again."

"Oh, Adam, is it?" she asked, clinging to his hand. "Truly, can I rely on you in all these things?"

He lifted her into his arms. "My darling, I'll make it my business to see that you are happy until the end of time."

"Well thank Heavens for that!" said Sophie, as they finally kissed. "Now, come on Adam, we are way behind. The cortege is forming, I must away to keep my Lady and her daughters company. Cordelia, I've packed this bag for you, wait here with Adam until the cortege departs, and then leave by the side door. Lawrence will have the horses waiting, I hope you bribed him well, Adam."

"I did," he replied, picking up Sophie's Bible and handing it to her.

"Oh, thank you, Adam. Yes, I do look grief-stricken enough. Oddly, I do feel for poor Gerry now. I suppose alongside his brother, he looks better. Cordelia, I shall tell them you have the headache and cannot think of leaving your bed."

"Oh Sophie, I'm sure all this deceit is wrong!" she cried.

"Courage, Cordelia. Only think of spending the night safe in Adam's arms, rather than Jack Hollingshead's."

"Be off with you, Sophie!" cried Adam, as Cordelia turned away in blushing confusion. "Before you undo all the good I've achieved. We'll meet with you tomorrow at Bickmarsh Hill."

"Indeed you shall," she replied. "Good luck, and God bless you both."

He closed the door on her and turned back to confront his betrothed. "If you are unsure of this, Cordelia, do say so. I've said I'll not force you into this, and I won't."

"Oh Adam, it feels so wicked," she confessed. "But I do so love you, and Sophie's suggestion is so temping."

"For us both, my darling," he replied with a husky laugh. "Come, we'll go a little way along the primrose path, and then double back to the steep and rocky way I promise you." ❧

Chapter Seventeen

The group of men got up from the table where they had been sitting in morose silence, brought about by Anthony Harcourt's bad manners. Jane Selby approached Hal and Justin as they conversed quietly with Sir Charles Wicliffe. "Never liked the fellow," Sir Charles was saying quietly. "Damned bad behaviour to speak ill of the dead like that."

"*Nil nisi bonum*," murmured Hal.

"Quite," he agreed. "Ah, Mistress Selby. Now here is one I can extend my condolences to." Then, as she expressed her thanks, he added: "How has my Lady faired, aye, and the sweet little bride? This is a terrible time for you all."

"Indeed, Sir Charles," she replied in subdued tones. "I came seeking Sir Henry because Mistress Sophie is so distressed…indeed, almost hysterical, and my Lady is concerned for her."

"Sophie, hysterical? Dear me, is Mistress Sandys not with her?" asked Hal, anxiety in his voice.

"No, Sir Henry, she has the headache. I did suggest I sought her out when Sophie grew distressed, but she'd not hear of it, and then she began to laugh and cry together. My Lady thinks it reaction to the events," replied Jane gravely.

"I'll go to her if Lady Harcourt will permit," suggested Justin.

"I'm sure she'll be relieved," said Jane Selby, looking dissatisfied as Hal made no move to accompany her. "There is something rather disturbing in her manner," she added.

"She has endured rather a lot of emotion of late. Perhaps Cordelia might be the one to assist in this, Justin?" said Hal frowning.

"I'll deal with it, Hal," replied Justin tersely. "You discuss Kit Withiam with Sir Charles."

Hal shrugged, guessing that Justin feared Sophie might reveal her feelings for Hal if she were indeed hysterical, as did he.

Jane Selby left the chamber with Justin following, and Hal continued the discussion with Sir Charles. They arranged a meeting for the next afternoon to call

all the evidence together in an informal hearing. Justin returned some minutes later as Sir Charles was taking his departure, and it was evident to Hal he was in no pretty mood.

"Ha, Mr Danvers. How is the sweet bride? Any more settled now? Poor little thing. It's not something any would wish on their worst enemy, to be wedded and widowed in a few hours. No wonder she's cracked under the strain."

"Indeed, I told Lady Harcourt, who is indeed preparing to leave, Hal, that we'd remove Sophie at once," said Justin curtly.

"Yes, she has enough to deal with, her and her daughter's grief," agreed Hal.

"Lady Harcourt is leaving, you say?" said Sir Charles. "Then, if you'll excuse me, Sir Henry, I'll escort her to the Dower House." He glanced to Sir Anthony who, with a group of younger men, was getting loudly drunk. "The sooner the ladies are out of here, the better. I don't think I'll take any leave of that fellow. Wasted effort, don't you agree?"

"Yes, one feels any attempt at good manners would be wasted," remarked Hal coldly.

"I expect you'll be taking your wards away too, Sir Henry?"

Hal nodded. "This very evening, Sir Charles. We go to impose upon Jack Hollingshead's family overnight, and then on to Bickmarsh Hall."

"I don't think we can, Hal," said Justin, as the older man, with a reminder of the appointment the next day, went in search of Lady Harcourt.

"Why not?" replied Hal. "I know he's not the liveliest of fellows, but Cordelia has agreed to…"

"Cordelia Sandys, so Sophie tells me, has eloped with Adam Blackwell."

Hal's jaw dropped. "Eloped? No…this is one of Sophie's jokes."

"I fail to see anything amusing in it," grunted Justin. "It makes you look foolish. Didn't you assure Madelaine Hollingshead the match was in the bag?"

"I indicated Cordelia was willing. This must be a mistake. Sophie was hysterical, you say? Doubtless you misheard her," he said stiffly.

"No," he replied evenly. "By the time I'd got to Lady Harcourt, she'd recovered her manners and was helping the poor widow and her daughter Kate, who is sadly distraught, to pack up their belongings."

Hal gaped at him. "Helping?" he repeated blankly.

"Aye. After I'd expressed my regrets, I got Sophie

away. I didn't feel in her present state she was to be trusted not to say something controversial. I took her to her chamber, expecting to find Cordelia there. Once we were inside, Sophie revealed what looked to be Cordelia sleeping as a bundle of clothing. She then confessed she'd organised Cordelia's elopement with Adam Blackwell. It seems that they left as the funeral cortege made its way to the chapel, and that by this time, if all had gone to plan, they would be married at Bickmarsh Hall."

Hal opened and closed his mouth a few times, a tide of rage growing within him as he realised how he'd been duped, and what a complete fool he'd look to Jack Hollingshead and his mother.

"Yes," observed Justin. "I was pretty miffed too. We are in one hell of a hole, Hal. It's going to take all your charm to get us out of this one."

"No, it's not!" he snapped. "We are just going to walk away."

"Walk away?" repeated Justin blankly.

"Yes," he replied. "Go home, leave them all to it. It's nothing to do with us. I wash my hands of both of them."

"You cannot legally do so, unfortunately. I agree, you have been badly treated by your wards, but a legal obligation is just that. You must assist Cordelia with her property, and there will be documents to pass over to Blackwell. As for Sophie, you can hardly leave her in that lecher Harcourt's care, whatever her offence. Any more than I can, laying aside any personal promise you may have recently given her." Justin couldn't resist the final jibe.

Hal gritted his teeth. "How could she do this to me? How dare she?" he raged.

Justin sighed. "I told you she was trouble. What shall we do? We can't accept Jack Hollingshead's hospitality. Shall we decamp to Bickmarsh Hall?"

"No," he snapped, then seeing others about the room glance their way, he got control of his fury. "No, we'll go to Tom Kingscott's. From there, I can send Sophie back to Aunt Margery's."

"The Kingscott's? Aunt Margery won't thank you for taking scandal there. Nor can Sophie be packed off back to Westwood. She must give evidence at the inquest, re-member. Indeed, Sir Charles will expect her to be pres-ent tomorrow. What are we to do, Hal?" he murmured under his breath.

"Do? I am damned if I know. What can we do?" He stared fixedly ahead for a few moments, then shrugged.

"There is no help for it, we'll have to impose on Tom Kingscott. We can't leave Sophie here with no other women in the house. I'd better go and make my apologies to the Hollingsheads and crave room from Tom to lay our heads."

He disappeared abruptly, leaving Justin to return to Sophie, who he found attending to their packing. She glanced to him, her face pale and her eyes red-rimmed. It occurred to him she looked the part of a grief-stricken widow.

"Where is Hal?" she asked quickly.

"Gone to arrange accommodation for us," he replied coolly. "We will hardly be welcome at the Hollingshead home now."

Sophie blinked. "No, I suppose not. But we are to go to Bickmarsh? Cordelia expects us."

"Most likely she does," agreed Justin. "But it will be better all round if we go to Tom Kingscott. Hal will quarrel with Adam Blackwell if we go to Bickmarsh."

"Is Hal angry?" she asked tentatively.

Justin laughed ironically. "I don't think angry fully covers his feelings."

"Why?" she asked, as Hal entered the chamber. "Why is he so angry?"

Hal looked at her in utter disbelief. "What did you say?" he demanded in a voice which made her jump.

Sophie sighed. Of course she'd known he wasn't going to like what had happened, that much had been plain. But, she'd forgotten how cold his eyes became when he was very angry and how, whatever happened he'd blame her, because he always did blame her. "I asked why you were so angry," she replied uncertainly. "I don't know why, really, because I knew you would be." She tried a tentative smile. "Perhaps I was hoping for a miracle."

"The miracle is I persuaded Tom Kingscott to allow us to lay our heads in his house for the next few days," snapped Hal. "So we are not the total social outcasts I feared we should be."

"Social outcasts? Pooh," said Sophie provocatively. "You begin to sound like Aunt Margery. Besides, we are to go to Bickmarsh. Cordelia and Adam expect us."

"I doubt very much Adam expects us with any degree of pleasure," remarked Justin dryly, as Hal appeared to be deprived of the power of speech. "You say they are probably man and wife by now?"

Sophie glanced to the window to mark the progress of the sun across the evening sky. "Yes, they must be by now, Adam had a licence and had prepared the vicar, but he'll be expecting your arrival for supper. I told Adam to tell the vicar you'd be riding over from the funeral to join them in a quiet supper, as it was unseemly to celebrate a wedding so close to a funeral." Suddenly, she found she was shaking again as reaction to all that occurred set in, and still Hal stood in ominous silence. "She only said she'd marry Jack Hollingshead to please you, Hal," she added, "in your heart you must know that. Surely you could tell she didn't like him? It was only because you persuaded her it was for her own good that she agreed."

"It was for her own good!" he replied, looking like thunder.

"I don't agree," she cried, relieved at least he'd spoken to her. "How can it be for her to marry a man she detests, instead of one she loves?"

"Do you dare to ask me such a question?" he cried wrathfully. "Can you not see the damage which is done? The marriage between Cordelia and Jack Hollingshead was the answer to all the legal problems, and probably the marriage her father would have chosen for her. Instead of which, she's run off with a penniless ale draper in the middle of a funeral, leaving me to pick up all the pieces and make excuses and explanations."

"Adam is not a penniless ale draper!" cried Sophie, stung. "He's a good man and he loves her dearly. He's prepared to sell his own land and move here to farm Cordelia's estate. And," she cried triumphantly, "she would never have had to run off in the middle of a funeral, if you hadn't pushed her into agreeing to marry Jack Hollingshead. You are the one at fault, in trying to make a match in the middle of a situation like this, Hal."

To her fury, neither of the men replied. Justin merely raised his eyebrows in an odious manner and Hal turned his shoulder to her.

"So what do we do?" asked Justin.

"I'm damned if I know," growled Hal. "A more uncomfortable situation I never expected to find myself in."

Justin shrugged. "In that case, we should depart in the best order we can. It's not as if we've anyone's feelings to consider now. Lady Harcourt and her daughters are leaving. Dury Southgate is assisting them. The place is left to Anthony Harcourt to bring to the Devil."

"As no doubt he will," snapped Hal. "I am merely waiting so as not to run into Jack Hollingshead and his mother as they leave. Tom said he'll give us notice once they've gone." ❧

Chapter Eighteen

They took their leave swiftly and made, in their heavy silence and sombe clothes, a suitably funereal procession. Justin, who rode alongside the heavily-veiled Sophie, behind Hal and Tom Kingscott, observed her crushed demeanour and the few tears which fell as the miles passed. "What did you expect? Surely you knew he'd be furious?" he asked, not unkindly, in an undertone.

She sighed and surreptitiously wiped her nose. "I hoped he'd let me explain," she said dolefully.

"No man likes being made to look incompetent. Hal had to go to the Hollingsheads and tell them that, far from contracting to Jack, Cordelia had eloped. That made him look as if he didn't know what was going on. Then, he had to explain to his kinsman that we needed lodgings because his wards had behaved so badly. How do you think he feels?"

"Not one half as badly as Cordelia would have felt!" snapped Sophie, sniffing.

Justin looked taken aback. "Why did the silly fool not say she disliked the man? Why let it go so far?"

"Oh, you men!" Sophie flicked away her tears. "You hypocrites! You knew she disliked Jack Hollingshead, both of you knew! You just saw the marriage as a neat solution to a tricky problem! It's always money, isn't it? None of you ever listen to what we want, you just decide with reference only to money."

"As I recollect the matter, your choice was entirely your own," he retorted, startled by this attack.

"Oh no! You knew my choice. You all did, but you all opposed it and made Hal feel that he should oppose it too. You all knew I loved Hal and that he loves me, but you were determined we shouldn't be happy."

"You forget your actions killed my sister!" he snapped, beginning to get angry.

"No, you forget, I paid you back for her life by saving yours," she retorted.

"If you two cannot ride side by side without quarrelling in an unseemly manner, you'd best split up," said Hal fiercely. "Sophie, come take my place beside Tom, and keep your tongue between your teeth."

"I am neither one of your wards, nor a child to be so addressed," remarked Justin coldly.

Hal dropped back beside him and Sophie rode forward to trot alongside Tom Kingscott. "Surely you could have behaved in an adult enough manner so as not to quarrel with her for a few hours!" snapped Hal, still furious.

"Strangely enough, I was trying to console her. I am aware she is upset and has endured a great deal these past days. Obviously, I have not your knack with women," he added sourly.

Hal grunted by way of reply and the remainder of the journey was accomplished in silence.

❧

Their arrival at Kingsholme, a rather elegant house built at the turn of the century in the new Baroque style, was as neatly accomplished as the house itself. In no time, Justin found himself in a tastefully-appointed chamber with hot water and towels laid out. There was a very comfortable bed and a splendid view out over the park. Everywhere he looked, he saw the home of a family who'd not made any mistakes in many generations. He felt depressed. He washed off the dust of travel, changed his linen and wandered next door to see what Hal was doing. He entered after knocking twice and found Hal sitting on the window seat, his chin cupped in his hand as he gazed from the window. "Nice estate," remarked Justin, following the direction of his gaze.

"They added to it considerably in the war," replied Hal, seeming to come out of a daydream.

"Money has never been a problem to them, then," observed Justin dryly.

"There has never been more than one son," sighed Hal. "Always a Tom Kingscott, going back generations. Just the one son."

"Or grandson, as in this case," said Justin. "That must have been a nasty shock to Tom, his son dying after a fall from his horse, as he did last year."

"Yes," agreed Hal. "Tom said they'd had hopes of a larger family this time. His son Tom was young enough, and his wife healthy, but they were left with just the one child. It was not to be."

"Some things aren't," said Justin. "Like this marriage between Cordelia Sandys and Jack Hollingshead."

"I was just wondering if I should have ridden after them and tried to stop it," he replied. "But I came to the conclusion that I didn't care enough. I am a failure as a guardian. You and Bess were married against the family's wishes when she was supposed to be in my charge. My sister, Mary married Guy without my father's consent. Only Hetta and myself married as we should, for even Ned married privately. Now both my wards have made disastrous marriages. I think I'll leave my children's marriages for somebody else to arrange."

"Time enough to worry about that when they are out of short coats," observed Justin dryly.

"At least we got away from Harcourt Park and brought Sophie away from the house, too, which is more to the point. What am I to do with her, Justin?" Hal added suddenly. "We ought to have another woman here for her, yet I dare not trust her to anyone. She frightens me, you know. She doesn't ever seem to stop. I thought we had an understanding. She knew I loved her and we agreed to be married once the fuss over this wedding calmed down. After a decent interval, we agreed it in that damned wood, standing over the body of that poor boy. Yet, the very next day, she causes another uproar by encouraging Cordelia to run off with Adam Blackwell."

"You don't know Sophie was behind it," objected Justin.

"I do," he replied. "As well as I know that I love her, and don't tell me she's trouble, I know that, too."

Justin sighed and sat down. "What are we to do?" he asked, bending his mind to the problem.

"I don't know. I am fast running out of ideas," replied Hal.

A tap came on the door and both turned to face it, unconsciously squaring their shoulders. Tom Kingscott entered with a smile. "Supper will be on the table in fifteen minutes," he said. "Not that you're hungry, probably, but by Heaven, that was a cheerless wake!"

"It left a bad taste in the mouth," agreed Justin.

"I, well, I wondered if you needed…" Tom began and hesitated. "I don't like to suggest…" He broke off and didn't complete his words.

"Suggest?" asked Hal warily.

"It occurs to me that there is a lady of my acquaintance who might be prepared to come to stay with Sophie…" Tom began in a tentative manner.

"Is she unshockable?" interrupted Hal in a wearily voice.

"Well, yes…she is," replied Tom with a quick grin. "She's a widow now, her husband died last year, and they had ten children, so she's used to young people.

She lives with her son, the Rector in the village, since her husband's death. It occurred to me she'd be the ideal companion for Sophie. She is a very sweet lady, with a good sense of humour and incredibly practical." He hesitated, and then added in a rush: "In fact, I've asked her to marry me as soon as she's out of mourning, only don't mention it to your Aunt Margery, will you? Poor Mary is terrified of her, and we don't want it spoken of until we're ready."

"She sounds ideal for Sophie," remarked Justin.

"Why should you worry what my Aunt Margery thinks?" asked Hal in astonishment.

"Well, she was my stepmother, remember, and is still rather formidable. By Heaven, I remember first meeting her as a lad, I was so terrified I could hardly speak! Mind, she is a very good woman, and always has one's best interests at heart," he added loyally.

"Even if they are not what one wants oneself," agreed Hal despondently, as he thought of the letter he'd be obliged to compose to his aunt within hours.

Tom laughed. "Poor Hal, you don't know how much I admire your tolerance. I am given to understand you often oppose her, yet she insists you have excellent manners."

"Oh, he does," agreed Justin, glad to lighten the atmosphere. "Hal never makes the mistake of disputing anything with Aunt Margery. He merely bows and declines to discuss the matter in the politest way."

"It is essential to have a method of protection from a frontal attack," agreed Hal, smiling slightly, "although, I'd be lost without Aunt Kate. But isn't Aunt Margery promoting your marriage to a near neighbour? One of her many kinswomen through marriage?"

"Yes, she was," he replied. "But fortunately, I was so unenthusiastic about the whole project, as to give the excellent lady a distaste of me. She married another last Lady Day. Your aunt was not impressed, but she had the arranging of my first marriage, I'll decide upon my second." His grin broadened. "I am minded to tell my stepmother I'm following your example, Hal, and suiting myself."

Hal looked horrified at the thought of being held responsible for Tom's actions, but Justin chuckled. "Excellent idea. She'll imagine another Sophie, and be so relieved when she meets your choice that you'll be back in her good books immediately."

Tom smiled too, but viewed Hal's face with concern. "Why, what is it, Hal?" he asked. "Are you truly concerned about Sophie? You don't think she murdered Gervase, do you?"

"No," he replied. "That is about the only thing I'm certain she isn't responsible for, but she certainly promoted Cordelia's elopement, and is somehow at the back of this whole debacle."

"Hal is feeling rather gloomy," said Justin. "He feels for the young fellow who was murdered and, quite frankly, we don't seem to be getting anywhere with finding the killer. All reason and inclination points to Anthony Harcourt. Sir Anthony, I mean, yet he was out of the country, or so he says."

Tom nodded. "He is the natural suspect, as he does so very well out of the result, but why kill the poor Withiam boy? It makes no sense."

"None of it seems to make sense at the moment," said Justin. "I must sit down and write it all out. I might make a table of suspects as I did at Chawcester, Hal, that seems to help."

"What, and see them all killed one after the other?" Hal snapped. "No, I think we should leave well enough alone. It would appear the Harcourts are not particularly pleasant people, as long as Sophie isn't a suspect, who cares who killed them!"

"As one sworn to protect the peace of this realm, you should!" said Justin sharply.

"I am protecting the peace of the realm," retorted Hal. "If you name suspects, they'll all probably die."

"So, we leave Sir Antony to his ill-gotten gains, and Jane Selby and Kate Harcourt to a life of poverty, do we?" said Justin, getting angry.

"Come, let's to supper!" said Tom peaceably. "We can discuss this over a cup of wine."

Recollecting their manners, Justin and Hal followed him down the splendid staircase and into the elegant dining parlour. Tom left them briefly for a conference with a servant and returned after a few minutes, smiling. "The maid says Mistress Redcroft has sent a message to say she has the headache and will take supper in her chamber," he said pleasantly.

Hal glanced warily to Justin. "Do you think we should make sure she's not runoff?" he asked uneasily.

Tom smiled. "I had the wench go and be sure, I knew you'd be in a fret, Hal. She said Sophie was asleep in her bed looking like an angel come down from Heaven."

"A Devil incarnate, more like!" replied Hal sinking back in his chair. "Thank Heaven for that, at least we can have supper in peace."

They proceeded to make an excellent meal, and as the wine sank in their costly glasses, Hal's spirits lightened. It was into the hilarity which frequently follows a funeral that a plumpish lady was ushered, about an hour later.

"Mary, my love!" cried Tom, getting to his feet and coming to meet her. "How good of you to come so promptly."

"Well, I understood from your message time was of the essence, and it's not that far across the park," she replied with a lovely smile.

"Hal, Justin, pray allow me to introduce my betrothed, Mistress Mary Fanshawe. Mary, this is my kinsman, Sir Henry Westwood, and his brother-in-law, Mr Danvers."

"We're delighted to meet you, Mistress Fanshawe," said Hal, bowing over her hand.

Justin bowed and looked shrewdly at her. "And obliged to you also, ma'am," he said, "for coming to our aid as you have."

"Is Mistress Redcroft not with you?" she asked, glancing to the table as she took a chair next to Tom and accepted a glass of wine.

"Alas, Mistress Fanshawe, she is worn down with the

various emotions of the past few days," said Justin politely.

"In truth, Mistress Fanshawe, I think she declined supper in a sulk because we are cross with her, and then exhaustion has overtaken her," said Hal sombrely.

"I'm sure it has, poor thing," replied the lady. "Tom, didn't you say she woke up to find her husband dead? What a shock that must have been. Married but a few hours and widowed like that, she must be mad with grief."

Hal sighed. "If you are not to be shocked out of all consciousness, ma'am, I must explain some unpalatable facts. Sophie claims she had made a mistake in consenting to marry Gervase Harcourt, and that she was never so relieved, after the initial shock of his death, as to not be married to him. In all fairness to Sophie, events and facts since discovered seem to indicate she was not wrong. But, of course, it leaves us in a tricky situation which, if you'd rather not be involved in, I quite understand."

"Yes, I can see it might," she agreed. "But Tom tells me Sophie is a good girl at heart, merely headstrong and prone to speaking her mind."

"Not a recipe for social success, ma'am," said Hal with feeling. "As you haven't, so far, fallen into a swoon at our feet, I am emboldened to tell you the worst. Not only left a widow after less than twelve hours of marriage, which leads to a complicated legal situation, Sophie then encouraged my ward, who was staying at Harcourt for the wedding, to elope with another suitor whilst I was in the midst of contracting her to Jack Hollingshead."

"Oh, this will be Basil Sandys daughter, I take it?" she replied. "Oh well, I'd say she was well out of it. Jack can be a difficult fellow, you know. I'd not have cared for him to marry one of my daughters, in spite of his land. Mind, my Betty might have improved his temper, a sweet girl my youngest daughter, is she not, Tom?"

"Indeed, Betty will make a perfect wife to any husband in the fullness of time. I shall be glad to welcome her as my daughter." Tom smiled at Hal. "See, I told you Mistress Franshawe was unshockable."

"I think even she will be shocked when she knows, as Sophie will undoubtedly tell her immediately, that she intends to marry me, and that she has done so since my wife died."

"I think I knew that, Sir Henry. Sophie's exploits and your Aunt Margery's fears for you formed the bulk of her correspondence these past six months."

Hal sighed. "Of course, how could it be otherwise? Everybody must know. I don't know why I am so concerned for my, or her, good name."

"Have some more wine, Hal, and don't worry so," soothed Tom. "I've never heard any say anything but good of you." ⚜

Chapter Nineteen

"Tom, it is kind of you to allow us to meet here," said Sir Charles the next morning as they gathered in the handsome library. "I don't think I want to set foot in Harcourt now that Sir Anthony has returned home. Your message came as I was sitting down to call everyone to my house, but this is more convenient for Sir Henry and Mr Danvers and the sweet little bride. So, you see me, and we wait for Southgate to join us on our council of war."

"War?" queried Tom with a smile as he poured mugs of ale for them all.

"Aye, 'tis a war we wage against evil," Sir Charles replied. "I know we only deal at the local level, but we are the grass roots of the army against wrongdoing. A good Justice knows his territory. He knows all the local felons and, what is more, he knows his neighbours and his neighbour's kin. 'Tis something you should consider, Tom. I'm not getting any younger, we've just lost Sir Edgar and I'll oppose Sir Anthony sitting on any bench with me."

"Thus illustrating the sound judgment required," remarked Justin, taking up his mug and handing another to the silent Hal.

"How is your ward this morning, Sir Henry?" asked Sir Charles. "I see you were prompt in removing her from that house, which I applaud, but isn't the legal situation difficult?"

"Extremely," replied Hal quietly. "We expect Sir Anthony to claim Sophie's dowry as part of the estate and know we'll have to go to law to prove there was, in fact, no marriage. It was of first consideration to get Sophie away, lest Sir Anthony consider her his lawful property, too."

"Yes, indeed," Sir Charles gave an almost maidenish grimace. "One shudders to think of her fate, abandoned to that wastrel…" He hesitated. "I don't know if you are aware of the wild rumours going the rounds, Sir Henry…" he began.

"Sir Charles, I am," said Hal shortly. "I regret to say, they are true. Mistress Sandys, the other ward left in my charge, has run off to be married privately with a young man of her acquaintance."

Sir Charles nodded. "Jack Hollingshead's like a bear with a sore head, they say. He'd been nursing that estate these last ten years."

"According to Mistress Redcroft, whom, it would seem, was the architect of the elopement, Cordelia, or Mistress Blackwell, as she is now, and her husband intend to reimburse Jack Hollingshead by the sale of Adam Blackwell's land," remarked Justin blandly.

"Do they, do they? Well, that's the honourable way, I suppose," Sir Charles replied mildly. "And Mistress Sophie was behind it all, was she?" He gave an indulgent chuckle. "Aye, I can see that makes more sense. Your other ward, Sir Henry, was such a quiet little mouse… but Mistress Sophie, she's the one with spirit. Such a beauty, too. You'll have your hands full with that one, Sir Henry."

Luckily for Hal, the door opened and Dury Southgate entered with Mistress Jane Selby on his arm.

"Mistress Selby!" cried the gallant Sir Charles, leaping to his feet. "My dear, are you fit to attend this meeting? I felt you'd all be prostrate with grief this morn."

"Indeed, sir," she replied quietly. "Both my stepmother and sister are. I've come in their stead, if you'll permit it."

"Mistress Selby insisted she come, Sir Charles, as she has information she feels might be of use, and thinks no private grief should stand in the way of justice," explained Dury Southgate.

"Such a brave little woman," said Sir Charles, patting her hand affectionately. "Your father would be proud of your courage, my dear. Come, sit here by me and tell us, in your own good time, what it is you want to say."

Jane took the seat and refused a mug of ale, accepting the glass of wine Sir Charles insisted she had, to bring some colour into her pale cheeks. Hal observed Jane Selby as Sir Charles fussed and coaxed her, his brow wrinkled as he tried to discover the difference in the woman. Naturally, she was shocked and grieved, but then she was shocked and grieved for her father from the beginning in her own quiet, unemotional way. Was that the change? Were emotions now stirred up under that sedate exterior? Certainly, she seemed in the grip of powerful feelings.

"Well, well, you tell us what you've come to say, my dear," said Sir Charles. "This is purely informal, you see, so there is no need at this point to swear an oath, or any such thing. You just tell us what is troubling you."

"My conscience, Sir Charles," she replied, and her glance flickered to Hal. "Yes, my conscience. I feel responsible for that poor young man's death."

"Which one, my dear?" asked Sir Charles. "Your brother or…"

"Mr Withiam," she said, her voice breaking and tears filling her eyes. "You see, I…I didn't tell Sir Henry the truth, not the whole truth."

"Did you not?" said Sir Charles, sounding surprised and glancing to Hal, who was eyeing her narrowly.

"No." Once again, she suppressed a sob, and fixed a beseeching gaze upon Hal. "I do beg pardon, Sir Henry, but…but, in truth, I was afraid."

Hal nodded, trying to banish the question at the back of his mind and concentrate on what she was saying.

"Well, and what if you were?" cried the good Sir Charles. "My dear Mistress Selby, when I review the events of the last few days, I wonder we are not all run mad. Naturally, you were afraid."

Jane Selby nodded, tears brimming over and running down the side of her nose. "Yes, sir, you are right it…it was like a night fear," she agreed. "But you see… you see…" Her voice choked with tears, and on Sir

Charles' insistence, she took a sip of her wine and tried to staunch her tears with a tightly clasped handkerchief. "I do beg pardon," she whispered, striving to regain her composure. "I feel so foolish, but…"

"Now never mind, my dear," Sir Charles patted her clenched fist. "If this is too much for you, we can leave it for another time. Mr Kingscott has invited a lady to chaperone Mistress Redcroft and she'll be glad to…"

"Mistress Harcourt, surely?" said Jane quickly, her head coming up to look to Hal again.

"No, Mistress Selby," Justin intervened before Sir Charles could agree. "As our ward, Mistress Redcroft was never a wife, but in name. As a married lady yourself, you'll know the marriage contract does require physical ratification to make it valid. Mistress Redcroft was never in fact a married woman, and therefore has reverted to her maiden name."

Jane Selby sniffed at the slight emphasis Justin put on the word 'maiden' and took another sip of wine.

"Well, well, that is a matter for you legal men," said Sir Charles placidly. "If Mistress Selby is too distressed, Tom, I wonder…"

"No, no, I must tell you, Sir Charles," Mistress Selby, plainly heartened by the wine, hastily resumed her tale.

"Sir Henry, when I brought you the message from Mr Withiam, I did not tell you all."

"Indeed?" replied Hal politely noncommittal.

"No, you see, as I said, I was afraid," she replied, her voice trembling. "I'd been talking to Mr Withiam earlier. He seemed troubled at breakfast and I asked him if ought were amiss. Mr Witham didn't seem to be sure, but eventually he told me how he was assisting you, Sir Henry, by talking with Gervase's friends to see if he could discover any information."

"Did he," said Hal, with resignation in his voice.

"Yes, he thought he'd discovered something but was doubtful about telling you, in case it had no relevance to what had happened. He kept saying that he wasn't a clever fellow and that he didn't want to annoy Sir Henry by telling you something trivial."

"Yes, this is what you told me just before I found his body," agreed Hal, wondering why she had come only to repeat her tale.

"Yes, but I didn't tell you that he'd told me the information first," she said quietly. "He, Kit, said I'd know if it was important or not," she glanced to them in appeal. "I know I should have come to you at once with it, but I was so afraid. Mr Witham had been killed to keep from telling you. I didn't know if the killer knew I knew, too."

"Well, of course that is perfectly understandable," said Sir Charles. "Good Heavens, which of us wouldn't know some fear in such a situation, let alone a poor defenceless woman, my dear."

"And what is the information?" asked Hal, as Mistress Selby smiled mistily upon her protector.

She bit her lip and turned her attention back to Hal. "The information concerns a member of my family," she admitted with some reluctance. "It is never easy to betray one's kin, especially those one has shared one's childhood with." She took a deep breath. "The truth, Sir Henry, is that one of the others told Kit Withiam they'd seen my brother Anthony on his way to Gervase's wedding. It seems the fellow stopped overnight at Grantham on his way here. After supper, hearing of a cockfight at an inn in another part of the town, he went there to see it. He said it was a filthy barn, full to bursting with men from all over the county, mostly drunk, all wagering in the most disgusting manner. But it seems he was willing to swear he saw Sir Anthony there, because he knew him well."

"It has a predictable ring of truth," said Sir Charles.

"Anthony is a great frequenter of low company."

"The implication being that Sir Anthony was in this country before your brother's wedding and therefore has no alibi," said Justin thoughtfully.

"It doesn't follow that Sir Anthony killed his own brother, though," remarked Hal. "I mean, I gather from Sir Anthony himself that there was no love lost between him, his father and your brother Gervase, but why choose his wedding to kill him? He could have done that any time in the past."

"Well, I imagine because he was marrying," said Sir Charles. "If Gervase was married and producing heirs, there was less and less likelihood of Sir Anthony ever inheriting. From his point of view, Sir Edgar's death was the honey on the cake, one assumes."

"Yes," Hal said, but with hesitation, glancing to Justin.

"It's too flimsy," Justin agreed. "Oh, I'm not saying it isn't so, Mistress Selby, but there is no proof. What if Sir Anthony was in the country at a cockfight? All Kit Withiam's acquaintance had done is to prove Sir Anthony a liar, which means he has no alibi. There are more people who could have done this deed than we can shake a stick at. We must return to motive. For what reason was Gervase killed?"

"So Anthony could inherit," said Sir Charles. "That's a good enough motive for me, and if he hasn't got any proof of where he was, then we need to find out exactly where he was."

"Yes," agreed Justin. "A sighting of him closer to Harcourt would be more promising."

Hal shook his head. "No, no, this is all wrong," he said. "Sir Anthony is no fool. Why would he take the risk of coming to Harcourt after dark? Scaling the creeper, if anyone did, for we can find no marks on the wall or window, or broken twigs, by the way. And then to select, at random, a knife from the table and throw the dagger a good twelve feet across a chamber to near impale his brother as he sat drunk in a chair?"

"Indeed, when you put it like that, Sir Henry, you have a point," said Sir Charles, much struck. "Why not just creep into the house, where if he were discovered, none could object, even if Sir Edgar were not best pleased. And then to stab his brother in the dark? He'd be closer, and more certain of reaching a vital spot."

"Which is, I am convinced, what did happen," said Hal. "Only Sir Anthony was not at the wedding." He frowned over a query which was in his mind and was about to ask a question then he thought better of it.

"Well, well, you've certainly given us cause for thought, my dear," Sir Charles said kindly to Mistress Selby. "I think now, if you are a little more composed, Dury should take you to sit with Mistress Fanshawe, and perhaps Mistress Redcroft, whilst we continue with our deliberations. We still have much to do, you understand."

"Will you not arrest Anthony?" Jane asked doubtfully.

"Well no, my dear, not at present. We can't arrest everyone who we think might have a reason for killing. Good Heavens, the prisons would be full to bursting! You run along now, and don't worry your pretty little head anymore. You've done your duty like a brave woman, and we'll attend to the matter from here."

"Come, Mistress Selby, let me introduce you to Mistress Fanshawe," said Tom Kingscott. "We'll leave Mr Southgate to help out. I swear, just listening to all those facts makes my head ache, so you must be very weary, what with everything which has gone before." ❧

Chapter Twenty

Hal got up as they left the chamber and went to the door as if in escort, but then stood listening at the panels after he'd closed it. "Sir Charles," he said abruptly, as the others stared at him, bemused. "Who inherits if Sir Anthony were to be found guilty of his brother's murder?"

Sir Charles blinked. "Well, good Heavens, let me think. Well, do you know, Sir Henry, it would go to Mistress Selby's lad, I do believe. She takes precedence over young Katherine, of course, being of Sir Edgar's first marriage. Although, if young Harry should die, it would be any male heirs of Katherine, I imagine."

Hal nodded. "Or any sons Mistress Selby might produce if she were to re-marry?" he suggested.

"Well, yes, although Mistress Selby has long been a widow...but then, if one considers her altered circumstances in such a case…good Heavens! What are you suggesting, Sir Henry?"

"I am not suggesting anything," he replied. "I am merely looking for motive, and not allowing myself to be blinded, as I have been, by appearances."

"But what you are suggesting is preposterous!" cried Sir Charles. "That good woman…"

"Is she a good woman?" asked Hal quickly. "Wasn't she quite as wild as her brothers? Didn't she run off to be married to a cousin, without consent of either Sir Edgar or his wife?"

"I don't think you are in any position to criticise, Sir Henry," cried Sir Charles, taken aback. "Your own wards have behaved in a like manner."

"Exactly," said Hal quickly. "That's what I am getting at! Justin, if Sophie had to plot a murder, how would it sound? Wouldn't it be every bit as theatrical as this one?"

"What are you saying?" cried Sir Charles, aghast. "That the sweet little bride did it?"

"No, no," cried Hal impatiently, "she would not have had so large a part in it if Sophie had plotted it. I'm saying it has a female touch. The timing, the dagger, the drama…"

Justin nodded his comprehension. "Yes, I see what you mean, if Sir Anthony had wanted to kill his brother, he could have done it any time these past few months, and none been the wiser. A dagger thrust in the dark, as Gervase was leaving an inn, a blow to the head on the road and a drowning in a convenient river. There'd be a hundred times easier a way of achieving his object if he had a mind to it."

"Exactly," said Hal nodding. "This is my point. This was a crime designed to shock and bewilder. To confuse and confound, so that none could make head nor tail of it. I imagine the death of Sir Edgar was not part of the plan, but who would an old man turn to, if both his sons were gone? Why, his daughter and grandson of course."

Sir Charles gaped at Hal in horror. "You can't be suggesting...good God, I won't stand by and hear that sweet woman...Sir Edgar was my friend, my stout-hearted companion-in-arms. I'll not have his daughter maligned in this manner!"

"Sir Charles," said Hal sharply. "This is a discussion amongst ourselves, I am not trying to insult Mistress Selby, but to find the murderer of Gervase Harcourt, Kit Witham and by extension, Sir Edgar himself. Would he not want the person responsible for this sought out and brought to justice?"

"Not if it is his daughter," replied Sir Charles in horror. "Think of poor Lady Harcourt…no, no, you must be wrong, it must be Anthony."

"I agree, he is a most unpleasant character," said Hal. "But surely, you can't seriously be saying that you'd sooner, if he were innocent, he were hanged than the true murderer?"

"Indeed I am not," cried Sir Charles, drawing himself up to his full five foot. "I am merely suggesting you are in error!"

"Well," said Justin, as both glared at each other. "It is something which will bear investigation. If you and Dury go after Sir Anthony and try to prove his guilt, Hal and I will try to establish Mistress Selby's innocence, and then we'll all be satisfied." He cast the frowning Hal a look, adding: "How is Lady Harcourt this morning, Dury? Is she well enough to talk to us, do you think?"

Dury Southgate, who'd sat open-mouthed throughout this, stumbled into speech. "No, no, not at all. Kate, that is, Miss Harcourt, is most concerned. The physician has been summoned again, although how we'll find the…however, that is neither here nor there.

Something will be contrived."

"Are matters settled badly for my Lady?" asked Sir Charles bluntly.

"Indeed, sir," replied the agent ruefully. "Sir Edgar considered himself a hale and hearty man. Gervase had made great inroads into the estate, but with the acquisition of a wife and careful planning, Sir Edgar fully intended to bring everything about. In the meantime, he'd mortgaged Lady Harcourt's jointure and Kate's dowry. He had no thought of death. 'It'll take us a good few years, Dury,' he said to me only last month, 'but I am confident we can bring it about. It means Kate can't marry for a while, but you'll be happy with that, and who knows, perhaps in the end you might be the fellow for her.'"

"I see," said Sir Charles, tight lipped. "Well, if you see the physician, Dury, tell him to send any physicking bills to me. I'll not have my Lady worried into an early grave."

"Indeed, there has been tragedy enough, Sir Charles," agreed Hal. "Let us not see if we can expedite this matter and bring a measure of peace to the family in some way. Dury, do you have time to assist us, or are you still Sir Anthony's agent?"

"No, it seems he's hired a new fellow to take my position. He'll be arriving within a few days," replied the man bitterly.

"Then Anthony's more of a fool than I thought!" cried Sir Charles angrily.

"What, are you to be turned off like a servant, Dury?"

"Without even my character," he agreed ruefully. "Indeed, Sir Charles, if I may impose upon you. I'd like you to witness my books, if you'd be so good. I made so bold as to remove them from Harcourt with my Lady, but as she is too ill to trouble…"

"Naturally, I'll do so," replied Sir Charles swiftly. "I'll ride back with you and Mistress Selby to pay my respects to my Lady Harcourt, and do so at once. Have no fear, Dury, none shall take your character within my earshot. Now, have you thought on future employment?"

"Indeed, sir, I am casting about in my mind for something which will keep me locally situated, for I cannot abandon Lady Harcourt, nor Kate, at this juncture, and we must get money to live. Luckily, Dower House is available as a home, although a sad step down for my Lady."

"Indeed, but these are matters we can discuss later," said Sir Charles. "Sir Henry, you have something further to propose?"

"Merely, sir, that all which has passed between us should be kept in confidence," Hal replied. "None suspected should be informed or forewarned of the fact."

"I have sat the bench these last twenty years or more," Sir Charles replied waspishly. "I can be trusted to keep my tongue between my teeth."

"Indeed, sir," agreed Hal smoothly. "I suggest we meet again two days hence to see what we have discovered."

"You've upset the old man, Hal," remarked Justin, once they were left alone.

"I've jolted up his ideas," agreed Hal. "It is a relevant point, Justin. We know motive is often the strongest pointer to guilt."

Justin nodded. "I agree, but I'd not take a wager on Jane Selby being brought to book. Nor on you not being her next target if she is the murderer."

"Indeed, I think that might be the only way we'd prove it," said Hal with a grimace. "That's why I cautioned Sir Charles so pointedly."

"So I guessed," he said with a quick grin. "Well, we could wager on the method she'll use, I suppose, if she were to make an attempt."

"Poison is a woman's favourite weapon," said Hal

cheerfully. "I must keep well away from her until we've uncovered the truth one way or another…" He stopped speaking as the door opened and Tom Kingscott entered followed by Sophie.

"Good morning Sir Henry, Mr Danvers," she said formally.

"Good morning," returned Justin, surprised as Hal darted her a sharp look.

"I trust you both slept well," she continued, in the same polite manner.

"Mistress Fanshawe begs me to extend her compliments and ask if it is your intention to be at Kingsholme today, or will your investigations take you further afield?"

"Well," said Justin, somewhat at a loss as Hal sat quietly with a sardonic look to his mouth. "I'm not entirely sure what Hal has planned, but I certainly need to get some things down in writing whilst they are fresh in my mind."

"And it is necessary for me to have some further discussion with Justin and our host," said Hal. "Pray extend our thanks to Mistress Fanshawe and tell her we are settled here for the immediate future. And, if the situation should alter, we will, of course, inform her immediately."

"Thank you, Sir Henry," she replied politely. "I'll be happy to pass on your message. Is it possible I might also have a discussion with you at some time convenient to yourself?"

"It is not likely I will find time today," he replied curtly. "Although I cannot speak for Justin."

"I wish to speak to you, Sir Henry," she replied quickly. "But I am happy to await your convenience." With a swift curtsey, she withdrew.

"Now what's afoot?" Justin remarked, glancing to Hal.

Hal shrugged. "More of her tricks, no doubt. She knows she is in my bad books over Cordelia's elopement, but surely she didn't think to gull me with womanly wiles."

Tom Kingscott laughed. "You two are so hard on her. Sophie is a sweet girl."

"No doubt Mistress Fanshawe tells you so," Hal remarked dryly.

"Why yes, how did you know?" Tom cried, surprised.

"An infinite knowledge of Sophie's ways," replied Justin. "If in doubt, use all your charm."

"And she has considerable charm," agreed Tom,

laughing and directing his glance to Hal.

"You'll not get Hal to agree with you," remarked Justin sardonically.

"On the contrary, I think Sophie has great charm," said Hal, taking a seat back at the table and pulling a sheet of paper toward him. "It's her ability to use it to achieve her own ends I view with suspicion."

"So, what are your plans, Hal?" Tom asked, when he'd finished chuckling. "In what way can I assist you?"

"At present, Tom, I am inclined to agree with Justin. We need to record our thoughts and formulate further steps to take. Until we've decided that, your assistance is not necessary. Only when we've decided what we must do next, will we call upon you to perhaps go with us to interview people."

"But what of Anthony Harcourt?" asked Tom doubtfully. "Shouldn't he be watched?"

"I think we're going to need more proof than watching him will provide," said Justin. "Sir Charles will, no doubt, send the Sherriff and his Constable to seek out this place where the cockfight took place, if anyone knows it, but I can't see much coming of it, to be truthful. What if Sir Anthony was in the country? He's not a convicted criminal, he may come and go as he pleases.

Neither is he a fool. He'll keep his head down and lead a quiet life for the next few weeks."

Tom nodded his comprehension and walked over to the window, deep in thought as both men began to make notes and try to put them into some order. He sat for some time, reviewing the past few days and then, as Hal stretched and yawned, Tom recollected his duties as a host. "This is a tiresome affair for you both. I have no doubt a mug of ale would settle some of the dust of your papers, if you'll excuse me."

Before Tom had time to do so, Sophie erupted into the chamber, stopping him in his tracks. "Hal!" she cried impetuously, all traces of her earlier demure manner gone. "That mealy mouthed Jane Selby has been talking such fustian! Do you think she is the murderer?"

All the men stared at her in astonishment, Hal amazed at her ability to invariably blunder on the truth without any reasoned argument.

"Oh, I do beg pardon!" Mindful of her earlier persona, Sophie's face was suddenly spread with embarrassment as she took in the expressions on their faces. "I forget my manners in…your pardon, Sir Henry, could I exchange a few words with you?"

"I rather think Tom has guessed your manners leave

something to be desired," replied Hal tartly. "Come in and shut the door behind you before a servant overhears your loose tongue."

"It doesn't matter, Jane Selby has just left." Sophie shut the door, her embarrassment fading a little. "I made sure of that, Hal. I escorted her, Sir Charles and Dury Southgate, both vying to protect the 'brave' little woman, to the stables myself and waved them off." Sophie spat the last few words in contempt.

"An epitaph Sir Charles frequently applies to you; only he calls you the 'brave little bride'," remarked Hal blandly, turning over a few sheets of paper.

"But how did she hit upon the same solution as you, Hal?" Tom cried, looking from one to the other in puzzlement at the tone of their exchange. "She's echoed almost the same words as you did, not half an hour ago!"

"Sir Henry called Mistress Selby mealy mouthed? I take leave to doubt that!" Sophie cried, unable to keep the triumph from her voice.

"I believe I expressed my doubts about Mistress Selby in a more rational manner, but was met with such disbelief, that I am reconsidering the matter."

"But you shouldn't, Hal," said Justin, laying down his quill. "In essence, your accusation is not amiss. Proving the matter will, of course, be difficult, but none other has the motive and the opportunity to effect her brother's death so easily."

"Other than, of course, Sophie herself," remarked Hal provocatively.

Justin smiled as Sophie glared at Hal. "Tell me again, Sophie, about the loving cup Mistress Selby brought to you and Gervase Harcourt."

"I told you already," she replied. "It was a two-handled cup with a beautiful design upon it, entwined about our initials and the date of the wedding."

"Was it full when she offered it to you?" he continued, writing down the details.

"Yes," replied Sophie, frowning. "Jane Selby came into the chamber just after Gervase was supported in by his friends. She followed them in with the cup, carrying it carefully. It was steaming," she added clearly, seeing the picture again.

"What did it contain?" asked Hal curiously.

"I don't know, just that it tasted very strong and was sweet with herbs. I thought sack, or perhaps brandy-wine. I'm not sure," replied Sophie thoughtfully.

"Did she say she'd mixed it, or had one of the servants prepared it?" asked Justin thoughtfully.

"No, she'd done it herself. She said so as she was picking up the pieces," replied Sophie. "She was angry with Gervase for smashing it. He called it a witch's brew, I remember now. Good Heavens! Why didn't I remember that before now?" she added in surprise. "Gervase sipped at it when she offered it, and cursed because it was still hot. She offered to cool it by adding more wine, but he said he wanted none of her witch's brews and drank it down all at once."

"So, she regularly brewed herbal drinks," said Justin with a pleased nod.

"Yes, but then so do I, so does Mary and Bess. Many women do so," said Sophie, frowning.

"Yes, but you slept heavily, you said you remembered nothing until morning," said Hal. "Could it be that the draught was drugged? Is that what you are thinking, Justin?"

"Why?" Tom asked. "Why drug Gervase if she was going to stab him?"

"I don't think she intended to," said Hal slowly. "I said from the start it was badly planned crime. I think she knew that you'd only sip at the loving cup, Sophie, for she will have observed over the months how you dislike most strong drink. But even if you'd drunk more, it would have merely drugged you more. It must have been done so that she could slip in to retrieve the cup, only he smashed it, so she was able to take it away. I suppose she wanted to check to make sure Gervase was dead anyway. Only, I don't think he was, so she had to resort to using a dagger to finish him off."

Sophie shuddered. "How horrible to think of it."

"Then don't," said Justin swiftly. "Think instead how we are going to prove the crime, for I can't see how it can be done. Even if you go and accuse her, Hal, there is still no proof. And don't talk about provoking her so she'll try to poison you, that is just not possible."

"Not impossible, though," he countered. "You forget she has a liking for me, 'tis possible I could get her to confide in me."

"It's too risky," said Justin. "If she doesn't kill you, Sophie will if she catches you making love to Jane Selby."

"I have no intention of embroiling myself," said Hal sharply, as Sophie's eyes flashed. "Merely inviting her to confide her troubles to me."

"Justin's right, it's too risky," said Tom. "There must be another way. Perhaps one of the servants might know something? Or Kate, or indeed Lady Harcourt."

"Both are too grieved to question and the servants are

either with them, or gone away," said Justin. "We need an item of substantial proof to lay before Sir Charles."

"We need a confession," said Hal stubbornly. "Without a confession, we are sunk, and I can't see us getting one. She's too clever for us."

"You admit a woman is too clever for you, Sir Henry?" mocked Sophie. "I cannot credit it."

Hal turned his considering gaze upon her. "Sophie, go back to Mistress Fanshawe and remain with her, if you please."

"But I don't please," she replied. "I can see you are about to plot something dangerous and I will not be sent away to be kept safe."

"I'm not sending you away to be kept safe," he replied coldly. "I'm reminding you of your duty to Mistress Fanshawe, who is your hostess, and has given up her time to come here to keep you company."

Sophie eyed him uncertainly. He knew etiquette was one of the mysteries she found difficult to fathom, and he never failed to use it. She felt her embarrassment grow as both Tom and Justin glanced to her.

"I am fully aware of my duty to Mistress Fanshawe," she stammered. "But surely, if you are going to put yourself in danger…"

"I intend no such thing," Hal cut across her protestations sharply. "Have we not indicated, Justin and I, that we'll be working on our reports for Sir Charles for a good few hours?"

"Well, yes, but I know you Hal…"

"Come, Sophie," Tom Kingscott took pity on her, offering her his arm. "I promised Hal and Justin a mug of ale twenty minutes ago. We are plainly in the way of their discussions, we'll go and fetch it."

"Promise me, Hal, you'll not go after Jane Selby alone," cried Sophie, feeling compelled to take Tom's offered arm.

"Have I not told you I am working on this report?" he replied curtly as Tom opened the door and ushered her through.

"You gave her no promise, I notice," remarked Justin, pouring sand upon a sheet.

"No more I did," agreed Hal.

"Hal…" began Justin uneasily.

"I shall take care, Justin," he said quickly. "I'm not going to seek Mistress Selby out alone. I thought I'd go to the Dower House. She'll be there for sure. What harm can come to me in a house full of other people?"

"The house was full to bursting when Gervase Harcourt died," said Justin, frowning over his papers.

"And I'll take great care not to eat or drink anything whilst I'm there. Also, I'll check my horse for broken straps and burrs under the saddlecloth. Are you satisfied?"

"No," he replied dourly. "But I know better than to dispute with you when you are set upon something." He glanced up. "I know you'll get more out of her if I am not there too, but do take care, Hal. I am convinced, the more I think on it, the more you are right."

"Good," Hal smiled as he got to his feet. "Then you'll be able to pursue the matter should I make a mistake and she kills me, too. My apologies to Mistress Fanshawe. I'll return as soon as I may. Do your very best to keep Sophie from following me, if you please."

Justin snorted. "How like you to take the easy task!"

Chapter Twenty One

"Hal!" Sophie stood up as he crossed the hall. "You lied to me. You are going off to see Jane Selby."

"Sophie, what are you doing here?" Hal demanded irritably. "Did I not tell you to remain with Mistress Fanshawe? Do you not understand we are not at Westwood, where you can come and go at your whim?"

"Well, of course I can," she retorted scornfully. "Tom has just bade me make free of his home."

"His words are but a courtesy," cried Hal in exasperation. "Everyone says the same, but it is recognised as only that."

"And only ignorant underbred people take them at their word, I suppose?" retorted Sophie, her cheeks reddening. "Yes, I can believe that. How false you all are."

"It's not falseness, exactly," said Hal, fearing his words had wounded her confidence. "I'm sorry, I should have explained it better to you. It's more of a..."

"It's more of a code?" she suggested tartly.

"No, not that exactly, just an unwritten understanding," he admitted lamely. "Look, I'm sorry I've been curt with you. I suppose you couldn't be expected to know all this."

"Oh, but I do. Aunt Margery spent weeks drumming such nonsense into my ears, and Lady Harcourt's manners were even more ridiculous," she retorted.

"You don't seem to be able to grasp what I am saying to you. I imagine it's the way Aunt Margery has held up the Kingscotts as the epitome of all that is perfect, but to me, Tom is a very nice, ordinary sort of fellow who happens to be wealthy. Yet, because I happen to have become involved in what you consider a 'social mishap' by getting my bridegroom murdered, it would seem your wits have gone a-begging."

Hal, who had been softening toward her, grew angry again. "And these circumstances make it imperative for you to insult me, I assume?" he snapped.

"I don't know," she replied mildly. "Would an insult waken you to the danger of the situation? If so, I am willing to try. Because, I cannot believe, having promised me you would not seek out someone we know to be a murderer, you are going to do just that!"

"Item: I gave you no promise," he corrected her.

"Item: You implied as much," she retorted. "You think you can get Jane Selby to confide in you because she is half in love with you, and that will protect you from her wickedness."

"I believe I have her confidence," he agreed.

"You fool!" she snapped. "She has taken you in with her pretty words and womanly ways. She flatters your ego and you step eagerly into her trap."

"Well, perhaps she finds it easier to persuade men to her company rather than using hoydenish tricks and a virago's strictures," he retorted, irked by the truth of her words.

"Indeed," she agreed, her eyes hardening. "I don't fawn upon anybody. Flattery is a falsehood, and Jane Selby is false, utterly false, we both know that."

"You know little of Mistress Selby," he replied sharply. "We could, perhaps, be wrong. She could be a woman maligned, that is why we must take care."

"You think you know Jane Selby, but she has you almost blinded by her meek, good-little-woman ways," snapped Sophie. "She's laid a trap and you'll walk into it because, you want to believe she's just like Libby. But she's not at all like Libby, and you insult Libby's memory to compare them. She was a far finer person in every way."

"You tell me my wife was a finer person?" he cried. "My wife, whom you drove to her death?"

Sophie turned as pale as she had been red before. "I didn't drive Libby to her death!" she cried angrily. "I was with her through the last months of her life. I hadn't deserted her, when she was ill and afraid. If they had but let me, I'd have been with her to the end. Libby was kind to me, probably the only person I've met who was truly kind to me!"

"Yet you desired her death!" he hissed, implacably angry that she should remind him of his desertion. "For your love of me was the greater."

She shook her head. "No," she replied. "That wasn't love, it was infatuation. In those months without you, I made you my hero against all the odds. I was infatuated, and had Libby's adoration of you to shore up the dream. It was later when you returned that I found the reality."

Hal looked disconcerted. He frowned and shrugged it aside. "This is neither here nor there. This is not the occasion for a discussion of your behaviour," he snapped irritably. "We are guests in…"

"There is no occasion in future for you to discuss my behaviour," she interrupted. "I am a half-married woman, no longer a child out of the schoolroom. The matter at hand is rather more pressing. Jane Selby must be caught. She is a very dangerous woman."

"You know the matter has been discussed and the majority don't agree with you. Indeed, Sir Charles is most insulted that such calumny could be thought possible of Mistress Selby," replied Hal stiffly. "I am to investigate my concerns further and to report back to Sir Charles tomorrow. Recollect: he is the justice here."

"Don't be silly, tomorrow will be too late for Sir Anthony," said Sophie impatiently. "Sir Charles is another man Jane Selby has convinced of her innocence. Don't you see? Sir Anthony is all that stands between Jane and her objective."

"Yes, I agree, that is one way of looking at it," Hal replied with exaggerated patience. "But Tom, Sir Charles and Dury have difficulty in believing Mistress Selby is guilty, and Tom and Sir Charles have known her all their lives."

"When has others' doubts stopped you from seeing a matter clearly?" she demanded. "You always bring fresh eyes to an affair, which, when they aren't blinded by flattery, tell you that Jane Selby is false."

"And what is it that clears your vision so effectively?" he demanded, disliking the lecturing tone she'd adopted. "Jealousy?"

Sophie stood very still for a few seconds. "You used to be bigger than this," she replied. "You most certainly have lost your eye. You are wearing the blindfold of conceit, I suppose." Abruptly, she turned and went from him without another word.

Stung, Hal followed her to the bottom of the stairs. "Sophie, I forbid you to interfere. Sir Charles is the Justice. This has nothing to do with you."

Sophie, halfway up the elaborately carved staircase, returned no reply or even gave any indication she had heard.

Hal stood in the hallway debating with himself. Her words hurt, just as she'd intended them to. Yet, like most of Sophie's utterances, they held precious grains of truth. He had enjoyed the admiration he'd seen in Jane Selby's eyes. Had it been flattery designed to disarm him? He hadn't thought so, but Sophie's words made him feel uncomfortable now. Was he conceited? He'd never considered himself so, but then he always discounted his personal attractions. He knew that Libby had fallen in love, initially, with his face, but it had been him, the inner Hal, surely, that she had adored? He hadn't realised until Sophie said it just how much that adoration had meant to him.

How, in the short years of their marriage, Libby's love had become the bedrock of his inner soul, and how since her death, he'd felt so lost and alone. Yes, it had been gratifying to see the look of adoration present in Jane Selby's eyes. Sophie never looked at him in blind adoration of his superior power.

Sophie expected him to be what he was, she recognised all his attributes, but they meant little to her. He would never be a wonderful being, a god to Sophie. She wasn't a worshipper at a shrine, but a mate, a partner who would walk shoulder to shoulder beside him through life. There'd be no blind adoration, more a mutual recognition of abiding trust and love. At least, so he imagined, as stripped naked of the cosiness of Jane Selby's admiration, he reviewed the situation.

There had been a look in Sophie's eyes as she turned from him, a disappointment in her voice. 'You used to be bigger than this, Hal. You've lost your eyes. You are wearing the blindfold of conceit.' The words came again, laid like lashes across his esteem. He couldn't deny the truth of them, even as he wriggled in shame. He thrust it aside. Never mind that sort of nonsense. He had a task before him, he had to find out if Jane Selby was false, as Sophie claimed, or perhaps just misguided. He shrugged his shoulders and made his way to the stables. ❧

Chapter Twenty Two

Hal rode swiftly out of Tom's estate and in the direction of Harcourt village. The Dower House was on the edge of the Harcourt estate, and he made this his destination, certain he'd find Jane Selby, Sir Charles and Dury Southgate still there.

In this, he was partially wrong. Dury was indeed in the tiny courtyard off the lane, and Sir Charles was closeted with Lady Harcourt, but Jane, it seemed, had walked up to the Hall.

As Hal jumped down to talk to Dury, he was aware of the beauty of the day and everything around him. All at once, it seemed at variance with his earlier ideas.

Dury, too, seemed inclined to put all thoughts of suspicion from him. He hastened to tell Hal of Mistress Kate's continuing distress and that Lady Harcourt was being stoical and helping Sir Charles with the accounts.

"Indeed," he ended, "on such a perfect day as this, one wonders how anything can be amiss with the world."

"Yes," agreed Hal, unconsciously relaxing some of his guard. "And Mistress Selby, she is also within with her son?"

"No, young Harry is with Kate," replied Dury. "My Lady has sent Mistress Selby up to the Hall, some trifling matter of her own silver, it would seem. I did volunteer to go, but my Lady thought it might provoke a further quarrel, so Mistress Selby offered."

Hal nodded in resignation. Plainly, Sir Charles's outrage had had its effect. "I am on my way to Sir Anthony myself," he said. "I'll see if I can't overtake Mistress Selby and take her up before me to save her the walk."

"She left some fifteen minutes ago," said Dury, frowning uncomfortably. "She would be at the house about now. Would you prefer me to go with you?"

"You are busy, I can see," replied Hal. "It won't take me long to talk to Sir Anthony, I don't anticipate any cooperation, so I'll merely call and escort Mistress Selby back."

Dury stood irresolute as Hal remounted, his doubts about his cousin Jane had been thankfully laid to rest by Sir Charles forthright manner, but now, in the face of Hal's unspoken fears, they arose again. "Wait, Sir Henry, I'll saddle up and join you," he said quickly.

"I'll be there and back by the time you've done that," said Hal pleasantly. "I'll return within half an hour, have no fear."

The journey to Harcourt was a matter of minutes. Hal paused at the tall iron gate which had been his destination the night of Sophie's marriage. Already, to his mind, the house had a rakish air. For the first time in probably years, the grass was unscythed and the sheep roamed right up to the house. He trotted down the avenue and dismounted at the door, which stood open. No servant came to take his horse, so he tethered him to a ring and entered the vast hall. Momentarily blinded, he stumbled and stared as a cry rang out.

As his eyes became accustomed to the gloom, he took in Jane Selby, stood over the body of her brother Anthony, bloodstained knife still in her hand, and an expression of fear on her face. "Good God!" cried Hal in astonishment. "What has happened here? Is he killed? Did you see who attacked him?"

Even as the last question fell from his lips, he knew, with a sickening dread, the answer. She turned on him, her lips drawn back in a travesty of a smile, showing the blood where it had spurted over the lace of her cuff and down her gown.

"Sweet Jesu!" he whispered. "Why?"

"Why?" she laughed with a terrifying chuckle, from deep in her throat. "Why? Why not? Why not make away with them all?"

"Mistress Selby…Jane, you cannot…no, this is all… no it cannot be!" Hal said, still unable to comprehend such wickedness, even though he had feared it would be so.

"Can it not?" she replied, advancing on him. "Do you truly see me as such a sweet, gentle creature? A pattern of sweet domesticity, as was your poor dead wife. Dear God! How you men sicken me."

Hal stared at her, transfixed, his worst fears confirmed.

"Oh, that shocks you, does it, dear Sir Henry?" she jibed. "How could I address the so august Sir Henry Westwood with disrespect? Yet, you have patronized me since you first saw I had a brain and might be useful to you."

"I thought you'd be only too happy to assist in finding your father's and brother's killer," he replied numbly.

She snorted her contempt. "Fool! I knew who'd killed

them, my aim was to mislead you, and possibly marry you, until I saw your eyes as you watched that trollop, your ward."

"Sophie is not a trollop," he replied grimly, understanding how Sophie has seen so much more clearly than he had. "And I must arrest you, Jane Selby, for the wilful murder of your brothers Gervase and Anthony, and the suspected murder of your father, Sir Edgar Harcourt."

"Oh, he was half-dead already!" she replied impatiently. "Who's to say if a little extra foxglove was for better or ill?"

"May God have mercy on your soul!" he replied. "I think perhaps your best recourse would be to consult a physician, for I fear your mind is lost."

"Nonsense, I am as sane as you!" she snapped. "And I'll need no recourse, for you'll die in a brawl with Sir Anthony."

Sophie, meanwhile, having set out in a mood of defiance, had, during the ride through the woods of Tom Kingscott's estate, decided to proceed with caution. It was thus that she entered Harcourt via the stables. She stopped to collect some of her linen from the laundress at the laundry, before making her way to the kitchens, to listen with sympathy to the cook's litany of complaints.

Mistress Tempy, the cook, greatly feared she could not remain in so ramshackle a house as the one presided over by her new master. Sir Anthony, it seemed, had not been sober since his father's funeral. He demanded his dinner at all hours of the day and night and kept a tribe of body servants, who were next best things to cutpurses, if she had any guess.

The whole house was being stripped bare by these rogues, indeed, most of the silver had already disappeared, and the cellars were drunk dry. Furthermore, now everything was going missing. Why, her good porridge pan, which had been in the pantry this past fifteen years had gone, and now her favourite knife with the long blade she'd got from the cutler at market was nowhere to be seen.

Sophie nodded and soothed, and suggested she took herself off to see Dury Southgate at the Dower House, where, if she had to work for board, she could at least be sure of an orderly house. Mistress Tempy sighed and said she didn't know what the world was coming to, but she hoped Mistress Jane might be able to talk some sense into her brother, she'd been with him this last half hour.

Sophie's heart sank abruptly at this news. It was not part of her plan to confront Jane Selby alone, however, she knew she couldn't walk away. So, she said she'd ask if Mistress Selby would like to walk back to the Dower House and hurried anxiously from the back of the house, her heart beginning to pound as she heard Jane's voice raised in anger and the scuffle of feet.

Fearing the worst, she hurried across an antechamber, snatching up a hideous blue and white Delft vase that Lady Harcourt had filled with fabulously expensive tulip bulbs earlier in the year, and tiptoed forward behind the screen set beside the hall door to keep out the draughts. Peeping around the side, a fearful sight met her eyes.

Anthony Harcourt was spread-eagled across the black and white floor, his blood stark against the tiles, whilst Hal retreated from the blood stained knife of Jane Selby, already clutching a bleeding forearm.

"Mistress Selby," he was saying patiently. "Please do think of your son. What good can this do?"

"Why, he'll take his rightful place as Sir Henry Harcourt," she replied. "Now I've dispatched those half-bred curs."

"Sir Henry Selby," Hal corrected her, then, as she gave a cry of rage, Sophie threw caution to the winds and flew across the hall, hurling the pot at Jane. It caught her a glancing blow on her shoulder and shattered on the far wall, as the gory dagger slipped from Jane's grasp.

She turned, her face a mask of fury. "You!" she cried. "That vase was Delft!"

"Not anymore!" replied Sophie, undaunted by the fury in Jane's eyes.

"I'll kill you!" screamed Jane. She glanced to her hand as Hal bent to pick up the fallen knife. She hit out at him with the full force of her hand, making him stagger, but he retained the knife.

Turning to her, he repeated his earlier words: "Jane Selby, I am arresting you for the murder of..."

"Oh, hold your tongue!" she snarled as both he and Sophie closed in on her. Then, suddenly all rage left her. "Very well, I'll come quietly, Sir Henry," she finished, and as they came closer still, she smiled her sweet smile up at him...Libby's smile...and snatching the knife again, plunged it into Sophie. ❧

Chapter Twenty Three

Hal's shouts for assistance brought the cook, her maid and one of the grooms who'd been in the kitchen in search of someone in authority. "Come quickly!" Hal cried, his arms clasping Sophie as, with one venomous look, Jane Selby ran out through the open doorway, into the avenue. "One of you, go after her! But have a care, she has a knife and is dangerous!"

The groom paused at the open door as the woman fled along the avenue, whilst the cook, with a cry of dismay, bypassed the body of her master, and helped Hal support Sophie into a chair. "Mercy upon us!" she cried, snatching off her apron and using it to wipe blood from Sophie's gown. "Never say she has murdered this pretty child!"

"I...I think it is but a flesh wound," stammered Hal in fear, "I am certain the knife hit the bone of her corset, and turned the blade aside."

The cook ripped the delicate silk of Sophie's bodice asunder and loosened the laces of her corset to find the wound revealed beneath the muslin of her chemise. "I think you are correct, Sir Henry," she said in relief. "The flesh is pierced, but not deeply." Skilfully, she ripped the fabric away, leaving the cut exposed. "Yes! It's little more than a scratch, most of the blood on her gown would appear to be yours."

"Yes, probably," he agreed. "I caught her with my wounded arm, so that I could apply pressure with my good hand if need be, but I was certain it wasn't a fatal wound. I think she fainted more from fear than from any hurt."

"I'd better attend to you both," she agreed, calling to the maid to fetch water and cloths, and not to forget her marigold salve.

"We are neither of us badly harmed," said Hal, easing Sophie in his arms.

"But, you there, quickly find some other men and go after Mistress Selby!" he shouted as the groom turned back to them. "She must be stopped before she kills again!"

"Did she kill him?" the cook asked, nodding to the

corpse of her master as the man ran off. She ripped the fine lawn of Hal's sleeve and tutted over the long cut which ran from his wrist to his elbow.

"Him, his elder brother and her father," said Hal with a shudder. "She must be mad. I cannot think what possessed her!"

"Greed!" said the woman, as the maid appeared warily, carrying a pewter basin, some cloths and a small pungent-smelling pot. "She were ever a greedy envious child, right from a little one. She never took any joy in another's happiness , always wanted everything for herself, and as soon as she had it, she had no use for it. Evil, she were, wicked, no wonder Sir Edgar wouldn't have her near him. Ah, there, my pretty, let me bathe away this blood," she continued as Sophie's eyelids fluttered.

Sophie opened her eyes with a little cry. "Oh, that hurts!" she said muzzily. Then, as she focussed on Hal's pale face, she cried: "Oh! Are you badly hurt, Hal?"

"No, just a cut to my forearm," he replied. "She opened up Durward's scar, which is why it bled so freely, but it's clotting now."

"Oh! That stings!" she cried again as the cook applied the salve. "I'm hurt? She stabbed me!"

"It is little more than a cut," he soothed. "Her arm

failed her at the last, although, as neither of us were drunk or drugged first, that isn't surprising."

"This really hurts!" cried Sophie fretfully, tears filling her eyes as the cook covered the wound with a cloth, and loosely retied her laces to hold it in place. She struggled to sit up, trying to gather up her wits and dignity. "Dear God, only look, I have a hole in me and my gown is ruined. And it's all your fault Hal Westwood! I told you not to come here!"

"And I told you not to come, too," he replied, as the cook set about tending his arm. He gave a grunt of pain and flinched. "And I am not responsible for either the hole in your side, or your gown. This good lady ripped your bodice in her attempts to rescue you from your own folly. I was merely trying to reassure you that the wound you sustained was not fatal."

"How like you, Hal, to dismiss everything as nothing, and not even to sympathise with me!" she wept, tears running down her cheeks

"Now, now, don't you fret, my pretty," soothed the cook. "Your nerves are all of a jangle, that's what, and Sir Henry's, too. Jenny, run and see if there's any of the master's brandy left. That's what's needed just now to hearten you, Sir Henry. Now, let me put some of my marigold paste on that nasty wound and it will heal up this time without no bother."

"Thank you, mistress," he replied, gritting his teeth as she started to bind the wound up. "A little tighter, if you please, I'll need to use my arm if I am to find Mistress Selby."

"Now you just bide a while, sir," said the cook, shaking her head. "The men are out searching for Mistress Jane, she'll not go far. Why this takes me back to the war, you know. The fighting about here were summat awful, it seemed we were forever binding up the hurts of one or another. Did you bring that brandy, Jenny, pour the lady and gentleman a little to help settle them down."

"A little it be, too, Tempy," returned the maid. "A bare quarter of a flask is all I could find." The girl glanced up through the window as she handed a glass to Hal. "There's men a coming up the avenue and they be carrying a woman's body between 'em."

"Are they now?" sighed the cook, tidying away her cloths and salves. "Happen this will be the end of the killing now. Fetch a cloth to cover Sir Anthony, and be quick about it, girl." ❧

Chapter Twenty Four

"Was she dead, Hal?" Justin asked later as they sat together in Tom's snug parlour.

"Not when they laid her down by Anthony's body," he replied. "The cook tried her best to save her, but I knew it was useless as soon as we pulled the knife from her chest."

Sophie laughed shakily. "Poor Mistress Tempy. I think she was more distressed over her good kitchen knife, than all the dead and wounded about her."

"People fix on strange things to angry about," said Hal. "Like gowns and such."

"I have every right to be cross about my ruined gown," snapped Sophie. "I am forever ruining my clothes, since I met you."

"That, I can't believe," he replied. "You must always have been a nosy, interfering child, ruining your gowns and annoying Master Benton's sister." The suggestion of a smile quivered on Sophie's lips, but she was still uncertain in her moods.

"Did Jane Selby say anything?" asked Tom tactfully.

"Apart from damning us all to Hell?" Hal replied in troubled tones. "Yes, I asked her about young Kit Withiam. I cannot deny I feel responsible for his needless death, I should never have asked one so vulnerable to help me." The teasing note had gone from his voice now, leaving it stark. "I have seldom met another with such a dearth of compassion or contrition as Jane Selby. It was plain she cared little that she was about to meet her Maker." He shook his head. "There was no real reason to kill Kit. He'd learnt that Anthony had attended a cock fight so that he was in the country when he said he wasn't, but she still killed him. Just because she could, she said."

"She cursed the Reverend Borwick, who Drury Southgate had hauled from his dinner, and died in no state of grace, with Hal praying for her, because Mr Borwick wouldn't," added Sophie, tears swimming in her eyes. It was horrible—horrible!"

"I prayed for her…and all of us," he agreed sombrely.

"A tragic waste," said Mistress Fanshawe.

Tom refilled everyone's glass. "What will they do,

the Harcourts, do you think?"

"Dury says Lady Harcourt will move back to the house with her grandson and Kate, and that he'll run the estate as before. Apparently, the Rector went straight to the Dower House to arrange the funerals."

"Sir Charles is helping her hush it all up," said Justin as a statement of fact.

"Yes," agreed Hal. "Gervase was killed by Sir Anthony and Jane took her own life in grief at her father's death whilst her mind was unhinged."

"Very neat," said Tom. "But it won't stop the gossip. Several of the village men joined the grooms in hunting Jane down, and she was spitting defiance to the end. She opened a wound in one fellow's leg before she turned that knife on herself."

Hal shuddered and drank off his brandy, refusing Tom's offer of more. "No, no, my wits are already muzzy," he said, "and I must be sober if I am to ask Sophie to marry me."

There was an abrupt silence at this and Justin took the bottle from Tom to refill his own glass and sat waiting, his eyes fixed on the pretty girl before them. Sophie kept her head down as she pulled at the bloodstained ruin of her bodice.

Hal made a face. "You say nothing, Sophie," he remarked, trying to keep his voice light. "You'll not spare my feelings, then, you'll make me, wounded as I am, kneel before you, and ask in form?"

Still, Sophie, to the surprise of them all, said nothing. Then, as Hal, taken aback, made as if to move, she said hastily: "No, stay, I beg you. Don't hurt yourself more on my account. Too many, it would seem, have been injured these past days," she hesitated, but still didn't raise her head. "Thank you for the offer of marriage, Hal, but I fear I cannot accept, and not only because I am, as Justin is about to remind me, still a widowed bride."

"Well, I didn't mean immediately..." began Hal, in shocked tones.

"I know," she nodded, and looked up to meet his eyes. "But even in six months, a year's time, however long it takes to free me from the Harcourts, I'll still not marry you. You were right, Hal, we are not suited."

"But I love you, Sophie," he said blankly.

"No, you don't," she replied. "You love Libby, you quite liked Jane until she started killing people. You don't know who you love, but it certainly isn't me. No, no, don't dispute it, don't you see that all we ever do is quarrel, and I am so tired of quarrels."

"You are tired, Sophie," said Mistress Fanshaw kindly. "Tired and shaken by the events of the day. Sir Henry is too impatient." She smiled across at him, and realised how deep his feeling were. "Sophie should go to bed and sleep. Things will look different in the morning."

"No," said Sophie. "It will all be the same. Other than, by your leave, Sir Henry, I'll go and live with Cordelia and Adam for a few months. It will make it easier if I am here should any legal problems arise, and I don't imagine you'll ever want to see my face again."

"But I do," he replied starkly. "Every day."

Sophie shrugged her shoulders and glanced to Justin. "Do I have leave to make my home with Cordelia and Adam?" she asked.

"For a month," he replied. "It will take that long to sort out the legal mess, although Dury seemed to think Lady Harcourt is eager to settle and be finished with everything."

Sophie shrugged. "Thank you. I'll send a message to Adam tomorrow. I fear I'll spoil his bliss, but Cordelia is insistent." Her eyes travelled to Hal again. "It is for the best, you know, Aunt Margery would agree with me."

"It's not," he replied. "But, if you won't marry me, then I can do no more." ⚜

Enjoy Chapter One

of the next book in the

Hal Westwood Series:

The Mistletoe Bride

1666

Prologue

Nicholas reined in his horse. "This is hopeless," he said, with a catch in his voice. "Merlin is lame, we'll never make it to Lincoln."

Bella gave a little sigh, and swallowed the sob in her throat. "I fear you are right, Nicholas, what shall we do?"

"The devil of it is, Bella, I don't know. It all seemed much simpler when I planned it at home," he confessed.

She patted his damp back kindly. "You couldn't have foreseen the weather."

"That's the point. At this time of year, I should have considered it. Maybe your brother is right. Maybe I am too much of an untried fool to think of marriage," he replied glumly.

He looked so miserable, with raindrops spilling from the rim of his dark hat and his once jaunty feather hanging limply to his shoulder, that her soft heart was rung. "I think you are wonderful, Nick," she confided shyly.

A radiant smile lit his face. He was at once transformed from a sulky schoolboy into a gay adventurer. "I adore you, too, Bella!" he said, his voice echoing his feelings. "I'm sure I'll think of something presently, but in the meantime, I fear we must walk. I am not willing to damage poor Merlin."

"Indeed, no, poor fellow! He has carried us so gallantly, too. I don't mind walking one bit. Only, do you know where we are, Nick?" she asked, looking doubtfully about her.

"No," he admitted reluctantly, as he slid from the saddle and reached up to help her down. "But we should hit the Lincoln road almost any time now. Mind those brambles, now, Bella. I am sure if we keep to this path, we must soon find the road."

He absently patted the nose of his horse and led the beast forward through the undergrowth of the wood, in what he trusted was the right direction. He hadn't lightly persuaded Bella Craven to elope with him. He was only too well aware of the difficulties of his situation.

Unless he could find the treasure hidden by his father, he would never keep his house and land. He had only until the last day of the year to pay off the mortgages which were due, or he'd lose everything.

He tightened his grip on Bella's hand and smiled into her inquiring eyes as she looked up at him. Her dark hair, misted with tiny droplets of rain, curled wildly about her lovely face. At least, if they got to Lincoln, that awful man Pridow wouldn't get his hands on her. Even if he did lose his fortune, he wouldn't let Bella be sacrificed to her brother's ambition. Pridow had made his late wife's life a misery with his mean ways.

Don't worry," she said with her sunny smile. "Once we are married, we'll soon find your treasure, and even if we shouldn't immediately, I'm sure Simon will give me my dowry. Shall we be married as soon as we get to Lincoln? You do have the licence?"

"It is all arranged. We shall be married at St Mary's, by a friend of mine who used to be the curate at St Cuthbert's chapel."

"Do you think I look old enough?" she asked anxiously.

He thought she looked a mere child, and couldn't help smiling as he replied: "Yes, none will suspect anything is amiss, provided you don't giggle."

"Giggle!" she repeated indignantly.

"Yes, you do, you know…ah, look! There is the road!" he cried as they pushed through the trees into a clear-ing.

"Is it the Lincoln road?" she asked anxiously.

"I don't think so…but it is a road…it must lead somewhere," he replied.

"As long as it's not straight back home," she agreed.

⚜

Hal looked about him. The Hall was definitely old-fashioned, Spartan almost, yet meticulously neat. The windows were high, built for defence, with stout shut-ters pulled back to let in the sparse winter light. The walls were recently washed to a dazzling whiteness, but devoid of any adornment. No tapestries to create the il-lusion of warmth or wealth. The floor was plain, flagged stones, which time had polished to a gentle sheen.

He crossed to the fire glad of its warmth, noting the logs piled high to one side, drying out, and took a seat on a bench set there, to warm his numbed fingers. There was but one chair, high-backed, dark and obviously old, in that it had seen better days, but had been carefully repaired to be of use for the new age. Likewise the padded cushions, which were placed gaily along the stone window seat, were neatly patched and darned, told a tale of their own. Money appeared to be short for the young couple.

"Sir Henry, please take the chair!" Adam Blackwell, returning with a mug of steaming ale, was insistent. "I mended it myself to take my weight. It will serve you easily."

"Thank you, Mr Blackwell," replied Hal, taking the mug from him and cradling it in his hands as he sipped the heartening brew. "It grows cold as the sun goes down."

"Yes," Adam glanced anxiously skyward. "I expected Cordelia to be returned by now. She has but stepped out to talk to the vicar's sister. The light fades so quickly at this time of year."

Hal nodded, and feeling weary and not inclined to put his host at his ease, slipped into silence. The fretting worries, which had driven him northwards at this inclement time of year, springing back into his mind.

Aunt Kate, and Aunt Margery too, to a certain extent, both had become part of the fabric of his life since his return from exile in France near seven years ago. Both in their very different ways had helped him adjust to the new life, so abruptly thrust upon him, and both were fond of him, as he was of them.

Now Aunt Margery was ill, very ill, if the truth were told, although she wouldn't hear of it. And Aunt Kate, although she was yet unaware of it, seemed to have a problem of her own. His errand at this time between Christmas and Twelfth Night was to collect Aunt Kate from where she was visiting in the neighbouring county and return her to Westwood. On the face of it, it was to help nurse Aunt Margery back to health, but in truth it was to get her from what could become a difficult, if not dangerous, situation.

And all this had to be done without any offence to those concerned, or any admission of what was going forward, a hellishly trick situation, which Aunt Margery was convinced only Hal could accomplish. Was it any wonder then, that he had decided to break his journey at the home of his erstwhile ward, Cordelia Sandys, making the excuse that he needed to transfer various papers to her husband now she was married, but in fact to gather his wits and plan how his objective was to be achieved without Aunt Margery's frequently repeated instructions.

"I'm sure Cordelia won't be long." Adam repeated uncomfortably, remembering how, from his very first meeting at the inn in Chawcester, Hal Westwood had the power to make him feel like an ill-educated clod.

"And how is my former ward, your wife?" asked Hal, disturbed from his reverie.

"Cordelia is—is well, replied Adam with hesitation. "I am sure both she and Sophie will be back directly. I've sent a lad after them."

"Mistress Redcroft—or does she go by the name of Harcourt in these parts—she is still with you then?" remarked Hal, although he knew it was so.

"Sophie is still called Redcroft," replied Adam frowning. "Mr Danvers came to insist it was necessary. She never took the Harcourt name."

"And she obeyed him? How refreshingly unusual of her! It is not a name one would wish to be associated with, most certainly." Hal agreed coldly.

"Definitely not in this location," Adam agreed with a sudden grin. "The gossip was dreadful!"

"I can imagine it was," replied Hal, "but something Mistress Redcroft is well used to, surely?"

"I don't know that anyone can become used to having lies spread about them," returned Adam, frowning.

"Such ill-natured spite must always hurt, I'd think."

Hal glanced sharply to the other man, a little surprised by his words. "Do you find your local minister to your taste?" he asked, his manner thawing slightly.

Adam gave a wry smile. "He's one of the old sort," he admitted. "He tends his flock with fire and brimstone! He considers Cordelia to be the spawn of Satan, even though she is trying her best to fit her beliefs to that of our English Church."

"Cordelia has renounced her Catholic religion?" said Hal surprised.

"She was never a convinced Catholic," replied Adam, defensively. "She decided it would be politic to embrace the Church of England if we are to remain here. Recollect she was brought up by nuns in France. What chance had she but to be a Catholic? Besides, in her faith, our marriage is no marriage at all, and she is little better than a fallen woman. She has been receiving instruction from the local man and hopes to be Confirmed at sometime in the future."

"And in the meantime, must pay lip service to the Rectory, and its inhabitants?" said Hal nodding his understanding.

"Cordelia will always be devout," replied Adam.

"Anything she does is the result of careful consideration and," he added, as Hal cast him a quizzical look, "the vicar's sister is a great favourite with both her and Sophie. They seem to have a sincere affection for each other. Sophie is so useful in helping Cordelia understand the English way of things."

"Yes, I can well see that one raised by French Catholic nuns, might find herself at a loss in Lincolnshire."

Adam pulled another face and came to sit opposite him. "It has not been easy," he admitted. "Cordelia and I represent all they fought against. The son of one Royalist and the daughter of another, brought up, as you say, by French Catholic nuns. Even Sophie, who is the only non-royalist, is spoken of with disfavour because of her disastrous marriage."

"So, none have called upon you, I suppose, or made you welcome?" Hal remarked, trying to keep the censure from his voice.

"Sir Charles Wicliffe came a few weeks after we'd settled in, to bring Sophie word of how things went at Harcourt, and Dury Southgate was a regular caller, until Lady Harcourt became so very ill."

Hal nodded. "Yes, it would be so," he agreed. "The local gentry would give you the benefit of the doubt and merely talk about you behind your backs, but your own people and the yeomanry, no. They'll make their feelings clear to your face."

Adam nodded grimly. "Not that I care for myself, but Cordelia doesn't deserve all the ill-feeling, anymore than Sophie."

"Scandal dies away eventually. Usually when another greater scandal comes along," said Hal. "I well recollect how it was when my uncle was killed. Many pointed a finger at me, and there were those who claimed Will Longstaffe had been a convenient scapegoat. And then, more recently, there was the gossip at the death of my wife and before that over the furore at Chawcester."

Adam nodded, recollecting the ferment of scandal which had spread in the sleepy market town whilst the Justice lay recovering from the wounds inflicted by a murderer who had run amok. "Yes, I remember it, too, Sir Henry, he nodded. "Yes and how suddenly, when the churchwarden of St John's disappeared with the collection one Sunday and was found dead drunk behind the abbey, it all disappeared overnight."

"No, it never completely disappears," said Hal. "People have long memories and are always glad to remember scandal, usually at the worst time."

Adam nodded again. "I am convinced Jack Hollingshead is at the root of all the ill-feeling," he confided. "Every time I give a direction to one of the people here, they straight away start on about what Master Jack would have done."

A faint rueful smile flickered across Hal's face as he recollected the first weeks of his return to England. "It is never easy to fill another's shoes," he agreed with reluctant sympathy. "But recollect, none had ever heard of Cordelia's existence. From what I have heard, her father, Sir Basil, wasn't the best landlord either. Most of his tenure was during the war, when he was at odds with the majority of the local population. Jack Hollingshead must have seemed like a dream come true to the tenants. He turned the property from a ramshackle—."

"Adam! Adam, are you there?" A slender young woman, her golden curls tumbled by the wind, rushed into the hall, her words, full of laughter, tripping from her lips. "You'll never guess what that…Oh…Hal!" She stopped in her tracks by the long, polished table, her hand going to her chest, as if to still her heart." Sir Henry, what a shock you gave me. I never expected to see you here!" ⚜

www.ingramcontent.com/pod-product-compliance
Lightning Source LLC
Chambersburg PA
CBHW031436240626
47154CB00001B/285